THE CAT, THE DEVIL, AND LEE FONTANA

"**T**his compelling departure from the Joe Grey series will have you flying through the pages, anxious to find out what happens next."
Reader to Reader

"**F**eline fans will enjoy reading *The Cat, the Devil, and Lee Fontana* and will await the next incarnation of this heavenly cat."
Iron Mountain Daily News

"Intriguing."
Booklist

PRAISE FOR
THE JOE GREY MYSTERIES

"**T**his is delightful entertainment. It would be a true cat-tastrophe if you let it pass you by."
Todd David Schwartz, CBS Radio (★★★★)

"**M**urphy's series is top-notch."
CATS magazine

By Shirley Rousseau Murphy

SHIRLEY ROUSSEAU
AND
PAT J.J. MURPHY

The CAT, the DEVIL, and Lee Fontana

a novel

AVON

An Imprint of HarperCollinsPublishers

AVON BOOKS
An Imprint of HarperCollins*Publishers*
195 Broadway
New York, New York 10007

First Avon Books mass market printing: November 2014
First William Morrow hardcover printing: February 2014

For Brennie and Max, Susan and Steve,
and every one of our Georgia friends,
you are each so very special.
And to Janet and Bob Thornton
for helping to bring alive
the Washington coast and for your
uncounted kindnesses and good cheer.

Authors' Note

THIS STORY HAPPENED before *Cat Bearing Gifts*. In that Joe Grey mystery, Misto remembers only scattered details of his moments with Lee Fontana. Now, in this interval between the yellow tomcat's earthly lives, he is close indeed to Lee. In his spirit form, he sees more clearly through time and space and observes more sharply the temptations of evil that haunt the old convict. Thus, his persistent feline spirit is able, in many ways, to intervene in Lee's battle against the powers that seek to destroy him.

1

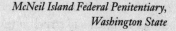

THE DEVIL ARRIVED at McNeil Island Federal Prison March 8, 1947,
bleating like a goat and looking like
a goat. He had taken the form of a
big buck goat with coarse brown fur,
a rank smell, spectacular accessories, and a drool-stained
beard. He was looking for Lee Fontana. Fontana, who was
considered not immediately dangerous to the other felons,
had been made a trusty and put to work on the prison
farm growing potatoes and mutton for the inmates. Satan
looked for him there. When he didn't find Fontana among
the pens and dairy barns and gardens, he turned his attention to a flock of nubile young sheep and for an hour
had his way with them, perplexing and then delighting
the young ewes. Afterward the goat stood in the muddy
pasture where it met the shore of Puget Sound, pawing
at the salty water that lapped around his hooves and star-

ing back toward the prison, watching through the thick concrete walls as Fontana left the mess hall wiping the last trace of supper from his grizzled chin. How old he'd grown since Satan had last looked in on him, his tall, thin body ropy and leathered, the lines etched deep into his lean face printing out a sour disappointment with life that greatly pleased the devil.

Galloping along to the prison and melting in through the high concrete walls, the goat materialized suddenly in the exercise yard, big, rough-coated, smelly, and causing considerable interest. He allowed a crowd of amused inmates to touch his thick heavy horns but when they started to touch other, more private parts, perhaps with envy, he butted and struck at them with his sharp hooves. They scattered. The goat disappeared, poof, into nothing, abandoning the form he had taken as he'd moved up through time and space from the flames of earth's fiery and turbulent core.

He was invisible when he entered the cell block, an errant swirl of sour wind pacing unseen beside the debilitated old train robber as Lee hurried along toward his cell, toward the ease of his iron bunk. Though Fontana couldn't see him, an icy aura made the hard-bitten old man clutch his arms around himself in a sudden and puzzling shiver, made him hope he wasn't getting the flu that was going around the cell blocks. That, with his sick lungs, wouldn't be good news. Whatever was the matter, he was aching with cold by the time he reached his barred door; he stood impatiently watching the uniformed guard leave his desk farther up the corridor, watched his rolling walk that accommodated his big belly as he came to lock

Lee in for the night. "You look beat, Fontana. You okay?"

"Cold, is all. Be warm in a minute," Lee said, looking hopefully down at his thin blanket.

The guard shrugged, but he shivered, too. "Does seem colder back here." He looked up above the three tiers of cells to the clerestory windows high beneath the ceiling as if to see one of them open or broken but all were shut tight, the wire-impregnated glass smoky with dirt where it caught light from the hanging bulbs. He looked at Lee puzzled, shivered again, locked the cell door and headed back to his desk, his gait rolling like a pregnant woman heavy with her burden. Beside Lee, the devil, too, felt the cold despite the fact that he had generated that unearthly chill, so very different from the normal cold of the cell block—he didn't like the damp cold of the cells any more than Lee did, he despised the chill of the upper world just as he hated its too-bright days and the vast eternity of space that swept endlessly beyond the spinning planet. All that emptiness left him uneasy, though hell knew he'd spent enough time up here on the naked surface enjoying his centuries of tangled and debilitating games. Watching Fontana now, he thought about the many times he'd returned to observe and torment the old cowboy—for all the good it did. Tempt and prod the old man as he might, and though he was always able to manipulate a few uncertain places in Fontana's nature, the end result was the same. Fontana would give in for a while to his prodding, would be drawn to the cruel and sadistic aspects of whatever robbery he was planning—but for only a short time. Then he would go his own way again, ignoring a more interesting treatment of his victims, as hardheaded and stubborn as the billy goat Satan had so recently sent butting through the prison wall.

But the devil wasn't through with the old man. He had infinite time. He meant to change Fontana, he meant to own Lee's soul for his own. Time was nothing to Satan, he moved through the centuries *as* he chose and *wherever* he chose, tending to the vast ranks of souls that teetered uncertainly on the cusp between evil and a bland life of virtue—but so many of them begging to be lost, beseeching him to take them with him on that last and fiery descent.

Lee Fontana was a harder quarry, but one he didn't mean to lose.

The guard sitting down at the desk crammed into his chair would have been an easier mark, but there'd be no fun in that game, with such a simple target. Satan had watched the round-bellied officer with distaste as he locked Lee into his cell, and when he'd touched the man with an icy hand the fat boy had shivered, hastily bolted the door and hurried away. Now, smiling, Satan slipped in through the bars of Lee's cell as invisible as a breath and stood waiting for Fontana to pull off his clothes, stretch out on his bunk in his skivvies and pull the blanket up, waiting for Fontana to ease toward sleep where his mind would be most malleable.

But as Lucifer watched Lee, he in turn was watched. The prison cat sat observing that dark and hungry shadow, peering out from beneath the guard's desk just as, earlier in the evening, he had watched the rutting goat play hell with the sheep out at the prison farm. The cat had known Satan even in goat form and knew why he was there. His silent hiss was fierce, his claws kneading, every angle of his lean body tense and protective. He didn't like the devil sniffing around Lee again, poking and prodding as he'd done ever since Fontana was a boy, showing up always with the same vendetta, willfully tormenting Lee, wanting what he thought was his due, wanting to get back at Lee for an effrontery that Lee had had nothing to do with. Lee had been only a child when his grandpappy faced off and bested the devil, but Lucifer wouldn't let up, he wouldn't back off, not until Lee gave in to his dark desires or, in death, went free at last, still unbound to the slave maker.

The yellow tomcat had lived at the prison most of his life, he'd arrived there as a tiny kitten in the pocket of a prison guard, had been bottle-fed by the guard and two inmates and, when he was old enough to be let outside, had learned to hunt from the resident prison cat. He had taken over from that aging beast when she passed on to enjoy another life. Indeed, Misto himself had died there at the prison, at a ripe and venerable age. That body, only one relic from his rich and varied incarnations, was buried just outside the prison wall with a fine view of Puget Sound, of its roiling storms, and its quiet days cloaked in coastal fog. The very night that a guard buried Misto, as fog lay heavy over the still water, the cat had risen again appearing as only a tangle of vapor mixed with the mist, and he wandered back into the cell blocks.

He wasn't ready to leave McNeil. The prison was home, the ugly cells, the exercise yard, the mess hall with its ample suppertime handouts, the kitchen with more scraps than a dozen cats could devour, the overflowing garbage cans, the dense woods and grassy fields, with its band of wild and amorous female cats and, out at the prison farm among the dairy barns and chicken houses, a fine supply of rats and fat mice to hunt and tease, and what more could any cat want?

During Misto's lifetime most of the prisoners had been friendly to him. Those who were not had been kept in line by the others. Now, returning as ghost, he had gotten his own back with those men in a hurry, driving a fear into them that would prevent them from ever again tormenting a cat or any other small creature. When, after his death, he'd materialized in the prison yard and let the inmates see him, some claimed another cat had moved in, likely one of Misto's kittens that was a ringer for him. But some prisoners said Misto himself had come back from the grave into another of his nine lives; *they* knew he wasn't yet done with the pleasures of McNeil, and he soon became a cell-block myth, appearing and disappearing in a way that offered an exciting and chilling new interest for the bored inmates: a ghost cat to tickle their thoughts, to marvel over and to argue about. Lee Fontana observed the ghost, and smiled, and kept his opinions to himself. As for Misto, it wasn't the comfort and pleasure of the island alone that detained his spirit there. He remained because of Lee Fontana.

The cat had lived an earlier life in Lee's company, when Lee was only a boy. A willful kid and hotheaded, but there was about him a presence that had interested the cat, a deep steadiness, even when the boy was quite young, a solid core within that had clashed with the boy's fiery nature. Drawn to Lee, Misto had, in the ghostly spaces between his nine lives, often returned to Fontana as he grew up and grew older. He had ridden unseen with Lee during a number of train robberies, greatly entertained by the bloody shootings, the excitement and the terror of the victims—though he never saw Lee torment, or seen him kill with malice. Lee had killed his share of armed men, but those shootings were in self-defense, meant to save his own life.

It might be argued that if Lee hadn't robbed the trains he wouldn't have been in a position to defend himself, would have had no reason to kill any man. Maybe so. But however one judged Fontana, the cat saw in him a strain of decency that the devil hadn't so far been able to touch, something in the hard-bitten cowboy that had kept the dark one defeated. If Misto had his way, that wouldn't change. He had watched as Fontana grew older and more stubborn in his ways and as he grew more sour on life, too. He had watched Lee's fear of old age and death settle down upon him, the fear that haunted most aging humans, and he didn't mean to leave the old man now, he would not abandon Lee so close to the end and to his last parole; he meant to stay with the old man to the final breath of his earthly journey, meant to follow Lee in his decline as the dark spirit made a last attempt at Lee's final and eternal destiny.

As a ghost, the tomcat had chosen perversely to retain the exact color and form in which he'd lived all his earthly lives: rough yellow coat, battle-ragged ears, big bony body moving with an ungainly clumsiness that belied his speed and power. When he made himself visible he seemed no more than a rangy prison cat lying on the warm concrete of the exercise yard soaking up the last of the day's meager heat or slipping into the mess hall under the tables bumming the inmates' scraps that were passed down to him by one rough hand and then another; the prison cat that lay now unseen on the cold iron shelf in Lee's cell, watching Lee's dark and shadowed visitor that stood at the foot of Lee's bed—waiting for Lee to be discharged in the morning, waiting to make one more try at bringing Fontana into his fold, waiting to play some final and unexpected card in his hungry game.

Out beyond the cell block the prison yard lay deserted, and a thin breeze scudded in off Puget Sound across the green and quiet island, touching the lighted windows of the guards' and staff houses and the small, darkened schoolhouse, touching the peaceful and forested hills—while there within the cell block the devil waited. And Misto waited, ready for whatever would occur tomorrow as Lee left the certainty of his prison home, as he moved out into a free and precarious world followed and hazed by that hungry spirit who meant, so intently, to steal the will and the soul of the lonely old man.

2

Easing onto his bunk, Lee pulled the rough prison blanket close around him, though it did little to drive the cold from his bones. Maybe he *was* coming down with whatever was sending men off to the infirmary, their faces white as paste, doubled over hacking up yellow phlegm. In the old days when he was young, death from the flu was common enough, it would take a whole family, half a town, in one violent outbreak and there was nothing much a doctor could do about it. At least now the docs had what they called wonder drugs, for whatever they were worth.

Well, hell, so what if he did come down with the flu on his last day in prison, so he died from the flu rather than be strangled to death from the emphysema. Dead and buried at McNeil in a convict's grave. As good as anywhere else, he guessed, because who would know or care? Reaching for his prison shirt and pants, that he'd left folded at the end of the small iron shelf, he spread them out over the blanket for extra warmth. They didn't help much. Damn screws didn't have the decency to run the furnaces, let a man sleep in comfort, the cheap bastards. The cell felt like a South Dakota winter, and he'd seen more than enough of those in his lifetime.

He guessed he should consider himself lucky to have a cell to himself, not shoved in with a bunch of young studs to hassle him, that he'd have to fight and then have to keep watching all the time because the bastards never would back off. Lucky to be on the ground floor, too, thanks to the prison doc. That climb to the upper tiers would take his breath, would make it impossible, on one of his bad days, to *get* a breath.

His cell was like any other, and he'd seen enough of those, too, stained toilet, stained sink, the narrow iron shelf to hold all his worldly belongings. His black prison shoes lined up side by side, just beneath. Smeared concrete walls where graffiti had been repeatedly scrubbed away. But it was better than some of the places he'd ended up, on the outside. Narrow sagging bed in some cheap boardinghouse, or the rotting floor of an empty miner's shack, his blanket spread out among the mouse and rat droppings. He thought with longing of a bedroll on the prairie when he was running cattle, the smell of the cook fire and boiled coffee, a steer lowing now and then, the faint song of a herder to soothe them and to keep himself awake, the occasional rattle of a bit or a horse snorting to clear dust from his nose.

Strange, tonight the whole cell block seemed not only colder but unnaturally dark, too. Though there was never any real night under the hanging bulbs, never the night's soothing blackness to rest your eyes and ease a person into sleep. New inmates, first-timers, found it hard to get used to, hard to sleep at all beneath the invasive lights running the length of the cell block ceiling like a row of bright, severed heads—though tonight even the overhead cones seemed blurred and dim, as if viewed through a layer of greasy smoke; and when he looked out through his bars, along the corridor, the four tiers of sleeping men were so shadowed and indistinct he wondered if his eyesight was failing. Shivering, he pulled the blanket tighter. So damn cold. A deep cold that had cut through his bones at intervals all day. He'd be warm for a while as he worked moving bales of hay, and then suddenly would be freezing again for no reason. He was so cold now that, staring up past the lights through the high, barred windows, he expected to see snow salting the night sky.

None of the other men seemed bothered. Nearby, where he *could* make out guys sleeping, their covers were thrown back, a bare leg or bare arm trailing over the side of a bunk, the sleeper snoring away happily, warm and content—as content as a man could be, caged in here like a captive beast.

Well, hell, he'd be out of here tomorrow. Leave the cold behind. Would be heading south to the hot desert, where he could bake in the hundred-twenty-degree sun, soak up all the heat he wanted.

His idea was to work a while down in Blythe, in the Southern California desert, the way his parole plan said, but to stay just a little while and then jump parole, pull one more job, and head for Mexico with a good stash tucked away. He wanted money for his last, declining years, he didn't mean to end up a pauper, with no money for his needs, that dread was always with him; hard as it might be, he meant to do something about that. A few hundred thousand was what he had in mind, enough to live comfortably for the remainder of his life, for however long that was.

Who knew, once he got out of this damp cold, got down into the hot desert and got himself some cash, once he was settled in a place of his own, maybe the emphysema would get better as it sometimes did when he was comfortable and not stressed. Hell, maybe he'd forget about dying, maybe he'd live forever.

His written parole instructions were to get off the train at San Bernardino before heading on down to Blythe, check in there with his parole officer. Maybe he'd do that, and maybe he wouldn't. Maybe just stay on the rattler until he hit Blythe, go right on down to the job, such as it was, tell the parole officer, when he showed up in a few weeks, that he'd forgotten about stopping off, or maybe that he'd lost the paper giving him any such orders.

The job in Blythe was supposed to be permanent, but even if his old running partner had arranged it for him, they both knew Lee wasn't about to work the vegetable fields for the rest of his parole time. That was migrant work, they had to like the hot, heavy labor just fine or they wouldn't keep slipping across the border, hiding in the trunks of rickety old cars half smothered to death, heading up to the States, men wanting better pay and better treatment than they got at home.

He meant to work at the ranch a few weeks so he

looked good to the parole board, get his bearings, lay out a plan to put his hands on some cash. Pull that off, and he'd be out of there, rich again and not a care to worry him. One big job, one nice haul, then on down across the border where he'd pick up a little adobe house and some land for a few bucks, enough to pasture a couple of horses. Find a little señorita to cook for him and take care of his needs, live on tortillas, good hot Mexican dishes. Maybe a last crack at good, hot Mexican love. If he could still handle that much excitement. He didn't like thinking how the years lay on him. Even his spirit felt flat, worn out, not fiery, as when he was young. He was giving out, his body giving out, aches and stiffness, and the emphysema made it so hard to breathe that when he thought of pulling another job, he wondered if he could handle it, if he could still bring off a job with the decisiveness and fast moves it would take and still get away clean.

But he had no choice. One more big job, or just wither away to nothing like an old horse turned out on barren, grassless land and left to starve to death.

He wondered, too, if he'd be up to the modern ways. He was coming out of prison into a world he didn't know anymore, a world of sleeker, faster cars than he was used to. Fast diesel trains that no man on horseback could take down the way you could halt a steam train, the way he used to do, and his grandpappy before him, neither of them ever expecting the steam trains to die out and a new kind of train to take over the rails. In the old days, in L.A., the vaqueros used to race their horses against the steam trains, their ponies faster in the sprint, but the locomotive taking over for the distance, leaving the riders behind.

With these new trains, a horseman didn't have a chance. This was the 1940s, everything fast and slick as he'd never imagined, the world turned into a place he didn't know, and, in truth, didn't want to know. The slick Chicago gangs all duded up in their fancy suits and greased hair, their high-powered machine guns and big fancy cars, their steel-fisted control of a whole city. Big crime, taking down millions of dollars, not the simple one-on-one robberies that Lee was used to.

The whole world had grown too big; it was overwhelming. The Great War, World War I, a war fought from the sky, from planes that, some said, would soon replace the trains, take you anywhere in the U.S. you wanted to go, in just a few hours. This was not his world. There was even talk of some new kind of camera invented, which one day soon would watch you enter a bank, watch your every move in there. A world of spying, more sophisticated fingerprinting, all kinds of technology the cops could use to trap you. It was hard to get his mind around the changes that had happened while he worked the prison farm, herded and cared for a bunch of sheep and milk cows. His own kind of life was fast vanishing, running cattle on thousands of miles of open range that were now mostly fenced, broken into puny little spreads, cut up and ruined. His kind of life had been sucked away into history like water sucked down a drain.

Tomorrow he'd step out into that world, a used-up old man. No new skills to cope with the changes, a dried-up old gunman with maybe nothing he *could* do but the field work where he was headed, hard labor that would leave him falling into bed at night aching in every bone and trying to get his breath. With all these fancy new ways, what kind of robbery was out there that he could even handle, anymore? When he hit Blythe, maybe he *couldn't* do anything else but fall into the same life as the Mexican pickers, work among them, eat, and sleep, and work the fields until one day they found him dead among the cabbages, and no one to give a damn.

THE CAT, AS Lee deliberated on his fate, dropped invisibly down from the shelf to the concrete and rolled over on the hard cell floor, watching Lee, knowing Lee's thoughts and not liking them much.

A mortal cat would know distress at the nervous unease of the humans he cared about. But the spirit cat saw more, he understood more and, too often, he felt drawn to do celestial battle on Lee's behalf. Now, flipping to his feet, restlessly pacing, he at last drifted up onto the iron shelf once more, above Lee's empty shoes, lay down across the iron grid, invisible ears back, invisible tail twitching as he waited for what was about to occur, as he waited for the dark visitor to make himself known to Lee, as was the devil's way.

LEE'S BATTERED WATCH said twelve-thirty, but he couldn't sleep. Still shivering, he dug the paperback western out from under his pillow and tried to read. He got through barely two pages before the print on the page began to blur, his eyes watering not from want of sleep but from the unnatural cold that shivered him, and from the harsh overhead lights that, even through the murky air, glared straight down into his face. He was idly turning

the pages, trying to stay interested in the cheap pulp western and wishing he had another Hershey's bar—he'd eaten
the last three—when a whisper from the corridor brought
him up startled, a voice as faint as a shifting breeze.

"*Fontana. Lee Fontana.*"

Easing up on one elbow, he looked out through the
bars. He scanned the cells across the way, tier upon tier,
but saw no one looking out at him, no one awake. Not a
soul stirred, the prone bodies seemed as still as the prod-
ucts of a waxworks, or as if they floated in a chill suspen-
sion of time.

"*Lee . . . Lee Fontana.*" A whisper closer than those far
cells, and as insidious as a rattler's buzz. He couldn't tell
the direction, it seemed to come from all around him, from
the ceiling, from inside the cell itself, and through the
concrete walls on either side of him. Whatever thoughts
slid into Lee's mind at that instant, he pushed away, whatever images arose he didn't want to consider. But then suddenly the prisoners' snores began again, the coughs, the
twang of flat metal bedsprings as some sleeper relieved his
tensions or rolled over. Maybe he'd imagined the whisper
he'd *thought* he heard, had imagined that seeming pause in
time, as well. Reaching for his book again, he stretched
out flat, pulled the blanket up, shivering, trying to get
warm and to read and not look around him, to pay attention to nothing beyond the cheap novel. He was turning
the page when the shadows in his cell shifted so violently
that he jerked upright, staring around him.

"*Fontana. Lee Fontana.*"

No one was there beyond the bars. But a shadow lay
across his blanket, the stark shadow of a tall man cutting

across the dark stripes that were cast by the iron bars. He squinted, but still the corridor was empty, unbroken by any figure. No one stood peering in at him, no one to account for the dark shape cast boldly across his blanketed legs. But a heavy malaise pressed at him, weakening him so he had to ease back, to lie supine, watching the dark imprint, watching the empty space beyond the bars, the empty corridor. He remained as still as if he faced a coiled rattler, as if the faintest shift of his body would trigger a flash of attack.

Frozen, slowly he made himself look up through the bars at the harsh lights, hoping that when he looked back, the man-shadow would be gone. The acid glow of the overheads blinded him, he stared until his eyes watered and then looked down again, mopping tears with a corner of his blanket, hoping the specter would have vanished. His vision swam with red afterimages, and only after some moments could he make out the shadow still cast solidly across his bed.

But now, as well, he could see a faint darkness suspended beyond the bars, a gray smear as ephemeral as smoke drifting and moving in the corridor, hovering with a life of its own, some terrifying form of life that was watching him—but how could that thin and shifting smear cast the harsh black man-shadow that cut so starkly across his bed?

Silently he slid his hand under the pillow reaching for the sharpened metal rod he kept there. Whatever threw the shadow, whether he could see it clearly or not, maybe it could feel the thrust of a blade. His fingers touched the cold steel, but when he tried to grip the homemade knife his hand wouldn't move, it was frozen in place. He tried to swing off the bunk but he couldn't shift his legs, his body was immobilized, he could no more move than could a slab of stone dropped onto the sagging bunk. When he tried to shout for the guard, his voice was locked to silence within his constricted lungs.

And what would he have told the guard? That he saw a phantom, that he heard a voice out of nowhere? That he couldn't move, that he was as silenced and locked in place as a sparrow he'd seen once, in dead winter, frozen upright to a telegraph wire. Phlegm began to build in his throat, phlegm from the emphysema, triggered by fear, mucus that would soon cause a spasm of choking that must bring him up off the bunk spitting, or would drown him. He began to sweat. He'd soon have to move or he would strangle. What the hell was this, what was going on? He wasn't going to die here frozen like that sparrow, die on a prison bunk drowning in his own spit, unable even to turn his head and clear his mouth. Fear filled him and rage until, angry and straining, he was at last able to turn enough to cough onto his sheet. But still he couldn't rise.

Hell, this wasn't happening, he was Lee Fontana, he could still hit a pigeon at fifty yards with a forty-five, could still see a train scuttling across the horizon small as a black ant, see it way to hell before the rails started to hum at its approach, could still jump a steam train and stop it cold—if there'd been any more steam trains. He had, in his prime, stricken men with his own brand of terror, there'd been a time when he had only to stare at a train engineer and because he was Lee Fontana the man would lay down his rifle and pull the engine to a halt. He had sent strong men cowering from him, left them rigid with fear. He didn't like it when that kind of terror hit him instead.

Sweating and straining, he was at last able to slip off the bunk, down to the cold concrete floor. Clutching the prison-made knife, he rose up, stood in the center of the empty cell facing the shadow—a naked, ludicrous figure wielding the knife as he glowered at the empty bars. A tall, flat-bellied old man, his tender white flesh tanned to leather only from his neck up and from his elbows down, where he rolled his shirtsleeves. Leathery brown hands marked by sixty years of rope burns and wire cuts, his face hard, wind-beaten, most of the rest of him pale and vulnerable.

When he approached the shadow, it thinned the way smoke thins when one walks into it but the chill deepened, and the instant he touched the cold metal bars, he faced not the corridor and the tiers of caged men, he faced a vast and empty space reeling away and soft laughter echoed inside his head, a sound that seemed to fill the world. *"You think you're something, old man. You're no more than a speck of dust, you're already a moldering corpse or nearly so. Dead soon enough, and no one to give a damn. You're a worn-out has-been without the cojones anymore to pull another job."* And the creature's laugh echoed coldly, deep into Lee's bones.

"Get out!" Lee spat at the emptiness. "Whatever you are, get out! Get the hell out of my space." Turning his back on whatever this was—and he knew too well what it was—he went back to bed, pulled the blanket up. He didn't look again at the shadow but he felt it watching him, felt the ongoing intensity of its interest.

This wasn't the first time he'd seen the shadow and felt its chill. The first time was long ago when he was only a boy. He was thinking back to that time when suddenly the prison cat appeared, lying on the shelf inside his cell, its yellow eyes on him, its yellow tail twitching as it looked him over. Leaning up, he reached to stroke it but the yellow tom leaped past his hand to the bunk, heavy and solid. It rubbed against him, its fur felt rough under his stroking, its purring loud as the tomcat settled down beside him, warm and yawning—and when Lee looked back at the bars, the figure had vanished. Across his blanket the spaces between the straight black lines were empty.

He heard the guard coming, making his regular round, his black shoes tapping on the concrete. The man glanced in at him, his fat face not changing expression as he took in every detail, looked at the sleeping cat, and shrugged. The cat roamed everywhere. How he got into the locked cell block was anyone's guess but he seemed to have no problem. When the guard had passed, Lee lay stroking the cat and looking around at his cell, the stained toilet, the dented steel sink with his toothbrush balanced on the edge, the graffiti-smeared walls, the familiar stain on the concrete floor where a previous inmate had lost blood in some self-inflicted injury. His book lay facedown across the stain beside the three empty Hershey's wrappers. Nothing was different, yet everything was different. The cell seemed without substance now, as if at any instant it might fade, and he with it. The intrusion of the specter had rammed his mortality home to him like a knife stuck in his belly. He lay the rest of the night thinking of that haunting, seeing his life vanish before its unearthly power like fragments of burned paper tattered on the wind. He lay there desolate and frightened, and with only the yellow cat to warm him, to somehow reassure and to comfort him.

THE DEVIL, IN human form, left the cell block pleased with his night's work. Moving unseen through the concrete walls, slipping through iron bunks and through the bodies of sleeping men so their dreams clutched suddenly at them and left them sweating, he drifted through the infirmary, the mess hall, the administrative offices, and down across the lawn that was kept neatly mowed by prison trusties, down to the edge of Puget Sound. There he stood, a wraith come out of eternity, staring out at the roiling waters that covered this small scrap of earth at this moment and at the distant smokestacks of Tacoma rising beyond—at the great bulk of Mount Rainier towering white and majestic over all that lay below, daunting even the devil in its rocky, snow-crowned dominance. Beside his left foot a rabbit crouched, so frozen with fear of him it was unable to run, riven with such terror that when he reached down and took it in his hands the little beast didn't twitch. It died slowly and in great pain, emitting one high, terrified scream before Lucifer at last broke its neck and tossed it into the bushes.

He had subtler plans for Lee Fontana. Unlike the rabbit, he meant that Fontana would provide his own pain.

3

LEE LEFT HIS cell for the last time dressed in a prison-made pinstripe suit a size too big for him, the sleeves hanging down to his knuckles, a red-and-yellow tie so gaudy that a dog wouldn't pee on it, and prison-made wingtip shoes that raised blisters before he ever reached the first door of the sally port, their squeaking soles providing his only fanfare as he headed out for the free world. Moving down the corridor of Mc-Neil for the last time, toward the double-doored cubicle where he would receive his belongings and sign out, his nerves were strung tight. He'd be on his own in less than an hour. His previous five releases from the federal pens didn't make getting out, this time, any easier. No one to tell him when to eat, tell him when and where to sleep, tell him where exactly to work each day and how to do his work. A man got out of practice making his own decisions.

At Admissions, a soft-faced officer with jowls like a

bulldog produced the usual brown paper bag with Lee's name scrawled on it, shoved it across the desk with a patronizing smirk. "Here's your worldly goods, Fontana." He looked Lee over, amused at the baggy pinstripe suit and fresh prison haircut, and at the one pitiful item he saw Lee take from his pocket and drop in the bag, the little framed picture of his sister, Mae, when she was ten. "Here's your train ticket," he said, handing Lee a plain brown envelope, "and your prison earnings. Don't lose them, old man. And be careful, it's a great big world out there."

Lee moved away from the counter wanting to smash the guy. As to his prison earnings, there wasn't much; they didn't get paid for working the farm, only for splitting cedar shingles that the prison shop made from the trees that grew along the shore—most of that pittance, he'd spent on razor blades and soap, on cheap dime novels the guards would pick up on the mainland, and on candy bars. He wondered if the money was still stuffed into the toe of his boot, from all those years ago when he was brought into McNeil and stripped of his civilian clothes, when all his belongings but Mae's picture were locked away as he changed into prison uniform. He hoped to hell the guards hadn't found it. He needed cash for a gun, for any number of essentials to start life anew.

Now, as Lee headed for the sally port, the ghost cat followed him unseen, his attention on the child's photograph that Lee had taken from his pocket, that he always kept close to him, the picture of Lee's little sister, Mae, from those long-ago days in South Dakota. The child who looked exactly like Misto's own Sammie, who lived now, in this time, in this moment, across the continent in

Georgia. Sammie, with whom Misto had lived a short but recent life, and with whom, as ghost, he still spent many nights, unseen, purring close to her as she slept.

The exact likeness of the two little girls continued to puzzle the ghost cat, for even now in his free and far-roving state between his earthly lives, the tomcat did not have all the answers. He knew only that there was a powerful connection between Mae and Sammie, an urgent and meaningful adjunct to their lives of which Lee was the center, a connection that, the cat thought, might ultimately help to save Lee in his conflict with the dark power.

Lee, clutching his brown paper sack and brown envelope, stepped into the sally port glancing at the officer behind the glass barrier. Receiving a nod, he moved on out through the second door. He knew he should be happy at the sound of the metal gate locking behind him. But he felt only unsteady at his sudden freedom, at being turned loose with no barriers, no limits or rules, adrift and on his own after years of confinement, lost and rudderless in a vast and unfamiliar world.

The sky was gray, the morning's heavy mist chilling him clear through. The small prison bus was waiting. He shoved the brown envelope with his ticket into his coat pocket, tucked the paper bag under his arm, climbed the three steps up into the stuffy vehicle, took a seat halfway back, nodding at the trusty who was driving and at the guard who sat angled where he could see the seats behind him. Lee was the only passenger. Earlier in the morning, and again in the afternoon, the bus would be full of schoolkids, children of the guards and prison personnel who lived on the island.

The bus rattled down the winding gravel road, past green pastures on both sides, past the reservoir and on down to the ferry landing where the SS *Bennett*, McNeil's forty-foot mahogany powerboat, was tied. The churning waters of Puget Sound looked as cold and gray as death, the hills of the distant shore vague beneath the overcast, grim and depressing, the smear of crowded mainland houses, with taller buildings rising among them, all generated the prisoner's fear of the vast and sprawling outside world. He knew the feeling would pass, it always did, but every time he was released he felt as off balance as if the cinch on his saddle had broken and he was scrambling to swing away from a bad tumble.

At the dock he left the bus, moved on down to the rocking launch where a uniformed guard and a trusty were coiling lines on the aft deck. The gray waters shifted and heaved as if forces deep down were restless. There was one other passenger, a prisoner chained to a bench on the foredeck sitting between two guards, a two-time felon who had made his third kill at McNeil and was being shipped off to Alcatraz. Lee crossed the wooden catwalk and stepped aboard, staying to the aft deck avoiding his prison mate. The hollowness in his belly was sharp with excitement but sharper with dread, leaving for the first time in ten years his secure cell, the farm where he'd felt comfortable, the animals he'd liked better than his fellow inmates—leaving the old prison tomcat, he thought, surprised he'd think of that. Leaving the old cat he'd come to care about more than he'd imagined. The yellow tomcat that had spent last night on Lee's bed, easing Lee's night-fears, somehow coming between him and the phantom that he hadn't wanted to see or to hear. Now he was leaving the old tomcat that was, it seemed to Lee, the only real friend he'd had at McNeil, the only presence he could really trust. The old cat that had, some said, died and returned again. Sometimes Lee thought he'd been there all along, that what the guard and prisoners had buried had been one of his offspring. Other times, he wondered. Whatever the truth, Lee had a pang of regret and knew he'd miss the old fellow.

He stood at the rail as the tall, lean guard cast off and began to coil line. One of the guards would have a shopping list in his pocket, they'd pick up needed supplies in Steilacoom before they headed back to the island, maybe food stores that had been trucked down from Tacoma, though most of their staples came by boat from there or from Seattle. Easing free of the dock, they were under way, the twin diesels churning the water in a long white tail boiling out behind them. Moving up to the bow, Lee stood chilled by the heavy mist and salt spray, riding the choppy waves liking the speed, and soon he began to feel easier.

Off to his left the overcast had lifted a little above the hills of Tacoma, the sun trying to burn through the murky cover. But it wouldn't burn away much, sun wouldn't blaze down on the land like the pure, hot desert where he was headed. As they approached land, the smokestacks from the iron smelters rose black and ugly, smelters that dumped their hot slag into the sound, souring the waters so nothing would grow along that shore. He could picture the streets and sidewalks of the city slick and wet from the mist and busier than he'd known: too many people, too many cars, not the quiet he'd grown used to on the island—the prison had been quiet most of the time, until a rumble erupted to stir things up, a dose of trouble breaking the monotony until armed guards stepped in and broke up the fight. Looking away toward the vast horizon of the mainland, he felt uneasy at so much freedom ahead, so much emptiness, so many choices, no one telling him what to do, no direction to his life except that he made for himself.

The prison counselor said that was what a parole officer was for, to guide him, help him over the rough spots until he'd settled in again. Well, to hell with that. He didn't need some wet-behind-the-ears social worker hardly out of diapers telling him how to live his life.

What the hell, the whole world lay open to him. What was he afraid of? He'd have free run at whatever he wanted. All kinds of robberies and scams were open to him, a chance at whatever he chose to take down, so what was he bellyaching about? Hell, yes, he'd get used to freedom again and to the new ways, even if life was more sophisticated, and people maybe harder to manipulate. The old habits hadn't all died. The old-fashioned, trusting ways would still prevail among the smaller towns and farms, among the honest people with their straightforward talk, their unlocked doors and innocent views, so many folks just waiting and ripe for the taking.

He tolerated the loud suit and noisy shoes for the half-hour boat ride to Steilacoom, was eager to get rid of them as they pulled up to the scrappy little community, coming in close to the tall pier that jutted high above them, the small prison boat rocking against the tall pilings. Couple of buildings up there along the pier, and he could smell coffee over the smell of dead fish. The boat nosed into the short catwalk that led to the shore. The train station was just on the other side of the tracks, dumpy wooden building, the town rising up the hill behind it, shabby little houses half hidden by the Douglas fir trees, the homes of lumber workers and maybe smelter workers from up around Tacoma. Ten years back, he hadn't seen much of Steilacoom, he'd been dumped off here from a marshal's car, handcuffed and in leg chains, after a silent ride down from the Tacoma jail through dense fir forests and past a couple of lakes. The marshal had handed him over to a McNeil guard. The guard had hustled him across the tracks, out along this same ramp he was descending now, and into the prison boat, had locked his leg chain to a wooden bench, and they'd been on their way over the rough, choppy water, McNeil Island looming ahead, dark green forests, pale green clearings, hard-faced concrete buildings—heading for his new and extended island vacation, courtesy of the U.S. Bureau of Prisons.

Now, stepping down off the ramp clutching his paper bag, he stood a moment watching the guards unload their prisoner—chained like a walking ghost of himself from ten years back. As they moved away into the train station he double-timed up a set of wooden steps and onto the wooden pier, separating himself as far as he could from the group. Heading out along the pier past a storage shed, he followed the smell of fresh coffee toward the lighted windows of a little café.

The room was dim inside, the shellacked walls made of beveled pine boards. Four wooden booths, two tables with Formica tops and stainless steel chairs, and a wooden bar. The woman behind it nodded to him, trying not to smile as she took in his pinstripe, pimp getup. Two men at the bar, plaid flannel shirts, heavy pants and boots, maybe lumberjacks. They turned to look and nodded briefly. Lee took a stool halfway down the bar, between the men and an old woman. He watched one of the men pour half his freshly opened beer into a frosted mug, and then tip in a glass of tomato juice and a big squirt of Tabasco; red beer was popular in this area. Lee didn't want to think how it would taste. The pudgy old woman down at the end, on the last bar stool, leaning against the wall, was dressed in several layers of clothes, none of them too clean. In his day you hadn't seen many woman hobos, but that was what she had to be. She smelled of sour urine, sour clothes, and a body that hadn't seen soap for a while. He ordered coffee and a slice of lemon pie from the glass case, then, hauling his paper bag, he headed for the men's room, holding his breath as he passed her.

Beside the door to the bathroom hung four wanted posters. Lee knew two of the men, they had left McNeil in the dark of night in one of the local residents' small boats. The boat had later been found adrift against the shore; the escapees were still at large. Lee took a good look at the other two pictures, at the men he didn't know. He was always interested in who was on the outside, maybe desperate and volatile, that might pose a threat if he ran up against them. And maybe part of his interest in the posters stemmed from when he was a boy, on those rare trips to town when he could enjoy the handsome photograph of his famous grandpappy.

Stepping on inside the little cubicle, he changed into his soft old Levi's and one of three shirts from the paper bag, removed Mae's picture and put it safely in his Levi's pocket. Feeling down into his right boot, he found the bit of paper with the folded bills inside, just as he'd left them. Seven hundred dollars, and he was mighty glad to find it all there. He left it taped in his boot, didn't shove it in his pocket along with the train ticket, his seventy-five dollars of prison earnings, and the prison-made knife. A bit of dried manure still clung to the sole of the run-over boot. He removed his rolled-up old jacket, shook the wrinkles out as best he could, then stuffed the prison clothes down in the paper bag. When he left, he'd drop them in the refuse bin out near the door of the train station—they wouldn't be there long, that old woman would fish them out again, sell the clothes for food or wine.

Coming out, he drew amused looks from the barkeep and the three customers, all of whom had likely seen, over the years, dozens of prisoners shed their cheap prison garb in just the same way. The barkeep set his pie and coffee before him and gave him a friendly smile, as if she knew exactly how good it felt to be back in the comfort of his own clothes. She was nearly his age, white hair smoothed back showing glimpses of pink scalp, lively brown eyes. How many departing inmates before him had she served, along with the locals, with the lumber and smelter men, and with the civilian residents of McNeil come ashore on one errand or another. He watched the lumberjacks down their red beer, still fascinated with how that would taste. He was just finishing his pie and coffee when he heard the train whistle.

Pushing some change across the bar, he rose, headed back along the pier for the station. He was just stepping across the tracks when the slow-moving engine gave a big blast and came into view ambling along close to the water, barely clearing the fir branches where they had been trimmed away, train huffing and clanging up to the station, squeal of brakes, shouts of the conductor. Lee dropped the clothes in the trash can, but kept the paper bag. He boarded quickly, with his ticket in hand, moved on in looking for a quiet space to himself.

He chose a half-empty car, took a seat away from the other passengers, laid his Levi's jacket and his paper bag on the seat next to him, to discourage anyone from sitting there. The car smelled of stale sandwiches and ancient dust. As he settled into the dirty mohair, a fit of coughing took him. He coughed up phlegm, spat it into his prison handkerchief. He could see through the dirty window half a dozen people hurrying down from the scattered houses above. The train waited in the station maybe fifteen minutes. Only four more passengers had entered his car when the train began to back and jerk, moving with a lot of hustle, and they were on their way. If this train made every little stop, it would be a slow, halting trip down across Washington and Oregon and into California—but then soon the train stretched out, moving fast, its iron wheels hitting a steady gallop that calmed and steadied Lee, the way speed had always calmed him.

When the vendor came by he bought dry sandwiches and coffee, the same sandwiches he'd live on for the next two days. He tried to clean the grimy window with his dirty handkerchief so he could see out, but he only smeared it worse. Irritated, he went out to stand in the windy vestibule between the cars, looking out at the waters of Puget Sound enjoying the sea while he could, the cool damp air, the green marsh along the inlets, before he got on down to the dry desert. He'd been up in this country a long time, away from that hot, parched land. He craved the dry heat, but he knew the muddy, sluggish Colorado River wouldn't be the same as the living sea, not like this surging water eating away at the lush and ragged edge of the continent. The overcast had followed them, but had thinned near the ground, enough to let him see an eagle soaring low overhead looking for dead fish. He stood clinging to the iron bar watching the dark waters and green marsh, and then looking out the other side, taking pleasure in the little farms, their cattle and fat horses knee deep in grass. When he was a boy on the dry prairie they'd never had grass like that, a man could only dream of feed like that for his stock.

Settling in for the long pull down to L.A., he gravitated between the dusty car, the narrow windy vestibule, and the men's room where he shaved and washed himself as best he could using their dinky little bars of soap, and paper towels. He slept in his seat, ate the dry sandwiches, read other people's discarded newspapers, and he thought too much.

The hitch at McNeil was the longest he'd ever served, he shouldn't have had a ten-year sentence. The only reason he got caught was sloppy work, and that had worried him. For the first time he knew he was getting old, afraid he'd lost his touch, maybe lost all talent for making a living in the only way he knew, the only way he liked. He'd give all he'd ever stolen or earned to be young and vigorous again, to be back in the early part of the century, back when the prairie was free and open, a good horse under him, nothing to think about but when the next steam train was due and what it carried, how much gold and cash—but then came the diesel trains, during the war, and you couldn't stop those babies by riding across the track waving a gun at the engineer. And those trains carried dozens of guards, soon there wasn't just one detective named Pinkerton to investigate a train job but a whole organization called Pinkerton, nosy, high-powered bastards, and his own times, his own ways were gone into the dust of the past.

After the steam trains were finished he'd worked cattle for a while, doing his first paid work in years. Then, long before America got into the war—but when many folks knew that day would come—he had taken a job in Montana, in Billings, breaking horses for the remount. Later, during the war, he'd heard that even the coast guard was using horses, patrolling the coastal beaches at night watching for German submarines.

For two years he had worked for the government breaking horses, he'd been straight then, no robberies, and he had, strangely, felt almost good about that. But then the itch for a thrill got him. When he left Billings he took on the Midnight Limited out of Denver, a diesel carrying military payroll. He'd planned every detail carefully, had even worn gloves to avoid fingerprints, accepting the annoying traps of modern technology. He had brought off the job alone without a hitch, had left the conductor and four guards tied up in the express car, had stashed the strongbox in the truck he'd hidden in an arroyo south of Grand Junction. But then, one second of bad judgment and he blew it. Blew it all, real bad. One second, standing beside that old Ford truck thinking how the money in the strongbox was meant for the new recruits at Camp Pendleton, thinking how those marines wouldn't get any pay, and he had turned away from the strongbox. Had left it in the truck and just walked away, knowing the sheriff or the feds would be on it within an hour. One weak minute, thinking how the leathernecks deserved their money more than he did, and he'd lost it all. Walked away, half of him feeling good, the other half shocked at the stupid waste.

And then, soon afterward, still pissed off at his own stupidity and with a lot of hustle and not the faintest plan, he'd stormed into that Vegas bank, leaned into the teller's cage and jammed the six-inch barrel of his forty-five into the girl's face, and before he could get a word out that feisty little bitch had slammed the brass window gate so hard it broke two fingers on his right hand. From that point on it was all downhill, the bank guard had him cold. The feds picked up a few prints on the train job, and on the Ford truck and the strongbox, where he'd been careless. They had him for both jobs though he never got a penny from the damned bank teller, and he knew he'd be doing time. He'd told himself bank robbery wasn't his line of work, but the truth was, he'd blown it bad. Suddenly, he knew he was old. An old man who'd lost his skill, and he'd envisioned the slow, confused end to his life, imprisoned by his own weakness, imprisoned by a fear far greater than he had ever known or ever wanted to know. Trapped by a mortality that seemed, every day, to draw in closer around him—and trapped by a heavier darkness, by a convergence of shadows pressing at him in a way far more lethal than simple fear of death, by a dark and terrifying aura that seemed to reach down from cold infinity, reaching to embrace and to own him, to painfully and endlessly devour him.

4

ON THE SHORT run down to Olympia beneath the snowy shoulder of Mount Rainier, they were soon skirting the vast and marshy shore of Nisqually Reach, where dairy cows grazed fat and content in their lush pastures. Among the tall green marsh grass at the water's edge, two bald eagles fought over a flopping fish, beating with angry wings at each other, tearing the silver body apart between them. But as Lee watched their hungry and brutal battle, the air inside the train, even through the closed windows, soon stank of the area's paper mills, a sour odor harsher than rotted wood, its thick effluence soon turning the land, the sea, and sky a dull, heavy gray, featureless and depressing.

But maybe, Lee thought, he'd better enjoy, while he could, even these pollution-bound inlets where the mills had soured the land, before he reached the dry desert, the pale dunes where the only water he'd see would be dark and sluggish, where he'd miss looking out every morning at the lapping waters of the sound washing against the ragged and wooded shore.

Now, suddenly, the world turned black as they pounded through a tunnel. When they emerged, the passengers around him strained to see the Cascade Mountains towering in the east, snowcapped, bright even against the graying sky. Only when, farther on, the manmade fog thinned near the ground, could he see the dense city buildings of Olympia, and the Olympic Range rising to the west. In the green surrounding fields, half a dozen eagles soared low over a pasture, homing in on something dead, then one lifted and left the group; he watched it rise on powerful wings to disappear into the overcast above, the great bird soaring free wherever he chose to go, his unfettered flight making Lee want to do the same.

Made him wonder, when he got to L.A. to change trains, if he should fly free, too. End the journey there, take off wherever he chose, never complete his parole plan. Buy a bedroll, put together a kit, hop a freight out of the city, never show up in Blythe, forget the job waiting for him, stop knuckling under to the feds.

Right. And end up back in the joint. Christ, that would be dumb. Besides, he wouldn't do that to a friend. Jake Ellson had gone to a lot of trouble to get him this job. Without it he might not have made parole, would have finished out his sentence right there at McNeil.

It didn't seem like twenty-five years since he and Jake had pulled their last train robbery, and now Ellson was married, to the woman they'd both wanted, was settled in a responsible job and had two grown girls—married to

Lucita because Lee had turned away from her, because he was too wild to want to settle down. Yet even now when he thought about her dark Latin beauty the heat would start to build and he'd wonder if he *should* have stayed.

Well, hell, that had been decided when they were young, Jake was the one who'd got himself tamed, and that was what Jake wanted. Lee hadn't cared to settle down, had no desire to be saddled with a family. Now he wondered what that would have been like, that life, children to love and to love him, Lucita in his bed, a warm, vibrant part of his life.

Leaving Olympia, the train was crowded. He tried to occupy both seats by spreading out newspapers but it wasn't five minutes, passengers pushing into the car, that a round little man entered carrying a briefcase, headed straight for the seat next to Lee, a nattily dressed little fellow in a baby-blue three-piece suit. Lee glared at him, willing him to move on, but brazenly he pushed the papers aside and sat down, his round blue eyes smiling behind wire-rimmed glasses. "Guess it's the only seat left." Still smiling, he made a short attempt at small talk, leaning forward to look myopically at Lee, his blue eyes too earnest, and the first thing Lee knew he had launched into a land-selling scam, intently pushing his worthless, five-acre desert plots. Lee tuned out the man's sales pitch, staring out through the smeared window at a red-tailed hawk lifting on the rising wind. The little man went right on, garrulous, so annoying Lee wanted to punch him. "You married, sir? You have children? Mister . . . I didn't catch your name."

"I didn't give it," Lee said shortly.

"Well, sir, if you have children, this land would give you a nice estate to pass on to them. Grandchildren? Think what you could leave to your grandchildren, why, this one piece of land . . ." But then as his blue eyes took in Lee's increasing irritation, his tapping foot and restless hands, he changed his tack. "What line of work are you in, sir? You look like maybe a retired banker."

Lee's temper flared. He rose, shoved past the man, and left the car, went to stand in the open vestibule trying to shake his anger. When he heard the door open behind him he turned, meaning to chase the little scum away.

Light glanced off the man's glasses revealing, now, eyes very different from the smarmy smile: cold, predatory eyes, a look that forced Lee to step back. Even his voice was different, grainy and hushed.

"You're getting old, Lee Fontana. You're old, and you're all alone. You have nothing," he said with satisfaction, "you have no one. No money to speak of, no possessions, no one who cares about you. Only the little cash you earned in prison, and the seven hundred dollars wrapped in brown paper in your left boot. How far do you think that will get you?"

Lee waited, chilled. As far as he knew, no one was aware of the seven hundred dollars. If the prison authorities had checked his belongings that long time ago when he first arrived at McNeil, they'd left the money alone—or maybe they'd missed it, tucked deep in the toe of his boot. But this little man had no way to know such a thing, and no way to know his name, either. The wind tugged at the salesman's seersucker suit and at his thin, pale hair. He watched Lee intently, his eyes as hard and penetrating as the steely stare of a hunting hawk, and an icy dread filled Lee. This was the shadow he had seen last night in his cell, the specter that had appeared to him now and again over the years, whispering, urging him, bringing out the rage and cruelty that seemed to dwell somewhere inside him, that usually he managed to put aside, to ignore. This was the shadow he had seen as a child, so long ago on the prairie, the chill presence that had frightened even his strong and powerful grandpappy.

"What do you want?" Lee managed, swallowing back a cough.

The little man smiled, his face and eyes cold as stone. "I want to see you prosper, Lee Fontana. I want to see you make it big, this time. I want to see you make a nice haul, enough money to take care of your retirement, just as you plan. I want to help you."

Rage filled Lee, the man was in his space, pushing him hard. He turned away, fists clenched, his anger nearly out of control, looked out at the calm green fields sweeping past, trying to calm himself, but still his temper boiled. He spun around to face the man, tensed to swing.

The vestibule was empty.

Neither door had opened, but Lee was alone. He stood for a long time, numb, not wanting to think about what he'd faced, wishing he had something steady to cling to.

When at last he returned down the aisle to his seat, he walked slowly, studying the faces of the other passengers. No one remotely resembled the stranger, no one looked up at him. On his empty seat the newspapers were strewn as he had left them, his sandwich wrappers crumpled on the floor where he'd dropped them. Still, he stood watching the rows of passengers, then at last slid into his seat. He sat with his eyes closed, but there was no way he could forget that icy stare; the man had driven a shaft of cold through him that left him sick with rage. He fidgeted, engulfed in a heavy silence, in a vast and growing solitude that was soon the silence of the empty prairie.

He was twelve years old, standing at the corral fence beside his grandpappy, the two of them staring out at the flat rangeland where there should be nothing to scare anyone, staring out at a moving shadow where there could be no shadow, at a shifting presence that turned his grandpappy pale. Lee had never seen Russell Dobbs scared, had never imagined his grandpappy could be afraid, but now Dobbs was afraid, something was out there, something beyond even Russell Dobbs's ken, something that the famous train robber couldn't have destroyed, even with a well-placed bullet.

Lee's grandpappy was his hero. When Lee was a boy, he hadn't spent much time with Dobbs, a few days once or twice a year when Dobbs would show up for an unexpected visit, yet the old man had dominated Lee's childhood. Lee's dreams of his grandpappy's adventures had shaped his hunger for fast trains and fast guns, for gold bullion, for the feel of gold coins running through his fingers. Russell Dobbs was known throughout the West for having taken down more train money than any man alive, and in far more reckless confrontations than any man. Young Lee had dreamed of even more dramatic robberies, had dreamed of far more wealth even than his grandpappy had stolen and had so recklessly spent.

From the time Lee could handle a horse well enough

to be of help, he had worked the ranch beside his daddy. His older brother was no good around cattle, and his two older sisters, Nora and Jenny, helped in the kitchen and in the vegetable garden—their parents didn't believe in girls working with the cattle. Lee worked the ranch, but every waking moment he dreamed of a more exciting life. Even that day leaning on the fence beside Dobbs, staring out at the prairie at what looked like a twist of smoke moving and approaching, the boy was even more alarmed by the old man's fear than by that half-seen specter, by the shadow of a man where there was no living figure. Dobbs had watched the figure so intently it seemed almost like it was speaking to him. Dobbs's cheeks were pale beneath the leathered tan and when, after a long while, the haunt vanished, his grandpappy had started as if waking from a dream. And had looked down at Lee, trying to know for sure if Lee had seen it, too.

Well, the five pastured horses and that old steer had sure seen it, they were spooked as hell; but for some reason, none of them had spun and taken off away from it, none of them ran, they just stood staring, twitching and dumb in their fear. That summer, more than sixty years ago, something had visited his grandpappy there at the home ranch. Lee never doubted that Russell Dobbs knew what it was, and that he had seen it before.

Lee had heard talk, back then, that Dobbs drew the devil to him like fire drawn to tinder, some said that Dobbs had made a bargain with Satan, but others claimed that Dobbs, having beat the devil in a wager, would never be shut of him. Whatever the truth, in the pasture that morning, Lee's grandpappy had been not only afraid, but angry.

After the steer and the horses had settled down, had stopped fidgeting and staring and gone to grazing again, and after his grandpappy had turned away, that was when Lee, still shaken, had turned and seen the yellow cat standing in the door of the barn watching him—and watching the empty prairie beyond, the cat's back humped, its yellow fur standing up stiff, its golden eyes blazing.

That yellow cat had been afraid of nothing. Lee had liked that tomcat that would kill a rat as big as itself and, fast as lightning, could kill a rattlesnake—the yellow tomcat that was a dead ringer for the McNeil prison cat, for the cat that had slept on Lee's bunk last night keeping him company after his visitor had vanished, the ragged and battered creature he wished was here now, beside him, to ease his fear of that little blue-eyed man, to calm the chill that, like a finger of ice, seemed lodged in Lee's very soul.

5

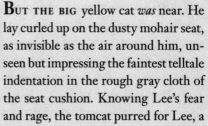

BUT THE BIG yellow cat *was* near. He lay curled up on the dusty mohair seat, as invisible as the air around him, unseen but impressing the faintest telltale indentation in the rough gray cloth of the seat cushion. Knowing Lee's fear and rage, the tomcat purred for Lee, a subliminal song too faint for Fontana to consciously hear, but a sound the cat knew Lee would hear deep inside himself, a purr that matched the rhythm of the rocking train, a rough-throated mutter of comfort meant to ease Lee's soul, a rumble generated not only by love but by the joy of life itself that, even in his ethereal form, the ghost cat carried with him.

But now Misto purred out of discomfort, too, out of concern for the old convict. A cat will purr not only when he's happy, he purrs when he's frightened or distressed. A mortal cat will deliberately purr to himself when he's hurt or sick, a muttering song to hold on to, perhaps to calm himself, to make himself feel less alone. Now Misto purred for Lee, wanting to hold him steady, wanting to drive away the old cowboy's sense of that little man's glinting, blue-eyed presence, to rid Lee of the evil that kept returning seeking to terrify or to win him, grasping hungrily for Lee's soul.

The blue-eyed man was gone now, the incubus was gone, his black leather briefcase gone, too, the satchel he'd left behind on the seat when he followed Lee out to the vestibule. The moment he'd vanished from the train, the briefcase had dissolved, poof, as completely as a mouse might disappear into the tomcat's sharp-toothed gulp. But though the man and his briefcase were no more, an aura of evil still drifted within the passenger car, a miasma as caustic as smoke, touching the other passengers, too. A sleeping man woke and stared up the aisle and twisted to look behind him, studying his companions, scowling at the tightly closed doors at either end of the car. Up at the front, a woman laid down her book and half rose up, looking around nervously. Two women stood up from their seats staring all around, seeking the source of whatever had made them shiver. Two seats behind Lee, a toddler climbed into his mother's lap howling out his own sense of fear. And beside Misto, Lee Fontana sat unmoving, still pale from the encounter in the vestibule, still edgy with the sense of the dark spirit that he knew wouldn't leave him alone, with the devil's curse that would continue to follow Dobbs's descendants.

Lee knew only rough details of the plan Satan had laid out for Dobbs's heirs those many years ago. He knew only what he'd heard rumored among his neighbors, back on the ranch. Gossip that, when Lee entered the room, would make folks go silent. Stories that the devil had set

Dobbs up to destroy a certain gang of brothers, but that during the train robbery as the devil planned it, Dobbs had turned the tables on Satan. That Dobbs's deception had so enraged the devil, he had sworn to destroy every Dobbs heir, to force or entice each Dobbs descendant to drive their own souls into the flames, into the pit of hell itself. To destroy the soul of each, but particularly that of Lee Fontana who had so idolized the old train robber. As far as Lee knew, he might be Dobbs's last heir, all Satan's vindication against Dobbs's supposed double cross could be focused, now, on Lee.

As the train slowed for the station ahead, Misto increased his purr, singing to Lee to soothe him; and as they pulled out again with barely time to take on one lone passenger, the cat purred until Lee settled back and dozed again; and beside him the ghost cat closed his eyes, lulled by the train's rocking rumble.

The ghost cat did not need to sleep, sleep was a healing gift left over from life, a skill comforting and warm but not needed in the spirit world—a talent the newly released ghost must reconstruct from memory, must willfully summon back until he established the habit once more, if he chose to do so, if he wanted that earthly comfort. The yellow ghost cat had so chosen and, drifting now toward sleep, he purred to comfort himself as well as to comfort Lee.

The tomcat didn't know what woke him. He rose suddenly, startled, half asleep. He shook himself and quickly left Lee's side, drifting out through the wall of the passenger car, leaving a warm dent in the seat behind him. For a moment he rode the wind giddily, lashing his tail as he peered back in through the dirty window watching Lee, the cat gliding with pleasure alongside the speeding train, and then he somersaulted up to the roof, banking on the wind as agile as a soaring gull.

Landing lightly atop the speeding train, he settled down, still invisible, looking about at the world speeding by him, at the green fields beneath the snowcapped mountains and, off to his right, miles of green pasture and the dull and gentle cows; and they had left the dark, cold waters of Puget Sound behind them. But now, in the cat's thoughts, he saw not the land that swept past the train, he saw back into a time long past, before ever that vast inland sea had formed, when all the land was dry, he saw into eons past, as it had been, saw a higher and mountainous shore, densely wooded, skirting the Pacific, a raised land with no hint of the deep bowl that would later be carved there to hold the deep waters of Puget Sound. He saw the great glacier to the north, easing slowly down over vast reaches of time, slowly scooping the land away, a gigantic beast of ice slithering and creeping down from the great northern ranges.

He saw a million years of time slip by as the glacier slowly toppled the ancient conifers and crushed them and dug away the land, as it dug the vast trench that would slowly fill with the waters of the sea and of the coastal rivers. He saw millions of years pass by, dwarfing all life into a speck smaller than the tiniest sneeze.

He shivered at the vastness of time, at the vastness of the earth itself, and at the short and tenuous span of life upon it. He perceived, as well as anyone could, that richly varied panorama of life forming and changing, that short span of the arrival of human life, of human evil and human good. He sensed as much of the grand design as his eager cat soul could embrace; but even so, he saw only a small portion of the grandeur which swept away to infinity, the vastness which no creature could truly comprehend.

Atop the train, the cat sensed when Lee woke. He knew when Lee sat up and looked around him, as the train pulled into the next small station. He knew Lee had been dreaming and that he was shaken, that he had experienced again an incident at McNeil that had greatly angered the old man. At once the cat returned to the passenger car, a whirl of air sweeping in through the dirty glass and onto the dusty seat: he was at once caught in Lee's rage, in the aftermath of the prison rape in which Lee had faced off young Brad Falon.

Falon, a surly man less than half Lee's age, had been Lee's enemy ever since that encounter.

He had been Misto's enemy far longer, yet for very different reasons. The tomcat had yet to make sense of the pattern between the two conflicts, but he knew that in some way they were linked together.

When Misto left McNeil for that short time after he died and was buried in the prison yard, he had fallen into a new life almost at once, he was born in a small Southern town, a squirming and energetic kitten who was soon picked from the big, healthy litter to be given as a birthday present to little Sammie Blake. He had grown up loved by the little girl and loving her, had grown into a strong, defiant big tomcat when he found himself protecting Sammie against Brad Falon and was murdered by Falon's hand.

Falon had been the cat's adversary in Misto's last life, and he was bonded in some indecipherable way to Lee himself and to what would happen to Lee. There was a pattern building, a tangle the cat could as yet barely see, a relationship between Lee, and Brad Falon, and Misto's little girl—the tomcat had yet to make sense of the pattern, but he didn't like it much.

Sammie was five when her daddy brought the tiny yellow kitten home to her, just before he was sent overseas in the Second World War. Sammie's mama worked as a bookkeeper in their little town of Rome, Georgia, and their small rented house seemed very empty, once Morgan had gone. Empty, and then soon vulnerable. The minute Morgan Blake left for the navy, Becky's and Morgan's old schoolmate began to come around, uninvited. Brad Falon was a well-muscled, pushy young man. In high school he had run with Morgan, but Becky had never liked him. Now he began to annoy Becky, coming to the door, frightening Sammie with his cold eyes and slippery talk. Becky never let him in, but he kept coming. The late night he came there drunk, pounding on the locked door, not beseeching anymore but demanding to be let in, and then breaking in, it was Misto who drove him off.

As Brad broke a window, reached in and unlocked it, Becky ran to the phone. Falon knocked out most of the glass, and swung through. He grabbed the phone from Becky, threw it against the wall. When little Sammie flew at him, he hit her hard against the table. He shoved Becky to the floor and knelt over her, hitting her and pulling up her skirt. As Becky yelled at Sammie to run, the big yellow cat exploded from the bedroom, landing in Falon's face raking and biting him. Brad tried to pull him off then flicked open his pocketknife.

The cat fought him, dodging the knife. Becky grabbed

a shard of broken glass and flew at Falon. He hit her, had her down again, cutting her. The cat was on him again when a neighbor heard their screams and came running; the wiry old fellow saw the broken window and climbed through, but already Falon had fled, banging out through the front door.

Behind him, Misto lay dying from a long, gaping wound that bled too fast, that bled away his life before anyone could help him. But even as Falon fled, Misto's ghost rose and followed. He followed as Falon dodged the police, gained his car and took off fast heading out of Rome, heading for Atlanta. The Rome cops didn't like Falon, they wouldn't be gentle if they caught him, nor would the county D.A. Some of the younger officers, having gone through school with Falon, observing the trouble he had caused all those years, might indeed have turned to law enforcement careers in an effort to right the wrongs of the world.

At the airport south of Atlanta Falon bought a plane ticket and an hour later, nervously drinking coffee from a paper cup, he boarded a flight for the West Coast, where he had connections who could be useful in whatever venture he chose to pursue. As Falon settled into the dusty seat in the DC-4, Misto drifted into the plane and settled unseen beside him, not too close, but unwilling to lose sight of him.

Falon had friends in a number of West Coast cities. Why, the cat wondered, had he headed for Seattle? Had that urge been formed simply at Falon's random choice? Or, by Satan's wishes? Why Seattle, not twenty miles from where Lee was doing federal time at McNeil? The ghost cat couldn't pretend to understand the forces at work here, but Falon's destination distressed him. Lee had no connection to Falon, and no connection to Georgia where Falon had grown up. Lee might have no family left anywhere, as far as he knew. He had lived his life on the run, had left the home ranch as a hot-tempered sixteen-year-old, and had not kept in touch with his relatives.

Misto, even in his ghostly state, couldn't know everything. There was, however, the one puzzling link: the mirrorlike resemblance between Lee's little sister, Mae, and little Sammie Blake. Mae Fontana, born a lifetime ago, before Sammie, whose old tintype picture, taken at their South Dakota ranch, Lee had carried with him all these years, in and out of prison, the picture he still carried among his meager belongings. Two little girls more alike than twins, the exact same wide brown eyes, same little heart-shaped faces, same dimples cleaving deep, the same crooked smiles, the same long pale hair so painful to comb free of tangles. Two little girls from two different centuries, more alike than twins could be. Misto had known of no connection between Lee and Mae, and Sammie. Until now, when in some inexplicable manner Brad Falon formed the connection.

When Falon killed Misto, when Misto rose as ghost to follow Falon out to the West Coast, Falon soon committed a bank robbery in which he shot a guard in the leg. He was tried, summarily convicted in federal court, and was sent from Seattle to the nearest federal prison, at McNeil Island. Though his sentence was shorter than the U.S. attorney would have liked, there was no question in the ghost cat's mind that forces beyond his ken had brought Falon and Lee together.

Did the dark spirit, with his persistent hatred of Lee's ancestor, mean to use Falon against Russell Dobbs's grandson, against the failing old man? But how was little

Sammie a part of his plan, this child so like Lee's sister? If she were in some unknown way also a descendant of Russell Dobbs, then she, too, would be in danger.

When, at McNeil, Lee's emphysema grew worse on cold, damp days, but then he felt good again when sunshine warmed the island, he grew increasingly desperate about his old age, grew more determined to pull off one more job when he got out; he did not mean to face his failing years with nothing to support himself.

With sympathy the cat remained near him. Misto was witness when, not a week after Falon arrived at McNeil, the prison rape occurred that so enraged Lee, the conflict between Lee and Falon playing, clearly, into the dark web Lee's adversary was weaving. As Lee confronted younger, stronger Falon, did the dark spirit expect Falon to kill Lee? More in keeping with the devil's plans, the cat thought, would be that Lee kill Falon in a passion of unbridled rage that would destroy Lee's own salvation.

Or was the confrontation between Falon and Lee intended to lay some pattern for the future, for a plan that would prove even more satisfying to the dark one? Though Misto could move back and forth within short periods of time, when it came to the complicated shape of the distant and tangled future, he was as lost as if trying to swim the heaving depths of Puget Sound.

But whatever the devil's purpose in bringing Lee and Falon together, it was surely no accident, and the yellow tom grew increasingly wary for Lee—just as he worried for Sammie herself, who was somehow entangled with Lee's own destiny.

6

AFTER LEE'S ENCOUNTER with Brad
Falon he'd found himself watching
the shadows more carefully, and he
didn't like this kind of fear. He had
been headed for the laundry that afternoon, had started to cut through
the exercise room when he saw half a
dozen jocks in there pumping iron. One of them, a new
arrival, had eyes as cold as a hunting vulture. Brad Falon
had already gathered a cluster of followers around him,
and Lee didn't want to mess with him. His good sense told
him to turn back and go a different way, to avoid trouble,
but he stubbornly pushed on in. Afterward, hours later, he
wondered why he'd done that. The men watched him
expressionlessly from where they worked the weights, the
press, their rhythm never ceasing but their eyes never
leaving him, their stripped bodies sleek with sweat. Lee
moved on past, knowing this wasn't smart, feeling Falon's
stare and not liking it. When, behind him, the rhythm of

the weight machine stopped, he tightened his grip on the knife in his pocket, didn't falter or let his glance flicker.

He entered the auto shop skirting a battered touring car set up on blocks waiting for a rebirth. No one entered behind him, and he could still hear the steady rhythm of the exercise equipment. Passing the touring car—a badly dented relic, one fender twisted, paint peeling over heavy rust, cloth top in tatters—he heard a faint moan.

Beyond the car against the wall lay a power sprayer beside half a dozen cans of paint. A motor block hung suspended from chains over a greasy tarp. He heard the moan again, a wrenching cry from among a stack of cardboard cartons. He glanced back toward the exercise room, then moved fast.

Behind the boxes lay a young inmate curled into the fetal position, his face covered by his pulled-up shirt, his naked ribs sucking in quick, shallow breaths. Bloody scratches covered his back. Lee had seen him around the prison yard. Randy Sanderford, a clean-faced boy doing three for an identity scam. His pants and shorts had been pulled down around his ankles, his blue shirt jerked over his face and mouth, likely muffling his yells. Bright red blood and semen spread from his rectum down his inner thighs.

Lee lifted and half carried him to the shower between the shop and the exercise room. Now he could sense a stirring among the jocks. The machines were silent. Listening warily, he stripped Randy down and turned the warm water on him, shoved the lye soap at him, told him to scrub, and where to scrub. The youngster hadn't spoken. He gripped the soap, shivering, began to wash, wincing at the pain. Above the shower Lee could hear the men moving around again, heard the outer door pop air as it closed. Randy whimpered once, then was quiet. Lee stood watching him, filled with rage at the useless jocks but with rage at the kid, too, for being so stupid, for letting this happen to him. The water stopped at last. Randy came out shivering. Blood still flowed, thinned by the water on his body. The boy stared at Lee, frightened and ashamed.

"What did you do, go in there to work out with that bunch? No one has to tell me this is your first time in the joint."

The boy began to cry.

"I'm going to tell you something, Sanderford. When you come into a place like this you'd better have one of two things with you, an ice pick or a jar of Vaseline. You're going to need one or the other."

Randy dried himself off with his shirt, staining it with blood. "I just came down to work out, I didn't . . . I was working the bench press when they grabbed me . . ." His face flushed.

"What the hell did you think would happen? You thought they were just a bunch of nice guys in there working out, that you'd waltz in, introduce yourself, and you'd all be friends?"

Randy looked so shamefaced that Lee wanted to smash him. Didn't the kid have any sense? Where the hell had he been all his life? What had he learned in his twenty-some years? "Hell, Sanderford. These prison turks aren't little kids playing dirty games in the barn." The baby-faced kid looked like he'd never been anywhere, like he'd had his nose wiped all his life by his rich mama. Sanderford wiped his mouth and smoothed back his hair.

"These men don't just rape, Sanderford. They'd think nothing more of killing you than of crushing a cockroach." Lee stared down at his own clenched fists, stifling an alarming desire to work Sanderford over, to beat the hell out of the kid, beat some sense into him. Shocked by his own rage, he stared hard at Sanderford, and turned away.

He had no reason to feel this boiling rage, this wasn't his normal response to a dumb kid, this kind of anger. He stood puzzled, watching Sanderford pull on his clothes. "You'd better do some thinking, kid, better decide how you're going to stay out of trouble in here, how you're going to defend yourself if you mean to survive in this joint." Trying to get his anger under control, Lee saw again Brad Falon's stare, felt again the cold threat, was so enraged that heavy coughing rose up in his sick lungs, choking him.

He walked Sanderford back to his cell, got him there in time for the afternoon count. He traded a pack of cigarettes to a reliable inmate for a small bottle of iodine, and paid a second pack to get the iodine smuggled in to Sanderford. Lee didn't smoke, the coffin nails were for trading. Tired and irritable, he went on to his own cell and lay on his bunk coughing and spitting up phlegm. The day hadn't started out good, and the next days didn't get any better. He was sick enough, the doc pulled him off farmwork for a week. Sanderford followed Lee like a lost puppy, after he was raped. The kid was grateful, but mostly he wanted protection. And, whether Randy was following him or not, Lee would catch Falon watching him from across the yard, a calculating coldness that made him want to waste Falon. He felt a threat from the man that wasn't just prison fear and wariness. Something more, as if the very shadows where Falon sometimes stood, watched him, too. And Falon's derision was magnified when Sanderford was hanging around. Lee sent Randy packing twice, but the kid kept coming back. He had lost patience when Sanderford, in desperation, began laying out scams to him.

Some of the moves were new to Lee, they were good ones and he found himself listening. The kid seemed to know his way around businesses and banks, though his easy life hadn't taught him much else. A dropout from UC Berkeley, whose pronounced heart murmur had kept him out of the service, the kid had disowned his family, hating their values, hating everything he called the establishment. He had blown the money his father gave him on women and on three expensive cars that he demolished one after the other while drunk. For kicks, he began ripping off the colleges his father forced him to enter. When he got into big trouble at Cal, his father at last threw him out and cut off his allowance. Within a week Randy had gotten a job as salesman at a small jewelry store. Within six months he had taken the owner for ninety thousand dollars and disappeared. Then, while living on the interest from the ninety thousand, he began ripping off banks. The boy had talent, Lee gave him that. He was clever and inventive, and Lee tucked away the scams for future use. If things were real changed on the outside, if he couldn't pull the kind of job he had in mind, maybe he'd have a go at the traveler's check operation.

"All you have," Randy said, "is the little transaction

slip you get from the first bank, with the numbers of the traveler's checks on it, to show the second bank.

"Two things are important at the second bank, the way you give your sob story, and the bank's willingness to please without checking out your story. You have to be subtle. Honest and quiet, and not too quick with the charm." Lee thought Sanderford, with that innocent face and big blue eyes, would have little trouble conning some young teller.

"I always pick large, busy banks in big cities," Randy said. "They want your business, they'll bend over backward to please the customer. If you need a few hundred bucks, that's the way to do it." The boy gave Lee an innocent smile. "Good idea, though, to have false ID. The second bank always wants to see something." He shrugged. "I've never been questioned. Every time, I just walked out of there cool as you please with the cash in my hand."

But Sanderford had been arrested and imprisoned for a different kind of forgery that, Randy said himself, was amateurish and stupid. He had been so intent on the convertible he had stolen that he had let his attempt to cash a simple forged check trap him, he said he never would have stolen the car in the first place if he hadn't been drunk. Lee thought maybe if Sanderford left the booze alone he'd make a first-rate con man. But Lee didn't like the kid. Sanderford was intelligent, very bright. But if he hated the world so much, why didn't he give up the booze, knuckle down, and *really* milk the humanity he despised? Watching the baby-faced boy, Lee felt only disgust for him.

7

THE ROCKING RHYTHM of the train and the stuffy heat of the car put Lee to sleep again in a luxury of malaise. He had no need to wake and hustle around, no prison job to go to, no lockdown time to think about, not even a set mealtime. He woke and ate his sandwich, and when the vendor came around, he bought another for later. He slept and woke as he chose, enjoying his freedom, looking out the window at the green pastures and at the long orchard rows fanning by so fast they dizzied him if he looked too long. Or looking down at the streets and into the windows of the small towns where the train crept through, or out at the boxcars crowded into the freight yards, and then as they gained speed once more he'd ease back, soothed by the green hills, or by the climb into the dark and wooded mountains, the train rocking and tilting, taking the narrow curves. He liked traveling, liked moving on, he liked the speed that made him feel suspended in time, with nothing to stop him or fret him.

Nothing except that sometimes when he woke he had dreamed dark dreams, would come awake planning crimes that were not his kind of brutality, actions against others that disgusted him, would wake to ugly suggestions and to the hoary presence that wouldn't leave him alone, that was more real than any dream. But then sometimes he'd wake feeling easier and was aware of the prison cat beside him, lying warm and invisible on the seat next to him—nothing to see, the seat empty except for his sandwich wrapper and his spread-out newspapers. But the cat was there, curled next to him. Reaching into the empty space, Lee could feel his warmth, and when he could feel the rough, thick texture of the tomcat's fur, and when he stroked the ghost cat, a gentle paw pulled his hand down closer, the big invisible tom enjoying the stroking just as much as he had in real life.

Lee told himself he imagined the cat, and that he'd imagined the dark presence in his dreams and in his cell that last night, told himself he had only imagined the evil in that puny little blue-eyed salesman. But he knew he had imagined none of it. He knew what he'd seen, that both the ghost cat and that chill shadow were more than real as they followed him onto the train.

He was happy to have the cat, he was good company, a friendly and comforting spirit to steady and embolden him. But he didn't need his darker traveling companion. Spirit, haunt, whatever you'd name him, Lee knew it was the same unworldly presence that had tormented his grandpappy when Lee was a boy. He didn't need this chill spirit that had made a bargain with old Russell Dobbs and for which Lee himself was now being prodded—being pushed toward the devil's due, as some might call it, that the dark spirit seemed to think he deserved.

IT WAS MAY of 1882 when Russell Dobbs, in the line of his work, relieved the Indiana Flyer of ten thousand dollars' worth of gold bullion just north of Camrose, South Dakota. Stopping the train where it slowed at a curve, Russell boarded with his partner, Samil Hook. Samil was a little man, wiry, and a crack shot. Dobbs towered over him, muscular and rough shaven. Between them they took down the conductor and the four crew members, left them tied in the express car while they loaded eight canvas bags of gold bullion into a small spring wagon.

Leaving the train, the two men separated. Samil drove the wagon, keeping to the deep woods along a narrow timber trail to a cabin hidden in a stand of pine trees ten miles north of Agar. Russell didn't worry that Samil would double-cross him, Samil feared Russell with a passion far more powerful than greed. Samil knew Russell wouldn't kill a train man if he could avoid it, but that he would kill a friend who deceived him as casually as shooting a rabbit for his breakfast.

Leaving Samil and the wagon, Russell rode alone to Cliffordsville where he holed up in the Miner's Hotel. The proprietress always took a keen pleasure in sheltering him. She would swear he had been there for better than a week. It was the next morning, early, one of the bartenders came to Mattie Lou's door to tell Russell a gentleman, a stranger, was asking for him.

As far as Russell knew, no one but Mattie Lou had

seen him slip in through the back entry, and Mattie Lou had told no one. He finished dressing, strapped on his gun belt, and went down the back stairs so as to come on the visitor from behind.

Halfway down, a man stood in the shadows of the landing. City clothes, fancy dark suit, embroidered cravat, soft black pigskin gloves—and the gleam of metal as his hand slipped inside his coat. Russell drew, fired twice point-blank, close enough to blow out the side of a barn.

The man didn't fall.

Russell saw no wound, no blood. The stranger eased up the stairs never taking his eyes from Russell, his Colt .36 revolver fixed on Russell as steadily as his smile. Russell fired three more rounds, again hitting the man square in the belly. Again, he didn't fall, didn't jerk, didn't seem to feel the impact.

"Perhaps by now, Russell, you have guessed who I am?"

Russell had seen his bullets enter a man and disappear into nowhere. Hadn't seen them strike anything behind the man. He fired again knowing the impact should put the man down, knowing it wouldn't. He looked toward the hotel lobby expecting that people would have heard the shots.

"No one can hear us, Russell."

"What the hell are you?"

"I think you know what I am."

Russell wasn't a religious man. If the way he lived sent him to hell, so be it. But he sure hadn't expected hell to come seeking him. "What do you want?"

"I want your help. In exchange, of course, I offer you a gift."

Russell waited.

"I can give you freedom from death and injury, I can make you impervious to any wound including those caused by a knife or bullet."

Russell had heard that old saw around a dozen campfires. But the man smiled. "Maybe you have heard it, Russell. This time, it's no tall story. Freedom from sickness, too. From pain. From death by any weapon. Freedom to live in health until you are an old, old man."

"An old man? How old?"

"Past eighty."

In those days, fifty was a respectable age. Russell waited. The man straightened his cravat, leaned comfortably against the hotel wall, and laid out his proposition.

"There are two families, brothers. The Vickerses and the Loves. Bad blood between them. With every coast-to-coast train worth taking down, it's a standoff who gets in position first to rob it."

"I know all that."

"Last week, the Loves robbed the mail train out of Topeka. The law was on their tail, and they had half a dozen lookouts when they buried the gold. Meant to return for it that night. The Vickerses found it, dug it up, then turned Lem and Cleve Love in to Pinkerton." The man smiled. "They did it to cut down the competition. You can imagine how that inflamed the feud."

"So?" Russell watched him warily.

"Cage Vickers is the only one in his family who doesn't steal. Some kind of throwback, maybe. Whatever his problem, he's pure as a newborn. And," he said, smiling, "he's fallen for Tessa Love, he means to marry her."

Russell turned away. This was of no interest to him. "I have a friend waiting."

He was stopped cold, couldn't move, he couldn't touch his gun in the holster.

The stranger continued. "Neither family would allow him to marry Tessa. He's decided to get rid of them all, to kill them all, including his own brothers. He tells himself they're all without virtue, that he'd be doing the world a favor."

Again Russell tried to move, but he was locked in a grip as tight as if he'd been turned to stone.

"When the next big gold shipment comes through out of California, heading east, Cage plans to set up both families to be caught red-handed when they try to stop the freight. Once they're locked up and convicted—he's hoping safe behind bars, on long sentences—he means to marry Tessa, leave this part of the country, and vanish."

"Fine. Then the trains will all be mine."

"I don't want that, I've taken a lot of trouble manipulating the Midwestern railroads. Through the right people in Washington I've been able to infuriate every settler who thought he was going to buy railroad land for a dollar an acre, I've worked to increase the land prices, to foment a strike against the railroad that has escalated into a small civil war. It's already cost the railroads a nice sum, and the public, enraged by the government railway, has turned to protecting the train robbers. No," he said, smiling, "I like things just as I have them, I want no change, I don't want the gangs stopped, I want Cage Vickers stopped. I don't like his plan. I want Vickers brought down."

"So do it, you're the one with the power." Trying again vainly to move his feet or to reach the butt of his gun though he doubted a bullet would faze the apparition.

"I can't stop him, the stupid boy is totally pure, he can't see me, can't hear me, he's beyond my influence."

Russell scowled. "I'm sure you'll find a way."

"I can't change events. I can only influence the players—some of them. There has to be a respectable amount of evil in a man before I can reach him."

"Hell, I'm not killing Cage Vickers, if that's what you want. And I'd be a fool to try to warn his brothers or the Loves. Any one of them would fill me full of holes."

The visitor waited.

"I gather this bargain wouldn't take effect until after I'd done the deed. That your protection of my life wouldn't begin until I'd already risked my neck for you."

"That is so. However, if you don't stop Cage Vickers, I'll take great pleasure, when the time of your death arrives, in seeing you suffer, eternally, in ways you can't yet imagine."

Russell said nothing.

"With the bargain I offer, you will have a long, pain-free, and profitable life, any kind of life you choose—youth and wealth and beautiful women, enviable power and superb health.

"You have only to stop Cage Vickers, see that none of the brothers are apprehended, and not go to the law yourself.

"If you refuse my bargain, I have within my power many creative ways to annoy and harass you for the remainder of your miserable life, runaway horses, train conductors who are fast and accurate and lust for blood, women who, once you have made love to them, feel an overwhelming desire to maim you as you lie sleeping beside them. Little things, Russell, accomplished through the minds of others, but oh, so effective."

Russell remembered stories of multiple calamities that beset some men over an entire lifetime, innocent men saddled with strings of disasters that defied all laws of probability.

"If you work with me," the dark spirit said, "you will know no sickness, no wound or pain, no bullet will ever touch you, you will not die of any cause until you are an old, old man and still healthy and vigorous. Even then, your death will be peaceful, no pain and no fear."

"And in exchange," Russell said, "I stop Cage Vickers from getting the Loves and the Vickerses arrested, so they can go on robbing trains. That seems simple enough."

"That is the bargain."

Russell was a born gambler, that's what robbing the trains was all about. But he'd never played for stakes like these. "Under what circumstances," he said softly, "would you consider that I had bested you?"

"Under no circumstances. If you do as I say, that won't happen."

"If Cage's plan fails, if neither family takes the train down successfully and no one of either family is arrested, I would be free of you?"

"You would."

"And you would uphold your bargain."

He nodded.

"Would you throw in that Cage and Tessa marry anyway, and live long and happy lives together, without the ire or retribution of either family?"

"Why would I do that? I told you that my powers are limited. I can only influence, I can't twist fate."

Russell looked back at him and kept his thoughts locked tight inside himself. He received so penetrating a look in return that he had to fight to keep from glancing away. He stared at the stranger until suddenly the figure vanished. The stair and alley lay empty.

Russell stood in the alley shivering. And slowly considering his options.

His question had not been answered. He had no real promise from the stranger. He thought about that a long time, then at last he turned and made his way back up the stairs, to his lady friend.

8

THE TRAIN BUCKED and slowed, waking Lee as the conductor hurried through calling out, "Centralia. Five minutes." Straightening up, he watched out the window as the mailbags were heaved off. Two passengers descended from the car ahead, hurrying inside the long, red-roofed brick building, then almost at once they were pulling out again, the white peak of Mount Saint Helens towering bright, to his left, against the heavy gray sky, bringing half a dozen passengers rushing to Lee's side of the train to look. But soon Lee slept again, only vaguely aware of the frequent hollow rumbles as the train crossed the railroad bridges that spanned Washington's swift rivers. When the sour smell of caged chickens filled the train, passing through Winlock, he looked out at the long, ugly rows of wooden chicken houses and, beyond them, a tractor and trailer spreading chicken manure on the vegetable fields. Not a job he'd want, not mired in that smell all day.

Soon, dozing, he woke again when they skirted the Columbia, the river's giant rafts of logs moving below him, down toward Lake Vancouver headed for the sawmills. How would it be to settle down here along the shore somewhere in a little shack, get some sort of job, maybe taking care of someone's horses, forget his grand plans for a hefty robbery and for that life-sustaining nest egg? Forget his urge to take on the feds one last time, to outsmart them once and for good? Along the green of the marsh, the train's approach sent restless flocks of shorebirds exploding up into the sour mist, sweeping away beneath low, heavy clouds. There'd be a twenty-minute stop at Portland, where Lee thought to get off and stretch his aching legs. Sitting too long stove him up like a stall-bound cowpony that was never let out to run.

It was stormy coming into Portland, the afternoon sky darkening, the streets slick with rain. Ignoring the drizzle, he moved out into the train's vestibule where he could get a good look. The streets were busy with fast, slick cars, so many of them, kicking up water along the gutters, streets lined with impressive new buildings sandwiched in between the comfortable old brick-and-stone structures from an earlier time. The train slowed approaching the three-story station, its peaked roof and the tall, handsome clock tower stark against the gray sky. But far ahead beyond the city, light streaked the sky where the storm looked to be clearing, to be moving on north passing over the train. The station lights glowed, the neon signs announcing, UNION STATION. GO BY TRAIN. Stepping back to his seat, he made sure his wrapped sandwiches were in plain sight on his two seats atop his neatly arranged newspapers, hoping to mark his occupancy.

Moving down the metal steps and into the station, he stood staring around the vast terminal, looking up at the high, domed ceiling towering above him, at its soaring structure of curved and interlaced crossbeams. The sound of other trains departing and arriving was only background to the loudspeaker's harsh and metallic commands. People hurried past him talking quickly, hauling luggage, shouting to others ahead of them. When he didn't move out of the way, they shouldered past him, scowling, busy travelers louder and more intense than a crowd of inmates, and way less disciplined. Women laughing, folks in little clusters talking frantically, kids running in and out between them not caring if they stepped on your feet. He wandered, pushing through, battered and pummeled. Maybe he should have stayed in his seat, quiet and away from people. Feeling in his pocket to be sure he had his ticket, he at last retreated into a small tobacco shop, a crowded little cubicle.

The smell of the rich tobacco was homey and welcoming though he'd never smoked or chewed, a heady scent that stirred something from the past he couldn't place. A woman stood behind the little counter, one hand on the cash register. Young, skinny, red hair to her shoulders, freckles heavy across her nose and cheeks. A baby in a carriage behind the counter, tucked up in its blue blanket and, when he glanced down over the counter, a little girl sitting on the floor playing with a set of jacks. He felt embarrassed coming in here when he didn't mean to buy anything.

"To get out of the crowd," he said shyly, looking at the young woman. "Too many people out there."

At the sound of his voice the child behind the counter looked up at him. Her gaze never wavering, she stood up clutching the edge of the counter, staring up at him with a steady, bold look that shocked him. Her look was so like his little sister Mae's, that he took a step back. Well, she didn't look like Mae, she had carroty red hair like her mother, a pale, freckled face that would have burned easily in that long-ago South Dakota sun. But beneath the child's black lashes, her brown eyes proffered the same challenging gaze as Mae's bold assessment: curious about him, unafraid but with a look deeper down that said if anyone reached to hurt her she'd kick and bite as desperately as a roped mustang. A look that put him in mind of the first time he put Mae on the back of a horse, a small old cowpony, back behind the hay barn where their mother wouldn't see. He'd started to lead her along, walking beside her, holding her firmly in the saddle—with disdain she had taken the reins from his hand, pushed him away, kneed the cowpony as if she'd done that all her life, and moved on out at a nice fast walk, legs and heels where they should be though her feet didn't reach the stirrups, a nice easy seat that told him she'd been watching the cowmen since she was big enough to look out the window, that she had absorbed what she wanted from them and didn't want his interference. Though later, learning to rein a cowpony, spinning him, hopping over logs, opening gates and then learning to rope, she'd listened and followed what he showed her.

This child wasn't anything like Mae but the same strong spirit was there in her eyes and a belated grieving hit him, a terrible longing for his small sister that nearly undid him. He bought two candy bars from the young mother, where she kept a little shelf of treats and a few

magazines among the cigars and cigarettes and cans of to-
bacco and bags of Dull Durham. He left the shop quickly.
When, once, he looked back, the child was still staring.
He hurried on to the train, hoping his seat wasn't taken.

LEE DOZED OUT of Portland, dreaming of his childhood
and of those early days when he left home at sixteen, horse
and saddle and a few coins in his pocket, going out on
his own. Leaving his little sister behind, and that was the
last he ever saw or heard of her. He didn't know why he
hadn't kept in touch, written to her once in a while. He
was young and hotheaded and too busy making his own
life, trying to survive among grown men, some of them
cruel as a hungry buzzard. He knew Mae was all right,
there at home, and he knew she could take care of herself.

He woke to darkened windows, night drawing down.
He ate another ham sandwich and the two candy bars. The
few farm lights he could see far off were dim and scattered.
The passengers around him snoozed, lulled by the train's
hypnotic rhythm. The crowding of strangers together into
a protected metal womb that raced free across the dark
land seemed strange and unreal, as if they were all caught
in the same inexplicable dream. The passengers around
him had pulled on sweaters, opened their traveling bags to
strew jackets and personal belongings out across the few
empty seats. The little toddler up front seemed the most
alive, whining and squirming. When the boy made a bad
smell, his mother grabbed him up, snatched up her carry-
all, and hurried him off to the restroom. That stink, mixed
with the stale-sandwich smell and the gathering odor of
stale sweat, grew so heavy that at last Lee returned to the

vestibule, where he could breathe, stood looking out at the night, sucking in the good cold wind.

He remained there alone, wary that the invasive shadow would return, but more caught up in the long-ago nights of the past when he rode balanced on a galloping train, waiting for the moment when he would enter the engineer's car, force the frightened man to stop the train, when he and his partner would tie up the engineer and the one or two guards, would relieve them of the mail and money bags, would step down again into the night and be gone before their victims could free themselves.

He remained in the vestibule until he was freezing, then headed back to his seat. Buttoning his jacket tight, he settled down, pulling the newspapers over him. When sleep took him, no dark spirit bothered him; waking sometimes, he saw only his reflection in the glass, against black emptiness—but then he woke suddenly to see the moon had risen, and he sat up startled, staring out.

A foreign land lay beyond the glass, a nightmare vision as twisted and unnatural as the face of the moon or of some distant and virulent planet: moonstruck lava ridges rising up twisted into phantasmic shapes casting unearthly shadows around them, towering, twisted specters sprung from bare earth where no tree, no bush, or blade could survive, only those monstrous twists of rising stone formed eons ago, by the ancient volcanoes that still marched across this land and north into Canada. The stark remnant of times long past held him, too fascinated to look away. How long he watched he wasn't sure before he felt suddenly the weight of the ghost cat pressing against him, warm against his jacket, and could hear him purring. When he looked down, Misto was there looking up at him; the ghost cat twitched a whisker, making Lee smile.

Did Misto mean to travel with him clear to his destination, clear to Blythe? Lee hoped that was his intention, though he didn't know why the big yellow tom would want to head for that parched desert, he didn't know why Misto was so determined to stay with him. Whatever the reason, the security of the big tomcat eased him—a bold guardian against the dark thoughts that too often pushed and prodded at him. Lee was learning to depend on that steadying sense of rightness that the burly beast lent him, that sense of stubborn protection that Lee found so comforting.

Misto dozed warm and close against Lee, purring as the cat idly dipped into his own memories, into thoughts of his own past lives. He thought about Lee and Mae as children, and then remembered lives lived long before that one, recalling dark medieval times when cats were thought to be witches' familiars, when he had barely escaped murder as one of these, and he remembered another time when he hadn't escaped, when he had been hanged with the so-called witch beside him, a lovely, dark-haired young woman whose spirit, too, had moved on into a happier realm.

How variable the fate of cats, and of their consorts, over the centuries, from those times of bloody cruelty, to the luxuriant idolatry a pampered cat knew in ancient Egypt. How indecipherable the vicissitudes of time, how mysterious the meaning of life for all living creatures. Drifting off into sleep, Misto wondered at how unfathomable life was, and of the far more vast spirit, wondered at the mysteries in all their eternal truths that not even the far-seeing ghost cat could decipher.

When Lee woke, the cat was gone. Only the sense of him remained and a lingering warmth against his jacket. The sun was up, the Oregon smog vanished, and the smell of the sea came strong. He looked out at the rolling waves brightening the Pacific, and at the green hills and tall forests north of San Francisco; and on a whim, knowing he shouldn't spend the money, he thought of having breakfast in the fancy dining car. Rising, he went to wash himself in the restroom. He shaved, cleaned up as best he could, and then headed up through the passenger cars and the sleeping cars with their little, closed cubicles.

In the dining car, he expected to have to stand in line but it was early, the waiters were just getting set up, laying out heavy silverware, fine glasses, and white napkins on bright white tablecloths. He was seated alone at a small table. The East Bay hills swept by on his left, a glimpse of the sea and dark redwoods across to his right. Sipping the best coffee he'd tasted in ten years, he ordered three fried eggs, hash browns, bacon, and a biscuit with gravy. He hadn't dined like this since well before McNeil, and he didn't expect to do so again, not in the foreseeable future.

He returned to his seat heavy with too much food, and as they made their way down the coast he tried not to sleep, he sat enjoying the bright green of the hilly pastures and the fat livestock. There were new calves everywhere, and a bull mounting a cow not a hundred feet from the train brought embarrassed giggles down the length of the car.

It was dusk as they approached the outskirts of L.A., too overcast to see the great letters marking the Hollywood Hills, but the nearer lights of the small towns swept by clear enough, picking out homelier neighbor-hoods, small businesses, and little wooden cottages tucked among tall Victorian homes. He tried to read the cheap dime novel he'd brought, but now he kept envisioning, at every scene he read, a crueler way to handle the action, a colder and more sadistic turn that the writer should have thought of himself.

Approaching the L.A. station, the train edged slowly through what seemed miles of lighted freight yard. As soon as they came to a halt and the conductor stepped aside, Lee swung out of his seat and down the steps, car-rying his few belongings. Inside the station he ignored the crowds that pushed around him as he walked the length of the big building trying to ease his aching legs, trying to come fully awake, after sitting too long on the train.

He had a long layover here. He asked questions, found the gate where he'd board, found a wooden bench to him-self, and at last he spread out his papers, and settled in. He'd be glad when he hit Blythe. Right now, he never wanted to see another train. Not as a passenger, shut in with a bunch of strangers, and not with even *one* whining kid. He lay down on the bench trying to sleep, trying to ignore the noise of people hurrying around him, but he had slept too much on the train. Restless, he read for a while, in the poor light, and then rose and paced the sta-tion again, trying to make the hours go faster. And then at last, tired out, he found another bench, lay down again covered with his papers and coat, lay waiting for morning, waiting for his train to Blythe.

9

LEE JERKED AWAKE as the train's couplings shifted, he could feel the engine straining as it began the heavy pull up Banning Pass, the passenger car rocking in the sharp wind that swept down between the mountains. He was glad to have left L.A. behind him and San Bernardino, too—he had stayed on the train during that two-hour layover there, hadn't swung off to report to his parole officer as his printed instructions told him to do, he hadn't felt like it. If the PO wanted to see him he could find him in Blythe, at work as his release plan told him to do. He had boarded the train to Blythe bleary-eyed and stiff after sleeping on that hard wooden bench most of the night; even a sprung prison cot would have been luxury. Breakfast had been a dry sandwich in the train station, at a little booth where the giggling shopkeeper must have had those dried-up ham-and-cheese treats stashed for a week or more.

As the train strained rising up the pass he looked out below him, down at the vast apple orchards, miles of green trees marching in straight formation across the high desert. Rising from his seat, he moved stiffly out to the vestibule, stood in the fresh wind smelling the heady scent of apple blossoms, the sweetness making him think again of Lucita, of old passions never fulfilled. One time, they'd been rodeoing, he and Jake and Lucita, not riding but just as spectators, just for the hell of it, sitting on a fence at Salinas watching the bull riding, but ready to swing off the rail fast if the Brahma turned in their direction. When the bull did head for them Lucita swung off but she caught her heel and nearly fell. They both grabbed her, pulled her up, but it was Lee she clung to. He'd felt her excitement, clinging close, both of them rising to the same urge—until she looked up, saw Jake's expression, and she pulled away from Lee straightening her vest and hat. She was so beautiful. Long, dark hair down over her shoulders, so slim in her leather vest, her pale silk shirt and well-fitting jeans, the silver jewelry at her throat and wrists exotic and cool against her deep tan. When Jake turned away, her dark Latin eyes were hot on Lee once more.

That look still made him wonder, sometimes. What if they had pursued what they felt, what if she had married him instead of Jake? What would life have been like? He thought for a while about that, Lucita in bed with him, his hands on her, the two of them in a little cabin just big enough to turn around in, cozy and isolated.

But how would he have made a living for her? Not farming, like Jake. Maybe breaking colts, or general ranch work—but that would have gotten them nowhere. Lucita slaving away in a primitive ranch kitchen, her long beautiful hands roughened, her dark eyes filling with disappointment when he didn't ever make more than the meager subsistence of a ranch hand. Her disappointment and anger when he began to yearn for the open road again, when he began to hanker for real money, when his thieving ways took hold again: the discouragement in her eyes, her bitter disappointment as she saw her own dreams wither.

But was her life any better with Jake? What had Jake given her, that Lee couldn't have if he'd settled down, if he'd abandoned his footloose drifting, as Jake had? Jake was ranch foreman, he made a good living, they had a nice house, saddle horses, he drove a new truck, and he'd written to Lee that Lucita had help in the kitchen, help with the housework when she wanted it.

Lee could have given her that, if he'd settled down and changed his ways. If he hadn't been so hotheaded, so *hardheaded* in what he thought he wanted. The train strained harder hauling up toward the summit, the apple orchards behind and below him now, down on the flats, but he could still smell their sweet scent on the fitful breeze that twisted up the mountain. Just at the top, the engine paused, the train hung there a moment and then heaved itself over, gathering speed until its tail of cars thundered down again, fast. All the green was left behind now. Ahead, down the mountain, the vast desert stretched away, a flat table of pale dry sand and raw rock, parched and faded where no water could reach it.

But then far ahead a line appeared sharply dividing the land: on the near side, the flat pale desert. Far beyond, a vast green garden of lush farm crops, brilliant green, melons, vegetables, the feathery green of date groves, hundreds of acres divided by the concrete aqueducts that carried water from the Colorado, water as precious as gold to bring alive the fields that fed half the state and more, some folks said—water the farmers fought over, their battles growing ever more violent. Water rights meant money, big money, inviting every legal and political grab, every scam a man could imagine.

When gusts of hot wind began to swirl up from the desert, spewing sand in Lee's face, he returned to his seat. Already the car was growing hot; it grew hotter still as they approached Indio. Off against the mountains he could see what must be Palm Springs, a little resort town patched onto the desert, its tall hedges and high rock walls hiding large vacation homes, he could see just their sprawling rooftops, and flashes of blue that would be swimming pools, oases for the rich. Beyond Palm Springs rose the dry mountains, their peaks incongruously capped with white, with snow that would remain all year, aloof and cold, high above the burning desert.

It was well past noon when the train pounded into Indio, the altered rhythm woke him, the train's slowing pace, the clang of metal on metal as they bucked over the crisscross tracks, then row after row of dusty freight cars. The temperature, by the big thermometer above the station platform, was a hundred and ten. Facing an hour layover, tired of stale sandwiches and of the stale smell of old food and sweaty passengers, Lee rose. Hanging on to the overhead rail, he followed the conductor, heading for the door. When they pulled up in the center of town he swung off the train, stood waiting to cross the fast highway that served as Indio's main street. Farm trucks loaded with baled hay and crated produce roared past him farting the smell of diesel. Across the highway an irrigation ditch seethed with fast-running water from the Colorado. Beyond this was a line of shops, a few restaurants, a couple of pawnshops. A reefer truck was pulled over to the side idling, the driver hammer-thumping its tires checking the air pressure that built up in the hot desert. In the bed of a rusted pickup, four migrant workers sat eating bread from torn wrappers. A stalled station wagon sat blowing steam from its radiator, two mattresses tied to its roof, its interior crowded with smear-faced little kids. Diesel fumes from the trucks started him coughing, and when he tried to cross the highway between them he misjudged his distance and had to leap back.

It took him three false starts before he got across, running. He followed the winking neon of taverns and hamburger joints, and soon enough could smell the garlic and hot sauces of a Mexican café. He followed the aroma down a side street until he saw ahead a splash of red and green neon announcing the Colima Café; the smell drew him like a kiss. Hurrying toward the small white house, he pushed inside.

Red checkered oilcloth covered the tables. The fly-specked walls were decorated with sombreros, faded piñatas, and beer posters. The hot, meaty, spicy smell made him think he'd stepped into heaven. He chose a small table, sat with his back to the wall, fingering the sauce-spotted menu, though he knew what he wanted. He sat holding the menu before him, surveying the room.

A man and woman sat two tables down: tourists, all dressed up. Three Mexican men in denim overalls occupied the table in the middle of the room, drinking beer and wolfing tacos from a heaped plate. At a table near the window were two young husky Mexican men dressed in flared jeans, tight T-shirts, and expensive boots, a dozen empty beer bottles on the table between them. Each had several self-inflicted tattoos on his arms, crosses and initials, the kind the peacock punks in the joint gave themselves with the help of a sharp instrument and blue ink. Lee tucked the scene away as he watched the waiter approach wiping his hands on his dirty apron. He ordered chorizo, two eggs over easy, tortillas, refried beans, and a bottle of beer.

The waiter grinned. "You miss breakfast, señor?"

Lee smiled back at him. "I missed this kind of breakfast."

"¿Qué clase cerveza, señor?"

"Carta Blanca. Pronto, yo tengo sed."

The waiter scurried for the kitchen, he was back at once with the beer. Lee tilted the bottle and let the icy brew slide down, then ordered another. The ferment they made in prison, from prunes and apricots pilfered from the kitchen, faded into welcome oblivion. When his meal came he covered it with salsa and savored it, too, trying to eat slowly and get the most from every bite, but too soon it was gone. He wrapped the remains of his beans and chorizo in the last fresh, hot tortilla. When finally he pushed back his chair and fished in his watch pocket for money, the two twenties and the five came out together. Annoyed, he peeled off the five and pushed the twenties back, but one of the Mexican boys tapped the other on the shoulder, watching him. Lee paid the bill and left quickly, knowing too well what was coming.

He was barely out the door when he heard it close a second time, and one of the young men shouted, "Hey, hombre viejo. Wait up."

Lee turned to face them on the empty side street. The two approached him side by side, walking with a belligerent swing through the green river of neon, the taller one casually tossing a small object hand to hand, and Lee caught the gleam of a switchblade. The young man's voice was soft, casual, and sure of himself. And they were on him, moving in close. "We want the money in that little pocket of yours, señor."

Lee smiled.

"If you do not give it to us, old man, I'll show you what this can do." Again he tossed the knife, watching Lee.

Lee judged his timing and distance. When the knife was in midair he stepped forward on his left foot, did a snap-kick that brought the toe of his right boot crashing into the guy's testicles. As the young man doubled over, grabbing himself, Lee dropped to a crouch and scooped up the fallen knife. He hit the button releasing the six-inch blade, swung it up in an arc at the man on his left. The blade traveled horizontally, hitting him just below the belt buckle to deliver a gut gash. Bright red blood splashed up across his white T-shirt and down the tight flared pants. The young Mexican looked down, gasped at what he saw, clutched his gut, and fled.

Lee knelt beside the fallen youth. He was curled up groaning, holding his crotch. Lee rolled the boy over, wiped the blood from the knife onto the boy's nose. "Old man, am I? If I ever see you again, you little pussy-ball scumbag, I'll cut your nuts off and cram them down your throat." He closed the switchblade, stuck it in his back pocket, stood up and headed for the train station.

Back on the train, as they got moving, Indio's industrial buildings edged past and then its small old houses, and then outside of town began the dizzying corridors of towering date palms fanning swiftly past, making him giddy if he watched for too long. Closing his eyes, he wondered if those two young *braceros* had signaled a new pattern in his life, one where he, an old worn-out gringo, stood at the mercy of the young and belligerent field hands with whom he would be working—but then suddenly the cat was with him again, easing Lee, curling up against his thigh, invisible but warm and purring, and Lee felt steadier. Ghost cat, spirit cat, perhaps from a brighter dimension, Lee was grateful to have Misto near him.

He guessed when he got to the ranch the big yellow tom would have no trouble hiding himself, moving about invisibly; or perhaps he would make himself boldly known among the barn cats and the other ranch animals. He just hoped Misto would stay with him; the tom had been with him at McNeil both as mortal cat and as ghost, the little spirit proving to Lee beyond doubt that a vast and intriguing universe awaited somewhere beyond, a realm far more intricate, and perhaps far kinder, than this present world seemed to offer. Lee thought the ghost cat might know almost everything Lee himself had experienced in his life. He wasn't sure what that added up to, but the thought was more comforting than annoying, that the friend from his childhood cared enough to know about him and to stay with him.

As the train picked up speed, the fanning of the palm groves so dizzied Lee that he turned again from the window. Dozing, it seemed he was a boy again, back with Russell Dobbs reliving, almost as if it were his own life, the tale of Dobbs's bargain with the dark spirit, with the haunt that visited Lee himself too often, cold and tenacious. All the long-ago gossip that Lee had heard as a child seemed to come together now, as the cat lay with his paws on Lee's arm, looking up at him, looking wise and all-knowing. As Lee dreamed, was it Misto himself who filled in the small, sharp details of the confrontation between the devil and Russell Dobbs? When Lee woke, he seemed to know the story more clearly, small details had been fitted into place. Could he still hear Misto's whisper—or was it Lee's own silent thoughts whispering, over the rattle of the train?

10

HAVING AGREED TO certain terms, Russell Dobbs spread the word quickly that the Northern & Dakota out of Chicago would be carrying a heavy payroll and that he meant to take it down. He put out that information in ways that would not be traced back to him, he let it be known that he would slip aboard at Pierre and work the job from inside the train, alone and that he meant to leave the train with half a million in cash.

His plan worked out very well. The five Love boys, and the three Vickers brothers lay in wait for the Northern & Dakota, stopping and boarding the train at different points, both sets of brothers unduly heated and aggressive with the promise that Russell Dobbs would already be aboard. Dobbs waited in the woods, quieting his horse as, inside the train when the brothers discovered each other, a small war fought itself to a bloody finish. When it was all over he rode away hoping he'd seen the last of the Loves and the Vickerses and of his phantom visitor.

Not until two weeks later, when Cage Vickers and Tessa Love were married, did Russell wake at dawn in his cabin to see the finely dressed figure standing before him, fancy black suit, embroidered vest, black string tie. He could not see the man's eyes. The elegantly groomed haunt put him at a distinct disadvantage. Lying naked in bed, Dobbs rose on one elbow, pulling the blanket around him.

"You have destroyed both gangs," the devil said coldly. "You knew I wanted them unharmed. You have, of course, lost the wager."

"I didn't lose anything. I agreed only to prevent Cage from getting them caught and arrested. Nor did I harm them. They harmed each other."

"The three who lived were arrested, you knew I did not want them arrested, you failed at your task."

"That wasn't part of the agreement. I said I would prevent *Cage* from getting them caught—Cage didn't cause that, they trapped themselves. That was the bargain," Russell said. "I didn't allow Cage to give up either gang, I kept that part of the agreement and you are bound to it. You promised me a long, healthy life, unwounded, unharmed." Though Dobbs had no idea whether the haunt would keep his end of the bargain. What made him think hell's messenger was bound by any code?

"Perhaps," said the dark one, "perhaps I will honor what you call a bargain. And perhaps not. Whatever I do, Russell, you have only one lifetime to enjoy the fruits of such an agreement—while I have all eternity to retaliate for your deception by twisting and manipulating the lives of your heirs, and never think, Russell Dobbs, that those who come after you will not suffer. Your heirs will be bound to me through your deceit, they will know me, Russell, I'll wield my hold over them in ways you have never dreamed."

"You don't have that much power. If you did, I would not have beaten you."

"You will see what power I have when you view the lives of your descendants, when you see them from the other side, when you witness the suffering and agony of your own kin that you have deliberately destroyed." But even as Russell rose, pulling the blanket around him, the devil vanished, was gone from the room, no faintest shadow remaining, the cabin dim and empty. Russell stared around at the log walls, the iron stove, his pants hanging over a chair. He got up, pulled on his pants and shirt, his boots, took up his rifle, and went to shoot some breakfast.

WHEN LEE WOKE, the passenger car was hotter than a bake oven, the midafternoon sun burning in through the train's smeared windows as they sped across the high desert. Far ahead, the land dropped down steeply onto the wide and ancient riverbed, dry now, forever waterless. And there lay Blythe, a jumble of faded rooftops, the end of the world, some said, the asshole of creation. He doubted the town had changed much, these twenty years. A small, ugly cluster of forlorn wooden buildings set along wandering dirt tracks.

But the dusty roads led, out beyond Blythe, to another

vast spread of brilliant bright green fields just as in Indio, another welcome oasis, and that was where he was headed, out among the farm crops, the miles of melons, summer vegetables, and alfalfa, huge fields that, even as far as they stretched away, were dwarfed by the endless desert that spread on beyond, parched and ungiving. He remembered too well, when he'd run with Jake, the sour salty smell along the dry washes where the tamarisk trees thrived, remembered the beery smell of the little town when you passed a bar, the high sidewalks above the one paved street, the cross streets of powder dust so fine it would splash up over your boot tops. Remembered the dirty faces of the little Mexican kids and the patient-eyed women with that deep, lazy Mexican beauty. Mexicans, blacks, whites, and Indians all working their tails off making money for the farmers, and what little money they put in their own pockets lasted only one trip to town, where they lost it to backroom gambling and to booze and prostitutes, and what they didn't spend someone waited to take forcibly from them.

But still the migrants kept coming, smugglers with overload springs on their Cadillacs rolling in from the border at night with trunks full of illegals who paid them two hundred dollars a head, innocents who blew their life savings trying to get a chunk of the American dollar, migrants who might end up treated like shit with the wrong farm boss, lucky if they got enough to eat for their stoop labor. And some of them weren't that lucky. Those who suffocated in the Cadillacs' locked trunks were stripped of what little they had and tossed out on the desert for the coyotes to finish.

Didn't seem like twenty years since he and Jake rode into California over the dry mountains to lay up after that Tucson train job, Jake nearly dead from loss of blood. And then a week later outside Blythe, when Lee was alone, the feds had grabbed and arrested him. Jake was holed up by then, Lucita taking care of him. And with Lee arrested and in jail, Lucita was all Jake had.

Thinking about all that had happened since, about the mistakes he had made, thinking how he'd promised himself not to get trapped in any more screwups, now Lee cursed himself for not getting off the train in San Bernardino. That could mean trouble, too. What the hell was he thinking? He'd better come up with a good excuse for his parole officer, he could have blown his release right there.

As the train slowed for Blythe, Lee stepped out to the vestibule. Peering around the side of the cars, he could see the town up ahead, a dry wart on the face of the ungiving plain. Stepping back to his seat, he checked the watch pocket of his jeans, fingering the tightly folded bills. Unlike the seven hundred more in his boot, this was clean money, money he'd earned in prison industries. But all together, enough—if the parole board got snotty with him—to get him a good distance away, in a hurry. When the train bucked to a halt, a heavy black cloud rattled against the windows turning the passenger car nearly as dark as night. What the hell was that? Not Satan's shadow, this was different. And not blowing leaves, there weren't that many trees in Blythe; and the black cloud made a clicking noise, hitting the glass, so loud he thought for a minute it was pebbles blowing—but this was clouds of something small squirming as they hit the glass, and some of them were clinging and crawling, were crawling up the glass . . .

Crickets. Swarms of crickets, thousands of flying bodies beating against the glass. And at a break in the swarm, when he could see the train yard, it too was black with them, they had turned the afternoon as dark as night. The station lights had come on, crickets surged in their glow, swarming, and where they swept against Lee's window they left trails of silver mucus. Peering down, where lights lit the track, he could see them fall and die there, glistening brighter than the slick metal.

Well, hell, he knew Blythe had these swarms now and then, over the years, like the grasshoppers in South Dakota. But did he have to arrive right in the middle of this mess? He rose when the car stilled; and as the rest of the passengers stood up, gathering their belongings, he felt a brush of fur against his hand. Sometimes, he couldn't understand why the little cat stayed with him. A ghost cat must have the whole universe at its disposal, must have all of time to travel through and to choose from, so what was he doing here? Had they bonded so well that the yellow tom simply wanted to be with him, wanted to remain where Lee was, or was there some other reason, some mystery yet to unfold? Moving on out of the train, stepping down onto the platform, his boots crunched dead and squirming crickets, the steps and sidewalk were alive with them, masses of dark, brittle insects swarming around his boots, swarming *up* his boots, creeping and flying up the walls of the station and inside whenever the door opened, swarming over the newspaper rack and shoeshine stand, dark stinking bugs crawling through the white powder that had been sprinkled along the street and sidewalk and across the thresholds of the shops to kill them.

It hadn't seemed to kill many, they were still thick on the varnished oak benches before the station, dark bodies crawling in and out the slots of the cigarette and candy machines, the sound of their beating wings against metal and glass like some dark prediction he didn't want to know about. The streets and gutters were dark with glistening bodies, crickets clinging to fenders and windshields, to tires, to license plates and chrome grills. Heaps of dead crickets had been swept up along the curb, the piles dusted with the killing white powder; crickets flew in his face or flew past him to beat their hard little bodies against the hot overhead lights—he wondered if the ghost cat was invisibly diving at them, swatting and gobbling up crickets. A shout made him spin around.

"Fontana! Lee Fontana!"

Lee stepped back out of the light, watching the approaching figure. Only when he saw the horseman's stride, the Stetson and boots and then the familiar face and crippled hand did he step forward, grinning.

11

JAKE WAS STILL lean, but he'd grown a bit of a paunch over his belt. Same grin, big wide mouth ringed with laugh creases. His thin face was wrinkled some from the sun, his dark hair was turning gray in streaks, and white along the temples.

"Didn't expect you to meet me," Lee said. "Damn glad you did. Crickets are about to crawl up my leg, swarm in places I don't want 'em."

"You look bushed, Lee. Suitcase?"

"Travelin' light," Lee said.

Ellson turned away quickly, maybe uncomfortable that Lee had done the jail time, and Jake hadn't, because the cops hadn't had enough to hold him when he had been suspected of robbery later. He led Lee through the crickets along the line of parked cars. On the curb a woman huddled cuddling a baby, ignoring the swarming insects as she held the child to nurse. Ellson headed for a red pickup that looked brand-new, its doors professionally lettered with the signature of Delgado Farms. Lee slid in onto the soft leather seat, shut the door quickly but even so half a dozen crickets slipped in. Lee caught them in his hand, threw them out the window and rolled it up again fast. The truck smelled new, the red leather thick and soft—a lot fancier than the old, rusted-out trucks they'd used to drive. Jake had been with Delgado Farms almost twelve years now, a big switch for him, staying in one place. Lee guessed he'd changed some after their messed-up train job. Jake and Lucita were married long before that robbery, he knew Lucita had come down hard on Jake about that. Jake looked more respectable now, calmer, more settled and sure of himself. He had to be doing well, head foreman of the whole Blythe outfit, which was only one of several farms Delgado owned. Jake did the hiring and firing. He'd said in his letter that Lee would be ramroding a crew of *braceros* and locals.

The Delgado family lived up in Hemet where they raised Steel Dust horses. They owned four big farms in the Coachella Valley, growing hay and dates and vegetables, land totaling over six thousand acres and stretching from the Chocolate Mountains to the Colorado River. Land that, before water was piped from the Colorado, had been dry rangeland, the grass so sparse it must have taken twenty square miles to feed one steer. Now, with water brought in, every acre was as valuable as gold.

Just a little speck of that wealth would set a fellow up real nice, Lee thought. Sitting in the new truck beside Jake, Lee wondered if Jake handled the Blythe payroll— then he turned away, angered at himself. What the hell kind of thought was that? Jake was his friend, just about his only friend.

As they headed through town, Lee began to see other changes in Jake, the calmer way he drove, the lowered timbre of his voice. As Ellson turned down a dusty side street, Lee could smell wet, burned rags from the town dump, and he grinned, remembering the night they had sat in there under a wrecked truck, passing the jug. Jake remembered, too. A little smile touched the corner of his mouth. Lee said, "What was that we were drinking?"

Jake laughed. "Homemade tequila, fermented cactus juice." They passed a line of feathery tamarisk trees crowded against weathered shacks and pulled up in front of a graying house, its window frames painted turquoise, its door bright pink. A neon Budweiser sign hung from the eaves. The smell of chiles and garlic mixed with the blaring jukebox rhythm of castanets and brassy trumpet stirred a lot of old memories. They got out, crunching crickets, moved past a young Mexican boy who stood outside the door with a broom, brushing crickets away. They stepped inside fast, but a few insects leaped in past them and under a table. Lee hoped to hell they weren't in the kitchen, but he didn't know how they could keep all of them out. He didn't let himself think too long about that.

The walls of the café were built of rough, dark wood. Down at the end, at one of three windows, a swamp cooler chugged away, keeping time to the Mexican brass, belching out cool, damp air. The tables were crowded with *braceros* and with a few dark-eyed women. They slid in at the only empty table, the oilcloth still damp from the waiter's towel. When Jake reached for the chips and salsa,

Lee tried not to look at the stump of his right hand where three fingers were missing, an accident Lee felt guilty for.

They'd taken down one of the last steam trains, a short run from San Francisco up the San Joaquin Valley. They got the only money bag they could find, had swung off the train when one glancing shot by a train guard hit Jake. Lee ran, in plain sight meaning to lead the cops away, hoping Jake would vanish around the far side of the train. He knew Jake had made it when he heard a horse pounding away. Lee made a lot of noise to draw them off, then slipped away on his own mount, moving silently in the dark.

He had ridden for maybe an hour, could still hear them behind him, but then their sound faded as they took a wrong turn. When at last Lee holed up, hid his horse in dense woods, and opened the canvas bag expecting a big haul, the bag contained a measly four thousand bucks.

Days later, when Lee thought the cops had eased off their searching, he'd gotten half of the money to Lucita. She kept it, but she was mad as hell. She wouldn't tell him where Jake was, she said his hand, what was left of it, was healing just fine. She told Lee, snapping out the words, her black eyes flashing, that this was the last job *they'd* ever pull, that Jake was done with that life, done for good, or she'd send him packing and divorce him.

Lee didn't hear from Jake for a long time after that, long after the marine payroll job and the bank fiasco when that damned teller nearly cut off his own fingers. Then, somehow, Jake heard where he was, maybe from someone they had worked with at one time, and Lee started getting a letter now and then, up at McNeil. A thin thread to keep in touch, but it had meant a lot to him.

Now, beneath the table, something brushed his leg, but when he lifted the red checkered oilcloth and glanced down, nothing was there. Only the faintest purr reached him, and in the shadows he saw a scrap of tortilla disappear into thin air. He dropped the edge of the oilcloth wondering, not for the first time, how a ghost could eat solid food.

But at McNeil when the cat had made himself visible in the prison mess hall, he'd gobbled up every handout he could beg. Well, hell, Lee thought, what did *he* know about the talents of a ghost? When the purring became louder, he scuffed his feet hoping to hide the sound; and then when the waitress approached, the cat silenced.

Not only was the beer ice-cold, the chiles rellenos when they arrived were light and fresh, the corn tortillas homemade. It was all so good Lee thought maybe he'd died and gone to heaven. If he could just make it from one small Mexican café to the next, without having to deal with the rest of the world, he could get along just fine. Jake, rolling beans and salsa into a tortilla, said, "Parole, rather than conditional release?"

Lee nodded. "Parole board didn't much like my record. I'm beholden for this job at the ranch, Jake."

Ellson shook his head. "Except for you, I'd have bought it when that guard shot at me, if you hadn't led them off they'd have grabbed me. I worried a long time, hoping you got away. The two thousand dollars you got to me, I did a lot of thinking, after that."

"And you took a lot of flack from Lucita."

Jake grinned. "That was a long time ago."

"More years than I like to count," Lee said. "I'm sorry

about Ramon, about losing your boy in the war. I'd like to have known him." He wondered how that must feel, to raise a fine son, and then see him die so young, so brutally. When he thought about how that must have been for Lucita, pain twisted his belly and he felt a warm longing to comfort her. Though he had never made a play for Lucita, once she and Jake were engaged and then married, he'd never been near her without being tempted, without the heat rising.

"She's up in Redlands," Jake said. "Her sister just had gall bladder surgery, Lucita's taking care of her. She'll be home next week. She's sure looking forward to seeing you, planning on cooking up a big dinner." Jake motioned to the waiter for another bowl of salsa. "Both our girls are married. Carmella's in San Francisco, her husband's a fireman. Susanne's in Reno." He grinned. "Married to a sheep rancher."

"Sheep?" Lee said.

Jake smiled. "He's a good man. Basque. Good people."

Lee watched Jake quietly. Jake's family had lived a whole lifetime, the girls grown up into their own lives, Ramon shot down by a German sniper, buried and mourned, while Lee had gone on year after year pulling a few jobs, getting older, getting slower, and then back in the pen scrubbing prison latrines, sanding prison-made furniture, eating prison slop, and then finally out working on the McNeil farm. He'd had no ties at all on the outside except Jake and Lucita, no one else who cared, no family of his own that he'd ever kept track of. Only the thought of his little sister, as if Mae were still out there somewhere, as if she were still alive. But if Mae *was* still alive, and grown old, where was she? What kind of life was she living? And why had she never tried to get in touch? But how could she have done that when he was always on the move, leaving as few tracks as he could, ever traveling on, aimless as a tumbleweed? And why hadn't *he* tried to get in touch?

Well, hell, he'd stayed in touch for a while. He'd write or make a phone call to the rancher, Sam Gerrard, who owned the land adjoining them, because Lee's family had no phone. Years ago he'd called Gerrard when he read in the newspaper that his grandpappy was killed. He couldn't believe it, shot to death during a train robbery, though Russell had taken three Pinkerton men with him. His grandpappy's death had set Lee back some, he'd been a long time getting over the demise of Russell Dobbs—as if a whole stretch of history had collapsed, as if the whole shape of the world he knew had shifted and changed.

He'd given Gerrard a number where he might be reached now and then, a hotel in Billings where he had a lady friend. That was how he found out when his daddy died, had a stroke, they thought. Died out on the range alone. Must have been a bad one, to make him tumble off his horse. Horse came back to the ranch, and they'd gone looking. They found his daddy two days later lying among the boulders at the edge of a stony draw. After that, Gerrard said, Lee's ma had left the ranch, sold it for what she could get, took Mae and their two older sisters back to North Carolina, to live with *her* sister. That was when he lost touch, didn't try to contact them. He knew Mae would be all right if she was with family. But he thought about her a lot, he hoped she had horses as she'd always wanted, and he'd carried her picture and would look at it, at that bold little girl who wanted to learn everything herself, wanted to do everything her way.

Mae and her older sisters were allowed to ride but only decorously, at a walk or slow trot, and they were kept as far as possible from the cattle and the cowhands. When Lee and Mae could sneak off alone, when he saddled a real horse for her and not the poky pony, she wanted to do everything, she wanted to learn to rope, she wanted to work cattle, she wasn't afraid and in a short time she handled a horse real well. Their mother didn't know half of what went on, working in the kitchen or around back in the garden, trusting Lee to take care of his little sister, thinking he was carefully chaperoning Mae on the pony when, in fact, they were off beyond the nearby hills, Mae learning to rein and work a good cowpony, to spin and back him, to chase a calf and learning to handle a rope.

What he didn't understand was, why did he still dream of her? Dreams so real, as if she were still alive, as if she were still a little child as he'd last seen her. In his recent dreams, she was in a house he'd never seen, or in a flower garden unlike any place where they'd grown up, and she was dressed in a way she wouldn't have been, back on the ranch, back in their own time. He was still wondering about those dreams as they moved out into the shabby street, both men full of the good Mexican dinner, the street darkening around them as evening fell. Along the row of little shacks, faint lights glowed behind curtained windows. They slipped into the truck fast, dodging crickets, tossing crickets out the windows. Moving on through the small town, they headed out a dirt road, its pale surface caught in the light of a rising half-moon, the long

straight rows of bean plants polished by the faint glow.
Now when they were moving fast and no crickets swarming in, Lee cracked open his window, letting in the musky
wet smell of the river, of the tamarisk and willows silvered
along the steep, silt banks.

Twelve miles out of town they turned onto a dirt lane,
cutting through a cantaloupe field, the smell of the fruit
sweet and cloying. Half a mile up, they turned into the
ranch yard under bright security lights, their dust rising
white against a row of packing sheds, long bunkhouses,
and small frame bungalows. Jake drove on past the big
mess hall with its long screened windows and deep porch,
past rows of assorted tractors and field trucks. He parked
in front of a cement-block house with a white picket fence.
A statue of the Blessed Virgin stood in the sandy yard, the
little, two-foot-high figure carefully outlined by a circle
of miniature cactus. Near the house was a paddock and a
small stable, and he could see a couple of horses. Beyond
were more packing sheds, then more ranch trucks and
some old cars. They got out beside the picket fence, but
Jake didn't head into the house. No lights burned there,
with Lucita gone. They moved across the dusty yard toward the cabins, where Jake turned up the steps of the first
one, the porch creaking under their weight.

The cabin door complained as Jake pushed it open,
reached in and flipped a switch so a sudden light flared
from an overhead bulb. The cabin held an iron bed, a
brown metal nightstand, a small battered desk, a small
wooden chest of drawers, and a straight-backed chair,
painted purple. An ornate wooden crucifix hung above
the bed, hand carved and gilded. There was a bathroom

with a little precast shower, and spotless white tile around the sink. A new bar of soap still in its wrapper, two clean towels and a washcloth, clean white shower curtain, all touches that spoke of Lucita, as did the little pitcher of wildflowers she had placed on the old, shabby dresser.

"Not elegant," Jake said. "You'll find a new razor and shaving cream in the cabinet."

Lee sat down on the bed to pull off his boots. "It's elegant to me. Clean. Private. Even flowers," he said, grinning. "No prison bars, and a real door I can shut. No screw coming to lock me in." He dropped a boot. "Bathroom all to myself, private shower without some jock elbowing me or reaching to feel me up, a razor I don't have to account for every day." He grinned up at Jake, as he dropped the other boot.

Jake looked back at him unsmiling. Too late Lee realized he'd hurt Jake, that he had rubbed it in that he'd been in prison all the time Jake had been free and making a life for himself. Lee didn't mean to do that. Jake turned toward the door, his white-streaked hair catching the light. "See you in the morning," he said shortly. "Breakfast in the mess hall, five-thirty," and he was gone, shutting the door softly behind him.

Feeling bad, Lee fished into the paper bag. He took out his few clothes, laid them on the dresser, and set the picture of Mae beside the flowers. He undressed, removed the seven hundred dollars from his boot, shoved that and his prison-made knife under his pillow. He turned out the overhead light and slid into bed, pushed down under the lightweight blanket, and stretched out to ease his tired body. It had been a long day, too many hours on the train, his muscles were all stove up—but not a moment later he felt the cat leap on the bed, landing heavily beside him, and this time he could see it clearly silhouetted against the shaft of moonlight that struck through the cabin window. How the hell did the cat do that, invisible one minute, and then there it was as solid and heavy as bricks, kneading the blanket and pushing him with its hind paws to gain more room, its rumbling purr rising as it settled in for the night. And now, for the first time, the cat spoke to Lee, its yellow eyes glowing in the thin moonlight, its yellow tail twitching.

"You're *sorry* you hurt Jake's feelings? You're *sorry*?"

Startled, Lee sat up in bed, staring at him. The cat had never spoken to him, not during all the years at McNeil, neither as a living cat nor later when Misto returned there as a ghost cat. Yet always Lee had had the sense that Misto could have spoken if he chose, that he understood the conversations of the inmates around him. By his glances, by the set of his ears, by the attention he paid to certain discussions, Lee had always felt that even the living cat was wiser and more clever than ever he let on.

"You're *sorry*?" Misto repeated with a hiss. "*Sorry*? Why are you sorry when, all through dinner with Jake you were thinking about ripping him off, and you were lusting after Jake's wife, you sat there laughing and joking with him while you lusted after the Delgado payroll, too, while you planned to double-cross Jake in two ways. And now, you're *sorry*? *Sorry you hurt his feelings*? What the hell is *that* about? What kind of friend is that?"

"I didn't think about it for long," Lee said crankily. The shock of hearing the cat speak was nothing to the realization that the ghost cat could read his thoughts—even if the beast did exaggerate, even if he did take an overblown view of Lee's short-lived temptation. When Lee moved uncomfortably away from the cat, to the edge of the bed, the tomcat remained relaxed and easy, glancing at him unconcerned as he casually licked dust from his paws.

"It's one thing," Lee said, "to travel with a ghost following me, with a damned haunt hanging on my trail. It's another thing when you start criticizing, telling me what to do, acting as if you know what I'm thinking, like some damned prison shrink."

It was unsettling as hell that the cat knew things that were none of its business, thoughts Lee wasn't proud of and that, facing the cat's righteous stare, shamed Lee all the more. The yellow tom stopped washing and looked back at him steadily, his wide yellow eyes stern and unblinking. Then he closed his eyes, twitched a whisker as if amused, curled himself deeper into the blanket, and drifted off to sleep as if he hadn't a care.

Misto was well aware that Fontana's defensive retorts, his anger and surly responses, had grown harsher as the cowboy grew older. But this was only a part of Lee's nature, a defensive shell to protect a normal human weakness. Lee's very temper was part of why the cat loved him. Lee's sometimes frail, sometimes volatile nature was why Misto guarded Lee so fiercely in wary defense against Satan, against the inroads the devil plied so adroitly in attempting to own Fontana.

12

MISTO'S DREAMS THAT night, as he slept at the foot of Lee's bed, were visions he knew were a part of Lee's future. And though he felt fiercely protective of Lee, staying close to him since his parole, his thoughts tonight were on Sammie, too, so far away in Georgia.

Brad Falon had returned to Rome after his prison time, escaping a dirty piece of business out in L.A., running from the law before the land scam he'd been involved in was uncovered. Now, he was too near again to Sammie, in that small town, was too interested in Sammie and in her mother and was a threat to them both.

Except that now, in Georgia, Morgan Blake was home again, he was out of the navy and back with his little family. Becky and the child need no longer face Falon alone, and that satisfied and eased Misto.

But Lee was alone, and just now he needed Misto. The ghost cat did not mean to leave Fontana as the dark spirit sought to own him. And in Misto's dreams, the connection between Lee and Falon and Sammie was building closer, their lives slowly drawing together, incident by twisted incident, toward a final and life-changing event that would shape the future of all three.

Only just before dawn did the cat stir from his dreams, and leave Lee, slipping out into the fading night to wander the dim ranch yard and then to stroll in through the bunkhouses observing the sleeping workers, their clothes and possessions strewn everywhere among the jumble of cots, a far less organized scene than a cell full of regimented prisoners. The breath of the sleeping men smelled strongly of chiles and garlic. He wandered and looked, amusing himself and then moved outside again where he chased half a dozen chickens, sending them flapping and squawking in panic; then he headed for the back door of the ranch house where, if he were lucky, Jake Ellson might have set out a bowlful of milk for the half dozen farm cats. The rancher had seemed pleased when he glimpsed a new mouser on the property, maybe a wanderer, maybe a drop-off, as often occurred in the open country. Misto, during his stay, meant to catch and leave a few fat mice on the porch, just to prove his prowess.

Yes, this morning there was milk. He lapped the bowl clean before the other cats got to it, and then looked up at the kitchen window, catching glimpses of Jake as he prepared his breakfast; the boss seemed to prefer quiet in the morning to that of a crowd of noisy *braceros*.

It was Friday, the end of Lee's third day on the job, that Ramon Delgado came roaring into the ranch yard in his big white Cadillac, kicking up dust, and Lee got a look at the two canvas cash bags that contained the ranch's weekly payroll, and then soon at the money itself. At enough cash to set him up real nice. And this payroll, to be doled out to more than a hundred men, was only one of four among the Delgado holdings.

The day was still hot as hell though the sun had already dropped behind the hills as they headed in from the fields. Lee had pulled into the ranch yard, the last in the long line of trucks, hot and sweaty after twelve hours of driving. He felt beat down to nothing, it took the last of his energy to get out of the truck, turn in his tally to Jake, walk across the dusty yard to his cabin and ease himself down on the top step, trying to get a full breath. The job itself wasn't hard physical work, driving the truck back and forth. Even the heat was to his liking—until it got *too* damned hot. But it was the stress of dealing with a few quarrelling *braceros* that would tighten up his lungs. He sat sucking air, slowly calming himself, watching the five other foremen stride across to their cabins, three gringos and two Mexican men, all brown from the sun and seeming comfortable in the heat, all of them at least a generation younger than Lee.

Well, he wasn't letting on how beat he was, he needed the job, and he liked it here. He had plans here, he didn't mean to move on until he was loaded with cash, and ready. But right now his shirt and pants stuck to him wringing wet, and his feet were swollen inside his boots. His eyes burned from the glare of the fields, from rows of broad melon leaves reflecting back the beating sun, and from sun bouncing off the hood of the truck. He was parched, dog tired, and his temper boiling from a run-in with the boy he'd picked for straw boss.

From the first morning, Lee had to work at establishing his authority. These men had different ways than the men he'd worked with at McNeil, and he was even rusty with the farm equipment. On that first morning, heading out of the ranch yard before daylight, driving a truck for the first time in years, following the line of trucks, he'd jerked the clutch so bad that the men, jammed into the truck bed, laughed and hooted and shouted good-natured Spanish obscenities at him. They'd eased along a dirt lane and sharply up the side of a levee to a thin track at the top, the old truck straining, then moving on fast through the darkness to keep up with the others. The thin ridge dropped steeply on both sides. The truck rocked and heaved as the field hands horsed around laughing and cuffing each other, thinking nothing of the drop, not giving a damn if they went over. Lee crouched over the wheel gripping hard with both hands, hoping to keep it on the narrow track. As the sky began to turn red, sunrise soon staining the fields, he could see an occasional turnoff angling down the bank on his left. On his right, almost directly under him, a concrete ditch surged with fast black water from the Colorado. He was mighty glad when he saw his own flag marker, ahead in the field below.

As he angled down off the levee, the rising dust from the trucks ahead filled his mouth and nose, dust crept into his lungs so thick that soon he was retching and gagging, coughing up specks of blood. Well, hell, maybe the emphysema would finish him right there in the stinking truck, and who would even care?

He slowed along the edge of the melon field and the men began piling out, lurching the truck harder, landing at a run to keep their balance beside the slow-moving vehicle, men peeling off into the melon rows. They got to work fast when they were picking on their own time, were paid by how much they could harvest. They didn't look up from their work as the sun lifted, as the sky slowly bleached to white and the rising heat slicked sweat across their bare backs. They stopped only to drink from the six water coolers that were wired to the back of the truck, then got to work again. Lee, driving along feeling the truck jolt as they loaded the melons, couldn't escape the sun's reflection from the fields and from the truck's hood and dashboard. The temperature inside the cab, even with the windows open, must be a hundred and thirty. He wished this were a horse operation instead of a farm, wished he were doing a job he cared about, something he could put his mind to.

By midmorning he'd pulled off his shirt. He felt cooked through. He grew bored with keeping tally on the pickers, marking down their loads as they dumped them into the truck bed. By noon the water coolers were empty and the truck riding low on its axles, its bed piled high with its first load of cantaloupes. Going back in for the noon meal, the men rode on the outside, clinging to the slats, their voices irritable now with heat and hunger, exploding in fast Spanish arguments, and the heavy, sweet smell of the cantaloupes sickened Lee. If he were twenty years younger, maybe he wouldn't mind this routine. At his age, with the emphysema flaring up, working all day in this damnable heat wasn't going to cut it for long. Where the hell had he gotten the notion that the hot desert was just what he longed for? It was early that afternoon when, observing the men at work, he picked out a straw boss to run interference for him.

Tony Valdez was a squarely built kid in his early twenties, with an easy way about him. Maybe too easy, but he looked like he could handle the men, and that was what Lee wanted. Valdez worked stripped to the waist, the silver cross hanging around his neck swinging as he bent to cut the fruit from the vines. Lee saw no prison tattoos on his sun-browned skin, and no sullenness in his face. "I'll pay you two dollars a day extra," he'd told Tony. "You'll keep the arguments down, and help me with the tally."

The boy's shoulders had straightened. "I can do that."

"Can you drive truck?"

"I can drive that truck."

Lee had nodded, thinking Tony would do. But it wasn't long before the kid was strutting like a Spanish rooster, goading the men. "*Estoy el segundo jefe*, you guys. Don't give me any shit," and the next thing Lee knew a fistfight erupted between Tony and a dark-skinned older man. Lee, jumping over a row of cantaloupes, grabbed the two of them and jerked Tony around to face him, his temper flaring hot.

"What the hell did I hire you for! To stop fights, not start them."

Tony looked at him innocently. "I was only keeping order, señor . . ."

The men snickered.

Lee shoved Tony toward the rows and whirled around, staring at the idle crew. "The bunch of you get back to

work or I'll run your sorry asses clear to hell off the place."
He'd burned with rage, almost out of control. The other
men looked at him, and quieted and turned away.

Lee didn't think he had the authority to fire anyone,
but they seemed to think he did. He looked Tony over,
trying to quiet the fire in his belly. "If you can't straw boss
like a man, Valdez, I'll pick someone who will."

Tony quieted, too, looking at him first with anger, and
then sheepishly. For the next three days Tony behaved
himself, he didn't goad the men, and he stopped two serious arguments capably enough. But then on Friday evening, when Lee moved to the right seat and let Tony drive,
heading up the levee, the kid double-clutched it, jammed
it into second and floorboarded it, shooting up the slope
so fast the front wheels left the ground and the rear end
skidded toward the drop-off. Lee grabbed the dashboard,
and the pickers laughed and cheered.

"What the hell are you doing, Valdez! Slow down!
This ain't no cayuse you're breaking!"

"Just getting the truck up the hill, señor."

"Yeah, and have the damn thing in the canal, on top
of the pickers." He wanted to smash the kid's face. "If you
can't do better than that, hombre, you'll ride in the back
from now on." Lee had been mad and rightly so, but in the
ranch yard as he swung out of the truck, he wondered if
that much anger was called for, wondered at the explosion
of blazing rage that had filled him.

Dusk was gathering as Delgado's Cadillac pulled into
the yard. Lee turned over his day's tally to Jake and moved
away to his cabin to sit down on the steps catching his
breath. Maybe he'd get used to this gig, and maybe he

wouldn't. On the hot evening breeze, the smell of beans and chili from the cookhouse drew him. Rising, he moved inside the cabin to douse himself with water, to gulp water, then he headed on out and down the steps, anticipating an isolated supper at the long tables, among the Spanish-speaking men.

Jake was just crossing from the house to the big white Cadillac parked beside the mess hall. There was no mistaking Ramon Delgado, as the boss stepped out. Looked like the fancy new car had been clean and shining when he left the home ranch this morning, before it picked up the day's collection of road dust. Lee could see the gleam of red upholstery inside. Along the back shelf beneath the rear window lay a handsome serape carefully folded, and on the hood, where other cars had radiator ornaments, Delgado had mounted a set of polished, brass-tipped long-horns that reached out just to the edge of the fenders.

Ramon Delgado was a big man, half a head taller than Jake and maybe twenty pounds heavier. He looked to be all muscle under his Levi's jacket and pearl-buttoned shirt. His boots were three colors of fine soft leather, heavily stitched in flower patterns. His black Stetson sported a sil-ver hatband. Lee imagined a nice home place up in Hemet, maybe an adobe house low and rambling, green lawns ir-rigated by the Colorado and shaded by rows of date palms. Everything about Delgado looked rich and successful; and beneath the wide black brim, his face, hard-angled and square, had the look of a man to be wary of.

Beside him, Jake looked thin and dry, the leathery look of a cowman, faded frontier shirt, faded jeans and cracked boots. Lee watched the two men head inside the

mess hall, eyeing the four bulging money bags they carried, bags marked with a bank logo that Lee couldn't read,
and each sealed at the top with a green drawstring and
a metal clasp. Watching Delgado with speculation, he
headed on in, to collect his pay.

The pickers, the minute they saw Delgado's car, had
piled out of the trucks laughing and talking and crowding
fast into the mess hall for their wages. They were lined
up inside, shoving and jostling, eager to pocket the week's
take, twenty to twenty-five dollars apiece, depending on
how fast a fellow worked, more money than they'd ever see
in Mexico. And the bags held, as well, the wages for Lee
himself and for Jake and the other five foremen.

He knew from Jake that Delgado made the rounds to
all four ranches every Friday, heading out from Hemet,
knew that Blythe was his last stop, that he'd stay with Jake
overnight, head back home in the morning. The same
drill, week after week. Leave Hemet at dawn carrying all
four payrolls, carrying enough cash to set a fellow up real
nice.

Maybe not as much as Lee would like to have on him
before heading for Mexico, but a nice start. And how could
Delgado miss a week's wages? The thought quickened
Lee's pulse, wondering where Delgado kept the money
until he headed out. In the local Hemet bank, maybe
picked it up the night before? Or in a home safe?

If the safe was one of those big walk-in jobs, that
would be a poser. He wished he'd paid closer attention to
the half-dozen master safe crackers he'd known over the
years in one prison or another. Though he had learned
some, all right.

But if there was a safe, what other kind of security did Delgado have? Dogs? Guards? Some kind of electronic device?

No, it would be better to hit him just as he started out in the morning from Hemet, wait until he was on the road alone, then force him over. He'd need firearms; and he needed to know what weapons Delgado carried, and where, what weapons he had stashed in that big Cadillac, and what weapons he carried on him.

But, picturing himself forcing Delgado's car off the road, a tremor of fear touched Lee. Was he up to this? Up to handling Delgado alone, as he had always handled his victims in the past, except for those years he ran with Jake? After parting from Jake, he'd blown a couple of jobs, and when he took a good look at what he was now, an honest look at how he'd aged, at how weak he'd grown compared to the man he had been, he didn't much like what he saw.

But then a dark sense of power kicked in, a sudden surge of certainty. He could do this. What was the matter with him? A dark vitality stirred his blood, strength burned in him, and a hard envy of Ramon Delgado, jealousy for all Delgado had that Lee had never had. A heady resentment boiled in him making him scoff at the idea he was too old to take down Delgado, that he was biting off more than he could handle.

He'd bring this off, he thought, smiling, he could take what he wanted and maybe—maybe he could set Jake up for the fall.

He thought about that, about laying the groundwork for Jake's arrest, setting up the clues, maybe lift one of Jake's guns from the house, with Jake's fingerprints on it, maybe something else of Jake's left "forgotten" under the seat of the Cadillac. He'd stash the money where no one would find it, return to the ranch innocent as a babe. And when the cops came nosing around he'd be there to sympathize with Lucita, to comfort her, to be enraged at Jake's betrayal of all they'd had together.

If Lee could hear the cat's whisper that Lucita would never believe such a story, that thought didn't last long. The dark presence told him more forcefully that he could do this, he could lay out a foolproof scenario that left Jake guilty beyond doubt, a plan that even Lucita would have to believe.

It would take time to work it out, to put every detail in place. But, thinking about the plan as he moved through the mess hall to the pay table, his certainty, his self-satisfaction, was a dark itch within him.

Taking his turn at the table, where Jake and Delgado were dealing out the week's cash, he collected his three days' wages, pocketed the meager change and left the mess hall. He could see the cooks working back in the kitchen, could see that supper wouldn't be set out on the long serving counter until the payroll had all been dealt with. Winding out between the lines of crowding men, he returned to his cabin smiling, liking his plan. He sat on the steps feeling bold and right, watching through the screens the crowd at the long table until a sudden sneeze behind him made him swing up off the steps turning, his fists clenched.

13

BUT IT WAS only the cat sitting on the rail big as life, lashing its tail, its ears back, glaring at Lee, a gleam in its eye that didn't bode for good. The big tom's yellow gaze burned into Lee as if seeing every detail of the plan Lee had embraced. When Lee looked deep, he imagined he saw in Misto's eyes every image of the robbery that he had envisioned, and none of that knowledge was the cat's business.

"Make no mistake," Misto said, "if you follow the passions that were fed to you tonight, you're lost for eternity, your soul will crumble to dust, there will be nothing left of you to move on and to know the joy of what yet awaits." The cat sneezed again. "He tells you lies you're too smart to believe. You're too smart, Lee, to suck up to the wraith's passions, when you know they will destroy you."

"Go to hell," Lee said. The cat was too nosy, too opinionated, too bossy. Turning his back, he sat down again on the step.

"You know, of course," Misto said softly, "that young picker's been watching you, that young Latino man standing in the shadows between the sheds, that young Tony Valdez, watching you with great interest, as *you* watched Jake and Delgado."

Lee lifted his eyes to scan the yard, watched Tony move away deeper between the cabins and disappear among the sheds.

"Valdez has a quick mind," the cat said, "he wonders what you found so interesting. The boy is full of questions."

Lee thought reluctantly that in the future maybe he ought to listen to the cat, after all, ought to swallow back his defiance and pay attention. And as Valdez disappeared into the night, Lee decided he'd better pay more attention, too, to who was observing him. Had better play it closer to the chest before Valdez had that whole crew of young hotheads nosing into his business.

"Maybe," the cat said, "you should take a better look at where those dark plans are coming from, before they take you down, Lee Fontana." The cat's challenge pulled Lee in one direction, while his thieving desire drew him in the other. Seated on the cabin steps, he watched Jake and Ramon Delgado leave the mess hall, striding away toward the ranch house. On the porch, they paused. Delgado moved on inside but Jake turned back, heading across the dry yard toward Lee's cabin. Jake paused at the bottom step, his boots coated with pale sand, the band of his tan Stetson dark with sweat. "Come on, Lee, join us for dinner.

Just a quick bite before Ramon and I start on the books, he'd like to meet you."

"Why? I can't be the first parolee he's hired."

Jake looked surprised. "You're my friend, he said he'd like to meet you."

"Sorry," Lee said, rising. "Just tired. I'll stop by in a few minutes, let me scrape off some of the dust."

Jake looked him over, nodded, and turned away.

Lee didn't want to meet Delgado. Besides a prickly conscience, he'd had a long, hard day, his legs ached, sand and dust made his eyes sting, couldn't Jake see he was beat? Jake took a couple of steps up, reaching to stroke the yellow cat. "Don't know where this one came from. Dozen cats around the place, new one shows up now and then, keep rats out of the seed and food stores. Most of them are half wild. This one's friendly enough, he makes right up to a person."

"Never been much for cats," Lee said noncommittally, wondering what that was about. He was right, the damned ghost cat was too nosy. He moved on into the cabin, glancing back as Jake crossed the yard and disappeared inside the house. He could see through the lighted windows beyond Lucita's lace curtains where Delgado sat at the dining table, the lamp lit and a thick ledger before him as if he had already started on the payroll and expenses. On the wall behind him where the lamplight shone, a painting of white roses made Lee think sharply of Lucita.

While he was cleaning up he thought about her, about being in her house surrounded by her little touches, her books, her flowers, her scent. He showered, put on a clean shirt, guessed he'd better wash the other one in the sink tonight. Feeling strangely nervous, he went on over.

The house was just as much Jake's house as Lucita's, Navajo rugs, leather chairs, agricultural and cowman's magazines, but with Lucita's touches everywhere, brightly jacketed books, potted violets, the lace curtains, the dining room furnished with an intricately carved Spanish table long enough to accommodate a dozen chairs, creamy walls, and above the dark, carved buffet the white roses as showy as Lucita herself. She loved roses, though he hadn't seen any out in that pitiful, dry yard where roses were never meant to grow. The painting made Lee uncomfortably aware of her, the petals as soft as her cheek, as creamy as the pale silks she liked to wear, Lucita in tight Levi's, a creamy satin shirt, fancy boots, her black hair sleek and shining, her dark eyes laughing.

Jake had folded back the lace table runner, out of the way, one end covered with a heavy mat, with bowls of beans, rice, and good Texas chili that a Mexican woman brought in from the kitchen. Lee took the empty place Jake indicated, accepted the cold beer Jake passed to him. As they dished their plates liberally, Delgado looked across at Lee.

"McNeil wasn't *real* hard time?" he asked casually. "More freedom than, say, Leavenworth or Atlanta?" The big man leaned back in his chair, sipping his beer from the bottle.

Lee nodded, taking in Delgado's bold, square features. Ramon Delgado might be a hard worker, but he was a man who lived well, treated himself well. What did he know about McNeil? What did he know about solitary, if you came in with a bad attitude, how you were stripped naked and locked into a pitch-black cell, five feet by five, cold as hell, no toilet, no sink, no bed to lie on, and what sleep you got was on the cold, damp concrete. They gave you one thin blanket, took that away in the morning, brought you a dinky little bowl of gruel, and you had to pick the cockroaches out of that. Lee had been in there only once. After that five-day stretch he was real careful, he stayed out of trouble, didn't make a move or say a word to draw the attention of the guards or, as much as possible, of the other inmates. If he had a beef with someone, he took care of it in a way that couldn't be traced back to him. After that stretch in solitary, he'd been a model inmate despite the hazing that was laid on him, and pretty soon he got what he wanted. "I worked the farm," he said shortly. "That part was easy time."

Though he hadn't lived in the farm complex like most of those who worked there, he'd gone back to the cell block at night. Even with Lee's attention to good behavior, he guessed he'd still made the warden nervous. But Delgado didn't need to know the whole story, the fancy bastard. What did he know about prison, anyway? Delgado's interest made Lee's temper flare but he did his best to swallow back his anger.

"What were you in for?" Delgado continued. "Jake mentioned bank robbery."

Lee nodded, drew his thumbnail down his beer bottle, crumpling the label away from the glass. "A job I messed up on." He had to try harder not to show his anger. He was, after all, working for the man, he guessed Delgado had a right to ask questions. "It was the first bank robbery I ever tried," Lee said, keeping his voice mild, trying to act like they were having a normal conversation. "And it was sure as hell the last."

"You liked the trains better," Delgado said, smiling.

Lee nodded. "The old steam trains. Those days are gone."

"Not many big shipments of gold, either," Delgado said. "All bank drafts or paper money, marked money, not like it used to be. And the diesels too fast for a man on horseback." His blue eyes burned into Lee. "You're thinking to stay straight, now? Thinking not to cross the law anymore?"

"That's my plan," Lee lied. "I'm getting too old for that life. My lungs are too sick, I can't take the abuse anymore." *But not quite the last job*, he thought, looking steadily at Delgado. As he watched this man, with his riches, with his great spreads of land and hundreds of men working for him, men under his complete control, Lee's dark urge pressed in at him, wanting part of what Delgado had, no matter who he hurt. If the other three operations, plus the date groves at Hemet, were as large as this ranch, that could total over six hundred workers. Say each man averaged around twenty-five dollars a week, depending on how much he picked, that would add up to some fifteen thousand dollars. Add in the salaries of Jake and the other ranch managers, and their foremen, and that still wouldn't be enough to retire on, even in Mexico, for whatever time he had left.

But then when he thought about betraying Lucita and Jake, he felt his face heat with shame. The cat was right, if he stole from Delgado he'd put a knife in the hearts of his friends. Shaken, not knowing what he wanted, he soon left the two men to their account books, the dirty dishes and empty beer bottles piled at one end of the table. Crossing

Lucita's comfortable living room to let himself out. Looking at the deep leather sofa with its tumble of soft pillows, he had a sudden vision of lying there with her, holding her close, a thought that brought heat again.

But which dominated? The heat born of lust? Or of shame? He'd never known himself to be so uncertain. Was this a part of getting old? Old, and too weak to know what he wanted? Too old and uncertain to resist whatever notion might, at any given moment, pass through his aging brain?

Dark of mood, he pushed out into the night, the day's searing heat vanished but the evening air still warm. A thin moon was rising over the melon fields, silvering the tamarisk trees beyond, along the riverbank. He could hear coyotes singing off in the distance, somewhere this side of the mountains. Looking out across the desert toward the wide Colorado River that fed the vast rows of crops, he had a sudden sense of what Jake had told him about Ramon Delgado, about how Delgado had built up this land by backbreaking hard work, and a sudden sense hit Lee of what Delgado might, in fact, feel for the land; and Lee felt a hint, deep inside, that what he had chosen to see in Delgado might be warped, twisted by the way he wanted to see it.

His cabin windows were black, but moonlight touched the porch. A tall shape stood waiting in the shadows beside the door, sending goose bumps up Lee's arms, a fear flashing through him that made him grip the switchblade in his pocket. The same fear he'd known back at McNeil when the dark wraith moved in through the bars to stand at the foot of his bed. He told himself it *was* only a shadow, that it had no power over him except that which he allowed it to have. He moved on up the steps and past it, stepped on in through his unlocked door, closed the door, and switched on the overhead bulb.

Nothing in the room seemed disturbed, everything looked as it should, his folded clothes and towels, Mae's picture on the white-painted dresser, the straight-backed purple chair standing where he'd left it, the quilted coverlet rumpled on the iron bedstead where he had sat to pull on his boots, the coverlet made by Lucita's hand. The yellow tomcat lay curled in the middle of the bed, blinking up sleepily at him. Again he was surprised at how glad he was to see Misto there, so pleased that Lee almost spoke to him, then thought better of that idea. He didn't feel like a lecture. Stripping off his boots and socks, his pants and shirt, he turned the quilt back as best he could without disturbing the beast, turned out the light and slid under the covers leaving most of the space to the cat. If, tonight, the dark spirit slipped into the room to torment him, so be it, he was too tired to care; he was too conflicted by the devil's hassling to deal with it tonight, he wanted only to be left alone, except for the ghost cat. He badly wanted Misto to stay. Though the big feline, who had taken solid shape tonight in all his shaggy glory, was damnably heavy as he stretched out across Lee's feet. Amused, but eased by Misto's boldness and warmth, reassured by the cat's presence, Lee drifted off into sleep, into dreams that made the dark spirit seem less threatening. That made Satan seem less powerful, tonight, than the spirit of the wily yellow ghost who lay wakeful, watching over Lee, though much of Misto's attention turned now, as well, to Georgia, to the dark spirit's keen interest in the family of little Sammie Blake.

14

It was hot in Georgia, too, but more humid. Earlier that same day, as a little breeze stirred the oak leaves, high among the branches Sammie sat straddling a gnarled limb, her bare feet swinging, her long pale hair tangled in the twigs and leaves. Life was good, her daddy was home now, at work at his auto shop just a few blocks away. Later in the afternoon she and Becky would walk down to join him and they'd head over to Grandma's for dinner. Below her at the picnic table her mother had laid out the monthly figures for Thrasher's Drugstore, her papers weighted with rocks, her ledger shaded by the sprawling tree.

Looking up, Becky watched Sammie with interest, the child completely absorbed in moving a little metal car along in the air above a leafy branch—she had attached a pair of paper wings to the car, stuck on with tape so it was now an airplane, and she had filled the hollow metal plane with white flour. Becky didn't know where Sammie's interest in flight came from, there weren't many planes around Rome, just a couple of small ones that enthusiastic young men were learning to fly. She watched Sammie pass the little plane over a branch, shaking it so the flour would drift down and cover the leaves. "Dusting the crops," Sammie said. Becky could swear Sammie had never seen a crop duster. Somehow, the child's use of the word, her knowledge of the word, made her uneasy.

She was probably reacting to nothing, maybe to some chance remark by a neighbor that Sammie had overheard, but still she wondered. With Sammie, any unusual reference, like so many of her dreams, might have far more meaning than seemed obvious. Sammie's dreams could affect their lives in ways that were far more real than the ephemeral world of nighttime fantasies.

Though many of Sammie's visions were small, unimportant events, a neighbor's truck breaking down late at night; the neighborhood cat who birthed five kittens, two black, three striped, just as Sammie foretold. Becky was used to those dreams, Sammie would tell them to her, then later would smile at her knowingly when the kittens were born just as Sammie said, or the truck broke an axle just before midnight and the neighbor called Morgan for help.

But some of Sammie's night visions were ugly. When she was barely four years old she dreamed that the courthouse was on fire and she woke crying that the tower was falling all in flame. A week later the courthouse burned, the tower fell blazing, its flying parts breaking ladders, smashing the hood of the town fire truck, severing a six-inch hose, and injuring four volunteer firefighters.

Becky and Morgan had told no one about their child's predictions, and they swore Sammie to secrecy. The same year she dreamed that her little dog was dead, the small spotted pup Becky had gotten for her from the animal shelter and for which she'd had a fence built to keep him from running in the street, the pup who slept with Sammie and spent every waking hour with her. Sammie dreamed that he followed their car to Main Street where a truck hit him, she dreamed his death in detail far too vivid for any child to have imagined, for any child to have to witness. Three days later the pup dug under the fence and followed their car when Sammie and her mother went shopping. He was killed on Main Street under the wheels of a delivery truck. The child's grief had already reached its peak before his death; now, her response to the fatal accident was numbness, a cold silence that deepened day by day, badly frightening Becky.

But not all Sammie's dreams were shattering, some were happy predictions, a new teacher she would grow to love; her grandmother Caroline's new sewing machine on which Caroline, a tall, handsome woman, would fashion bright new clothes for Sammie. She dreamed the tale in a brand-new storybook, knew it nearly word for word before it was read to her. She dreamed of a school party with papier-mâché elephants and giraffes and a cake with a zebra on top, her school "circus party" about which she knew nothing at the time.

But now, this past week, a stranger vision had begun: Sammie had started dreaming of an old man, someone neither Becky nor Morgan had ever met. Sammie called him the cowboy, she would wake worried because *he* was worried, because he was frightened. "Scared because he's growing old and weak," she told Becky. It seemed that only by sharing her dreams could the child deal with her fears; and this old man seemed as close and familiar to Sammie as if she had known him all her life. Becky tried to say something reassuring about people getting old, how natural that was; she would hold Sammie and rock her until the child's sadness seemed to ease, until Sammie's pain and fear for the old cowboy drew back, the distress in the little girl's dark gaze to soften, though she would remain pale and unnaturally quiet.

But now Sammie, flying her crop duster over the leaves saying the cowboy would be happy about the plane and that it would make everything all right, that the airplane would bring him what he wanted, the connection of Sammie's play with those night visions indeed disturbed Becky. The powerful juxtaposition of dream and waking play left Becky warily on edge, left her waiting nervously for whatever would happen next, for whatever was destined to happen, for the inevitable conclusion to her little girl's strange and unnatural predictions.

15

LEE'S FIRST SIGHT of Lucita nearly undid him, he was driving a loaded truck in from the fields, the men clinging to the sides cutting up as usual, when he saw a cloud of dust a long way off coming up the dirt road toward the ranch. As it drew near he recognized the green Chevy station wagon that Jake said he'd bought Lucita last Christmas. "Got it just in time," Jake had said, laughing, "before her old Ford fell apart." Lee watched her park before the house, step out, and open the tailgate. He'd expected that after so many years she'd be changed some, maybe a bit faded, maybe having gained a bit of weight. He hadn't thought she'd be even more beautiful, still slim and long waisted, her sleek black hair wound into something complicated, her pale, silky shirt open low at the throat, her breasts high and firm, her jeans just as narrow and smooth-fitting as when she was a girl. He was so intent, watching her haul out packages and a small suitcase, that he nearly ran the truck into a toolshed; behind him the men exploded shouting and laughing. He braked fast and they leaped off, heading for the mess hall.

Killing the engine, he sat in the truck watching her carry a load of groceries into the house, balancing the bags, swinging the door open with her foot. He wanted to go over and help her, to talk to her, but instead he moved on into the mess hall behind the pickers. He loaded his plate at the long counter, found an empty seat alone at the end of a long table where he could see the ranch house, see her unloading the last packages. He ate his meal quietly, and then followed his crew out to the truck again and headed back to the fields. Seeing Lucita had put him off his game so badly that twice he let the truck swing too close to the edge and almost went off the levee. Trying to pay attention to his driving, he thought about dinner tonight with Lucita and Jake, feeling as nervous as a lovesick boy, felt so unsettled he had half a mind to beg off, to say he didn't feel well.

But that would hurt her feelings, and would make Jake wonder. He sweated nervously through the afternoon. Evening came too soon, and not soon enough. Hurrying in from the fields, parking and crossing to his cabin, he showered, cleaned and polished his boots, put on the one clean shirt that he had washed the night before, spreading it out on his towel to ease the wrinkles before straightening it onto a hanger to dry. He should have gotten off the train in San Bernardino if only to buy himself some new clothes.

Leaving the cabin, walking across the yard, he was foolishly aware he was getting his boots dusty again. He'd started up the porch, was reaching to knock when she flung the door wide and threw her arms around him, startling and embarrassing him. She smelled like roses and she was so warm, her cheek soft against his, her kiss on his cheek sisterly and tender, and then she held him away, looking him over.

Her golden skin was without a wrinkle, except for the laugh creases that had deepened around her dark eyes and that made her seem somehow easier and more comfortable. She still wore her black hair long, pinned up with a silver clasp, but now it was touched with streaks of white, a bright touch that added a new charm. Her low white Mexican blouse and flowered skirt clung in a way that made him want to pull her close again, to keep on holding her. Seeing his look, she backed away, her dark eyes laughing. She took his hand and led him on inside, closed the door behind them. No dog greeted them, though she and Jake had always had a dog or two around the place, Lucita's own dog close and protective of her. She saw him glance around and knew exactly what he was thinking.

"My Aussie was poisoned, last fall," she said. "I can't bear to get another dog, to have that happen again. Someone poisoning coyotes," she said, her voice breaking, "and my dog found the bait."

She led him into the living room where Jake was setting down a tray before the leather couch, she pulled Lee to the couch and sat down beside him. "Nearly twenty years, Lee," she said easily, as Jake passed him a beer in a chilled glass. Lee would have been more comfortable drinking from the bottle, would have felt easier, too, if Lucita would move away a little, and if she hadn't dressed up for him. But she had always loved a party, loved any excuse to get dressed up. In the old days she served her party meals on cracked pottery, not the fine china and expensive silver that now graced the Ellson table. Beside him, her sweet scent mixed sharply with the spicy smells of a Mexican dinner, a combination that brought back long-ago evenings, brought back so many times for the three of them, when he and Jake had sparred good-naturedly over her. A flowered plate sat on the table, piled with miniature tamales served before dinner with the beer. It took two days to make tamales properly, and Lee was more than flattered.

"From the freezer," she said, laughing. "I made a big batch at Christmas. Do you remember, Lee, that Christmas in Flagstaff, ten feet of snow, and the young horses all playing and bucking, where we'd cleared the road, chasing each other like kids? And when the truck broke down and we couldn't get into town, all we had to eat, all that week, was the oats for the horses, until you and Jake shot that big buck?"

Lee smiled, remembering how good that venison stew had tasted, after a week of oat porridge. They'd lived on oats and venison until they'd got the truck fixed, had finally jerry-rigged the broken part with bailing wire.

When she led them in to dinner, he watched Jake seat her at the table, gently pushing in her chair; and the meal she served, concoctions of chiles and cumin, of onions and garlic and lean, roasted meat, would entice the angels right down from heaven. She talked nonstop, and that was unusual for Lucita. Was she as uncomfortable as he, afraid of the silence between them? Or maybe she didn't want to mention his prison years, bring up a painful subject. They talked about the cowponies Jake used to break, on that five barren acres she and Jake had rented, with the one-room squatter's shack. Jake had broke some good colts that year. Lee remembered Lucita's gentleness with a wild new colt, always patient but never backing off when the youngster needed to be worked, never stopping until the colt had finished his lesson.

He remembered how Lucita had found four baby rabbits in the hay barn, and had shut the dogs out, wouldn't let anyone fork hay from that part of the barn until the rabbits were grown and gone. Sitting with her and Jake remembering the old times, the good times, he remembered, too, the times when their skuzzy friends had shown up, had stayed for maybe a week or two holing up from the law, remembered how irritable Lucita would grow, angry at Jake for letting them stay, for ever running with them—angry at them both for attracting what she considered scum, the dregs of humanity. And that thought turned him quiet. If he lifted the Delgado payroll, and destroyed Jake's job, he was no better than those others.

He told himself Delgado had more money than any man had a right to, told himself he could pull this off without ever hurting Jake or Lucita, but he knew that wasn't true. One way or another, such a theft would spill over and hurt them, bad. The truth was, when he looked at it squarely, whatever wealth Ramon Delgado had, he had earned with hard work and sweat and he had every right to it. Lee might rob a man, but he had never before fooled himself that he had a right to what he stole. What he took by force was just that, robbery. That was the game he'd played, steal and get out, vanish where the cops couldn't find him. Now, taking an honest look at himself, he didn't much like what he saw. And that night, leaving Jake and Lucita, leaving the nearness of her—but still thinking about crossing her and Jake—he lay on his bunk confused, badly conflicted, tossing and unable to sleep.

He'd never felt this kind of uncertainty. In the old days

he'd known exactly what he wanted and had gone for it. Had made his plan, carried it out, and, more times than not, had got away clean, with a nice haul. But now he tossed all night, drifting in and out of sleep, thinking with shame of betraying the two people he valued most in the world, but then his thoughts drowning in darkness as he coveted the Delgado money, so near, so easy to lift for his own.

He came awake before dawn to the clanging bell from the mess hall. He looked out at the stars, rolled over, and wanted to sleep again, he was worn out, so tired that even his mind felt bruised. In sleep and in wakefulness he had fought himself, and fought the insistent urgings of the dark spirit. And as he twisted and turned, as the dark voice whispered to him, the ghost cat pressed close, sometimes rising to pace across the blanket, standing bold against the invasion that sought to mold Lee to its design.

Now, this morning, even as Lee woke more fully to the second clang of the breakfast bell, the yellow cat sat at the foot of the bed looking hard at him. This time, the cat didn't have to speak, Lee knew exactly what he was thinking: Lee had won *this* battle, he had awakened knowing he would not betray Jake and Lucita, and the cat was pleased.

Rising, hastily washing and dressing, he thought about choosing a new mark for his retirement stash, about surveying the ranches and businesses in the area until he found one that kept sufficient cash on hand to be of use. The gypsum plant, maybe. Or one of the big cotton or alfalfa farms. These were places he knew nothing about, he didn't know how they were run, he would have a lot to learn about their operations, a lot to catch up on. You didn't just walk into an office, wave your gun, and expect to walk away with a haul. He'd have to know the layout, see where and when the workers moved about, have to know what they did in their jobs, as best he could find out. Needed to know how the staff was paid. In cash? If they were paid by check, that put them out of the running. If by cash, he had to know who transported the money and when, where it was dealt out, and on what day. He'd have to work out the timing, have to know the whole drill, and that would take time. Time, and a degree of energy and stamina that he wasn't sure he could still muster. He had already blown one job because of poor planning. That had sent him to McNeil, he wasn't doing that again.

The local motels and restaurants wouldn't have the kind of cash he needed, not there on the premises. And if he hit a bank, pulled a federal crime and got caught, he'd spend the rest of his life, for sure, in the federal pen, would most likely die there, breathe his last gasp on some hard prison cot with no one to give a damn. The minute he got stressed trying to work out a plan, his breathing got worse; he knew that only part of his coughing and lack of breath was the dust. Why he had thought the blowing desert sand wouldn't irritate his lungs, he had no idea. And the Federal Bureau of Prisons wouldn't care, why the hell would they? He'd agreed when they said the heat would help him, and he'd thought it would be easy work, driving the truck back and forth, he hadn't thought any further than that. But now, with a new robbery to plan, he could feel the pressure constricting his lungs again, and he knew he'd better get on with it, better figure out what he wanted to do before the emphysema took a turn for the worse and he wouldn't have the strength to even hold a gun steady.

16

THE HARDER SATAN pressed Lee, the stronger the cat seemed to grow. No matter how Lucifer tried to manipulate Fontana, either the cat or Lee himself found a way to best him. Misto's exuberance for life, even when he traveled between lives, the ghost cat's love for the living human spirit was poison to Satan, Misto generated a joy so willful and strong, so stubborn, that the dark spirit at last backed away—for the moment. Repulsed and defeated, Satan melted from Lee's cabin out into the night where he restlessly wandered the ranch yard looking for lighter entertainment, seeking some mindless diversion to cool his seething rage.

At last, smiling, he took the form of a coyote, rank and mangy and flea-ridden. Slipping in through the walls of the nearest bunkhouse, he amused himself for a while weaving terrifying dreams among the sleeping workers, bloody nightmares that stirred memories of childhood hunger and beatings in the tired men, of adolescent atrocities, the pain from knives and attacks with broken bottles. He rekindled terrors that made the dreaming men shudder and cry out and made the shaggy carnivore smile, yellow toothed, grinning with the lusty evil that was so easy to press into the simple minds of these otherwise happy-go-lucky men.

When he grew bored with these mind games, he wandered across the ranch yard leaving no tracks in the sand, and in through the locked door of the Ellsons' house, into Jake and Lucita's bedroom. They slept twined together, dreaming, after a long and easy lovemaking, and here again he sought to drive fear into his quarry, to shatter their happy slumber.

But in the cloying atmosphere of happiness, his attempt at nightmares failed. The two slept undisturbed and peaceful except for Lucita's occasional soft moan, her hand brushing Jake's cheek but then pulling away again, tucking her hand under her own cheek. Her dream was a scenario Lucifer couldn't read or seem in any way to alter, and that, too, maddened him. The night had not gone well. If he were a human trespasser, armed and in a killing mood, if he had entered the room to shoot them in their sleep it would have gone better, though even then he thought he might have had a battle, eyeing the pistol Jake kept beside his bed.

Annoyed with the recalcitrant attitude of those in the upper world, Satan left the Ellsons' at last and quit the Delgado Ranch, abandoning this world for the moment in a swirl of wind to vanish down through packed sand and desert rock, through miles of stone and undersea rivers and molten beds of plasma. Fast as the wind he fled down and down into the hot and fiery regions where he could nurse his frustrations in his own surroundings. There, taking his ease among the familiar fires, gathering strength from hell's searing flames, he laid out plans for his imminent return.

The devil is not one entity. Like the hundred eyes of the fly multiplied ten trillion times, he is everywhere he chooses to be, everywhere at once, growing stronger where he is welcomed, fading and weakening when he is willfully rebuffed. Now down among the flames and comfortable once more, he thought that when he returned to the world above he would attend once again to the events in Georgia, to the Blake family where the scenario he had set in place was developing nicely, to the little family that was so interestingly connected to Lee Fontana. Though he would continue to haze Fontana, too, of course, searching for weaker elements in Lee's nature. The pieces were coming together very well, the results of his work were gathering in myriad ways toward an explosion of satisfying destruction. With the help of Brad Falon, that lustfully eager pawn, a final retribution was building, a last determination for the heirs of Russell Dobbs, a crushing conclusion to the lives of the final descendants of this one distasteful enemy. Soon he would destroy the last trace of Dobbs, would turn to dust all that Dobbs had begotten in his defiant human life.

THE CAT, HAVING faced off the devil with a power that seemed to Misto greater than he alone could have mustered, smiled with pleasure at Lucifer's departure. Whatever had happened tonight, Lee and the cat together had bested the dark one with a triumph that made Misto feel he could whip immense tigers, could defeat blood-hungry carnivores from far crueler ages, long past.

Once the devil was gone, Misto waited on Lee's bed only long enough to see that Lee slept soundly for the few hours remaining of the night, then he left the old convict and faded out into the cool dark. Above, on the roof of the building, digging his claws into the heat-softened shingles, he was still smiling a sly cat smile at the dark wraith's retreat, at knowing that he and Lee, armed with a fierce anger born of love, could weaken the prince of malevolence. From the rooftop he watched the coyote enter the bunkhouses, watched the devil's cold manipulation of the work-tired men, watched Satan's failure to reach or make any impression on Jake and Lucita Ellson. Above Misto the stars sparked and gleamed, and a low moon hung over the desert hills, its thin curve picking out mirrored reflections in the black and glassy surface of the great Colorado River that flowed away beyond the ranch. Happily twitching his tail, the ghost cat immersed himself in the glory of the earthly world, a world so intricate, so complicated, so dazzling a panorama with its billions of living forms all so cleverly designed, all unique and all so freely given. To the cat, this world was a great and ever-changing wonder, he felt now the same joy he had indulged in while riding atop the southbound passenger train down the coast, a giddy madness of pure pleasure. And now again he let his thoughts turn back in time, let his vision sweep back into a past when this whole vast valley lay deep beneath the sea, when these fields and low hills were part of the sea floor, grazed by fishes instead of sheep, the undersea hilltops scoured by schools of Pleistocene sharks hunting their fishy prey. And then his vision leaped ahead to see the earth heave up and the sea floor violently lift, mountains rising as the earth's plates buckled, the wrinkled coastal range pushing up and up and the sea draining away from the newly emerged land, sucked away in foaming rivers.

Sitting on the cabin roof, the cat reveled in those vast changes over eons of time. He knew a heady amazement that he, one small and insignificant cat spirit, could be privileged to witness such miracles, that he, in this time between his various lives, could look out upon whatever aspect of existence he chose, on huge events and small, all come together into the endless sum that formed life's unfathomable tapestry.

Thus, on the roof, Misto waited out the night contemplating the earth's richness but looking down often, too, beneath his paws through the cabin roof to make sure that Lee rested peacefully, praying that Lee wouldn't falter, in the future, in his defiance of the dark one.

Only in the matter of Lucita was Misto uncertain, wondering how Lee's resolve would endure—and well the cat should wonder, for in the days that followed, Lee found any excuse to be near her, any pretense to stop by the house at noon on some trumped-up errand, a need for clean towels, a request to borrow a broom. Or he would stop by the stable as she groomed or worked with the horses, or in the evening he would have an excuse to speak with Jake. Lee was more convinced each day that Lucita welcomed his attention and that she returned his feelings. The cat watched, lashing his tail, but for the moment he kept his remarks to himself; he only knew that Lucifer was not finished yet, as Lucita's slightest smile, her smallest glance heated Lee's blood. And though Lee stuck to his commitment regarding the Delgado money, Satan was busy honing Lee's resentment that Jake stood in his way with the woman he wanted; Lee didn't like seeing the two together, often so wrapped up in each other that they were aware of no one else.

Lucita kept her Appaloosa mare turned out in a half-acre paddock with Jake's big sorrel gelding, and they often rode in the evenings, out along the levees. Lee would watch from his porch as she went off with Jake, sitting the mare easy, sleek in a Western shirt, her shining black hair tied in a knot at her neck beneath a white Stetson, and as Lee watched and coveted her, Misto sensed the dark wraith easing in to make his move.

If Satan couldn't force Lee into the robbery that was against Lee's deepest instincts, then he would see that Lucita was the cause of Lee's downfall, he would stir Lee's lust for her until Lee, one way or another, moved to destroy the Ellson family and so destroy himself.

On a Sunday night when Lucita had made a pot of chili and invited Lee over, the ghost cat followed him. Wanting to see how Lucita responded to him now, he trotted invisibly on Lee's heels into the Ellson house. The smell of chili and of chopped cilantro filled the cozy rooms, making Misto lick his chops as he gravitated unseen to the top of the refrigerator, as he looked down on the three where they sat at the kitchen table drinking beer, laughing about old times. Misto could as well have made himself visible, could have walked right on in as he had done often these past days as he worked at befriending Lucita, as he sought to establish a bond with her, to gain an inside look at the little, easily missed moments that might arise between her and Lee.

The tomcat found Lucita just as charming as Lee did, just as pleasant to be near, beautiful, tender, soft-voiced. He would come to the back door to beg for handouts, would rub against her ankles, purring when she stroked him, and she always had a kind word. But tonight he remained unseen where he could observe the mood and preoccupation of the three players more closely, could listen and perceive without Lee's wondering why this sudden, intent observation.

As they served up their bowls in the kitchen and moved into the dining room, where the rest of the meal was laid out, the cilantro and onions and salsa, the rice and beans, the ghost cat drifted to the top of the carved china closet. There he sat tall and bold and invisible looking down at the three, offering no telltale shadow, no hint of a purr to give himself away. He watched them sprinkle cilantro and onions onto their chili, sip their beer, watched the interaction between the three of them: Lee longing for her, Lucita aware but ignoring his glances just as, when they were alone, she did her best to ignore his heated looks though she was indeed drawn to him. Jake remained as unresponsive as if he sat at a high-stakes poker table, no clue to what he was thinking, even when Lucita tried to breach an uncomfortable silence recalling a cattle drive the three of them had made over in Kingman that, for some reason, brought color to her cheeks. She was passing the bowl of chili when they heard, from the nearby pasture, a horse squealing with fear, the Appaloosa mare's shrill cry. Lucita bolted from her chair and was out the door. Jake grabbed his forty-five and was on her heels. Lee followed wondering if coyotes were prowling outside the paddock, or possibly a cougar, which were seen occasionally. Or maybe a stranger wandering in bothering the horses. Lucita's leopard Appaloosa was showy and worth stealing, and the sorrel gelding was a registered Thoroughbred worth good money.

Only Misto, following them to the paddock, knew what was there. A dog would have known, would have barked wildly—if Lucita had seen fit to have another dog. In the paddock the mare and gelding were circling and wheeling at a frenzied gallop, white eyed and crazy with fear, rearing, spinning, and ducking as if attacked by hornets, so terrified they were ready to jump the fence or crash through.

Jake, as he passed the tack room, had grabbed his lariat. He managed to rope the gelding, and now he stood quieting him. Lee moved beside the mare as Lucita fought to halter her. When she'd buckled the halter on at last, trying to calm the mare, she led her rearing and snorting through the gate and toward the stable. Jake had quieted the gelding. He brought him to lead beside the mare, helping to steady her. Lucita got her into her stall, still white eyed and fighting. Jake nodded to Lee to stay with her, threw a saddle on the gelding and bridled him, and headed out—hunting a varmint that Lee knew he would never see, and could never kill.

As Lucita tried to soothe the mare, Lee moved quietly into the stall. The Appaloosa seemed to accept him, she didn't shy away as he stood beside Lucita smoothing her mane. They talked softly to her, and at last the mare eased into Lucita, her shivering calmed, she didn't flinch when Lee found a soft brush and began to brush her neck, to softly brush her face. Lucita rubbed her ears, and scratched a favorite spot on her withers. Slowly, slowly the mare calmed. If Lucita was aware of Lee's closeness, she gave no sign. Only when the mare had settled enough to snatch a bite of grain, only when Lucita turned to look directly at Lee, did he see the fear in her eyes.

"What was that, Lee? What's out there? That was no animal. Where is Jake, is Jake all right?"

Lee knew there was a shotgun in the kitchen, that he could pretend to go looking, but he wouldn't go out there in the dark when Jake didn't know he was there. And what was the point? What Jake hunted couldn't be shot. Lucita looked at him, so shaken; they stood close together, the mare crowded against them for reassurance. "That was no man," Lucita said. "You saw it, Lee. A shadow, a man-shadow. But not a man." She turned, pressed her face against the mare's neck. The mare turned, nuzzling her.

"Something moving," Lucita said, "something . . . transparent. You saw it." She turned to him, reached to touch his cheek. At once his arms were around her, holding her. "You saw it, Lee. That wasn't anything living," and she was trembling in his arms.

"Lucita . . ."

She lifted her face to him, he held her close and kissed her, a long kiss, felt the heat of her, they remained as close as one being, the mare pushing into them, pressing her nose to them, the three of them needing each other, until they heard the sound of hooves, the gelding coming into the barn. Lee turned away, letting her go. When he looked back, her eyes searched his for a moment, still frightened, still needful. She started to speak but then she, too, turned away, burying her face against the mare's mane.

"I don't know what frightened them," Lee lied. Jake was coming, his footsteps in the alleyway.

Lee knew that this moment with her would lead nowhere, that it was fear that had done this, that she would not have touched him otherwise, would not have clung to him. The dark spirit had done this, and silently he cursed the haunt—and yet he would not have missed this one perfect moment even if he burned forever in Satan's hell.

It was now that the cat appeared beside Lee's boot and then leaped to the manger and into the partially filled grain box. He didn't startle the mare, in fact only then did the Appaloosa settle down completely, nose in beside the cat, and begin carefully to nibble up her oats. The cat rubbed against her then he slipped out of the manger again and down into the stall. Wading across the straw bedding, he rubbed against Lucita's ankles, his purrs calming the three of them as Jake opened the stall door and stepped in.

"I found nothing." He looked pale; he looked at the mare, so quiet now, and reached to stroke her neck. "They're both calm now. Whatever was there, it's gone." He looked at Lee, at Lucita. "Whatever that was—a cougar or whatever the *hell* it was, I hope it doesn't come back. I took the electric torch, looked for tracks, couldn't find anything. I'll try again, at first light." He touched Lucita's cheek, took her in his arms as Lee turned away and moved out of the stall.

17

Lee had been at work for nearly two weeks when he discovered the perfect escape from whatever crime he ultimately planned, a foolproof way to vanish from Blythe, to slip from the cops' grasp without a clue for them to trace. It was midmorning, he was inching the truck along beside the field below the levee keeping pace with the pickers, when above him atop the levee an unfamiliar truck came rattling along fast. It passed him and, some distance beyond, turned down the side of the levee onto an open dirt strip, stopping in a swirl of dust. Two men got out, began dragging heavily loaded burlap bags out of the truck bed. He was trying to make out the lettering on the truck's door when a buzzing sound made him look up, the racket grew to a deafening roar and a yellow biplane flashed so low over him that he ducked.

The plane banked steeply, flying treacherously low as it swung back toward the strip. The engine cut to an idle, the left wing dropped, the plane side-slipped at such a steep angle Lee was certain it would crash. The pilot in the open, rear cockpit looked down unconcerned. At the last minute he straightened the plane, touched down, and rolled lightly to a stop just beside the truck.

Lee put his own truck in neutral, got out, and walked over to take a look, watching the truck driver and his partner as they began to empty their bags, one after another, into a hopper in the front cockpit, releasing a heavy white powder that smelled like the bug poison they used in prison to keep the roaches down, or like the white cricket bait scattered like snow on the streets of Blythe. The name on the truck was Valley Dusters. The pilot slid out of the rear cockpit, pulled off his helmet and goggles releasing a tangle of brown curly hair. A young man, fancy white scarf tucked into the collar of his black windbreaker, clean tan slacks, black boots. He looked at Lee questioningly, not quite belligerent but with a lopsided half-smile.

"I thought," Lee said, "you were going to drive that booger straight into the ground."

The young man smiled. "I guess you're not a pilot. These babies are handy as hell, you can outfly a hawk in one of these." He looked Lee over. "You look like a horseman. You ever been up higher than a bronc's back?"

"Never have, never intend to." In prison he'd watched pilots buzz the walls once in a while, that always brought men out into the yard, staring up, wishing they could grab on, catch a lift out of there. Some guys claimed that in the future huge planes would fly all over the country, more and bigger even than the planes that had helped win the war, planes that would carry hundreds of passengers clear around the world. Already there were a few such flights, out of San Francisco and L.A. But this little yellow plane seemed a different breed, so small and handy it was free to land anywhere, in a pasture, an open field, the pilot could come and go as he pleased.

"It's a war surplus trainer, a Stearman," the young man said. "I'm Mark Triple."

Lee put out his hand. "Lee Fontana. I work for Delgado."

Triple nodded. "Come take a look."

Lee moved around to study the big radial engine, then stared into the open cockpit at the worn canvas seat cushion, the black instrument panel with its cluster of dials that looked only confusing to him. He couldn't imagine leaving the earth in this little machine, a man would have to be crazy. Yet the idea, the freedom such a plane offered, deeply excited him.

"I put a bigger engine on it," Triple said. "Four hundred and fifty horse. Carries a good load, but I'm going to get a new plane that will carry more dust, handle more fields without reloading. There's a growing demand for crop dusting."

Jake had talked about how much this method of distributing insecticides saved in produce, about the higher yield to the fields when the crops weren't ruined by insects. It looked like a good business, all right. It would have to be, if this young a man, who couldn't have been in business long, was already buying a new and bigger plane. How much, Lee wondered, would that set him back? Compared to a car or truck, a plane had to cost a fortune. He smiled at the kid, encouraging him. "Looks like you're doing all right."

Triple laughed. "Just getting started. Going back to Wichita in a few weeks, there's an aircraft plant there, and there's a guy back there wants to buy the Stearman."

Lee studied the pilot. "Which way will you go to Wichita?"

"Up through Vegas, to say good-bye to a girl there. Then on direct to Kansas."

"Saying good-bye's kind of final."

"I'm going on to Florida, hook up with a friend. Tired of working for others, we plan to start up our own dusting business."

"You won't be coming back to California?" Lee asked with interest. "How long would a trip like that take?"

"Here to Vegas, a little over an hour. Vegas to Wichita, given good weather, maybe nine or ten hours."

"Nice," Lee said. "Time was, it took folks months to make that journey. I guess, the way you work, on your own and all, you don't keep time schedules like an airline would, you're not beholden to anyone?"

Triple smiled, studying him. "I don't keep any schedules, and I work my own hours. As long as I do the work, my time's pretty much my own. I have my own hangar, I work when and where I'm needed. I check in with the home office once a week and send them a bill, and that's about it."

Lee nodded. "Your hangar . . . You keep your plane nearby?"

"The abandoned military airfield—that flat stretch west of town up on the butte. I contract to Valley Dusters out of San Bernardino. I'm pretty free now, I guess, but I want my own operation, I want to do things my way." He glanced up at the two men, who had finished the loading. "Have to get moving," he said, swinging up into the cockpit. "Nice meeting you, Fontana."

"Will you be back this way?"

"Next week," Mark shouted, revving the engine. "Dust again next week."

Lee wanted to ask him more but Triple was on his way, the engine roaring. Lee stepped back beside his truck, watched the yellow plane taxi, gaining speed, watched it lift at the far end of the field like a great bird leaping up, even with the weight it carried. He watched it bank sharply, heading back low, dropping its nose along the far side of the levee, where acres of young bean plants stretched away.

With its wheels just above the green rows it spat a white cloud of dust that settled quickly down on the long lines of bright leaves. At the other end of the field, Triple flew under a power line then climbed and turned, came back under the same line to make another pass. Lee stood with his hand over his nose and mouth, choking on the insecticide—but deep in thought, thinking where that plane could go without any record of takeoff time or destination. Soon he was coughing hard, but the idea that gripped him was more urgent than his sick lungs—a crazy idea, but he thought it might work, and a hot excitement surged through him. Mark Triple and his yellow plane could be, Lee thought, his one sure ticket to freedom.

All the way back to the sheds, driving the straining truck with its load of melons and pickers, and all the rest of that day driving back and forth he thought about Mark Triple, about the airplane that could put him over the mountains clear to Vegas in an hour or so, a four-hour trip or better by car. Looking off toward the hills, where the plane could so quickly vanish, he started counting the days until Triple would return, until he could bring Mark Triple innocently into the scheme he was building. He needed to get into Blythe, he needed to look the town over with more care, and to study the surrounding area. It had been many years since he'd spent any time there, things change, new and different businesses opening up. Now, with the anticipation of a perfect getaway, he found his excitement growing; this heist would not involve Jake Ellson, and that made him feel lighter, easier in spirit. Even his lust for Lucita settled into a dull ache as his common sense kicked in and his thoughts rallied to a more sensible robbery.

In the next days there were fewer times when he couldn't get his mind off Lucita, fewer nights when his dreams were filled with her, when he tossed and fought his pillow—or when the dark presence returned to wake and hassle him and urge him in his lust. If he did lie wakeful, he would instead sort through various schemes, ever impatient to get into town and take a look, get the lay of the place and pick out a new mark, now that he had an inspired and, he hoped, reliable getaway. And then, on the nights when the dark presence came stronger, pushing him to pursue Lucita more forcefully and to follow the more certain path to the Delgado payroll, the ghost cat would crowd close to Lee. Then, Misto seemed almost to become one with Lee, fighting the dark force, hissing and snarling and even seeming to grow in stature as he sought to ward off the evil that would crush Lee. The power of the cat beside Lee strengthened him so much that some nights he would scoff and laugh at Satan; and as the dark and angry spirit drew back, Lee would stroke the cat's rough coat, and smile at Misto's rumbling challenge.

But Lee feared, and perhaps rightly so, that there would be times ahead when his own strength wouldn't hold, when, alone perhaps, he would be overwhelmed, when he must watch Satan take the lead and, try as he might, Lee would be unable to best him, when it would be too easy to let the dark wraith bully and intimidate him into following the devil's plan.

18

WHEN MORGAN BLAKE was mustered out of the navy, the minute he got home he had floated a loan to make the down payment on the old Wilson gas station. Working from early dawn through the evenings, it didn't take him long to convert the building into a spacious automotive shop. He kept one gas pump, removed the other three, turned the remainder of the open, roofed area into parking for his repair customers. The shop itself was a white frame building with two bays and two hydraulic lifts. There was an office attached, a storeroom behind that, and a small bathroom. The little office, with its plate-glass window looking out under the overhang held an old metal desk, three wooden chairs, and a small wooden table cluttered with automotive catalogs. Both the shop and the office smelled comfortably of grease, metal, and the sharp scent left by the arc-welding equipment.

Now as he moved away from the raised lift where he

had been greasing a forty-two Plymouth, a white delivery van pulled into the drive and parked to the left of the bay entrance, emitting the scent of fresh bread and pastries that traveled with it. He watched his mother-in-law step out of the cab, waving and smiling in at him. He grinned and waved, and lowered the Plymouth to the concrete, as she went on into the office. Caroline Tanner was a handsome woman, tall like Becky, her dark hair peppered with white, her Levi's fitting her lean body easily, her white shirt freshly starched. She carried a white bakery box, she set it on the table, balanced on a stack of papers. It was just noon, she had obviously come to share lunch, and he wondered why. She was more than welcome, but she didn't do this often. He stepped into the little bathroom to wash up, and retrieved his lunch bag from a shelf among boxes of small automotive parts.

In the office he spread some paper towels on the desk as Caroline drew up another chair. They had exchanged no word, nor needed to. He laid his sandwiches out on the paper towels, one roast beef, one tomato and bacon. Caroline accepted half a roast beef sandwich, and poured coffee from his thermos into the two mugs he had rinsed out. He watched her with apprehension, and when she looked up at him, her gray eyes were filled with something so unpleasant that before she could speak he reached out, put this hand over hers. "Caroline, I already know."

"Brad Falon's back in town," she said softly.

He nodded. "I heard he was out on the West Coast. L.A., I think. I wish he'd stayed there."

"You haven't told Becky?"

"No." He sat looking at her, remembering the pain he

had caused Caroline when he and Becky were going together in high school and he ran with Falon. In those days he wouldn't listen to Caroline, any more than he'd listen to his own parents.

She looked at him steadily. "Brad's mother was in the bakery yesterday, we sat back in the kitchen, had a cup of coffee. I don't like the woman much, she's so . . ."

"Righteous," Morgan said.

Caroline smiled. "But she's been through hell with Brad. And now, knowing Brad, it'll start all over again."

The Falon house stood three blocks from the house where Morgan had grown up, Morgan and his parents had gone to the same church as the Falons. Morgan's mother had lost many nights' sleep over his friendship with Brad, over the scrapes they got into, and there was a lot his parents had never known, the stolen car radios and batteries they had fenced outside of town. When Morgan went in the navy, Falon was already in jail, he had been in and out of jail ever since.

For Morgan, the trouble they got into had all been boyhood pranks. When he joined the navy, he was done with that. But for Falon, that early beginning had added up to more than pranks. Long before Falon went to jail as an adult for the first time, he did a hitch in Juvenile Hall for trying to kill a little girl's puppy. He was stopped only just in time, but the judge said the intent was there. With Falon's previous juvenile record, he wasn't cut much slack.

That was when Morgan took his first honest look at Falon, saw Brad for what he was—and saw himself mirrored there. But even then, even in high school, he wouldn't stop running with Falon.

Now he watched Caroline cut her homemade pie, the blueberries oozing juice. She had brought a container of whipped cream, which she spooned liberally onto the pie as he refilled their coffee mugs. Caroline had spent plenty of sleepless nights when he and Becky were kids. Becky wouldn't stop seeing Morgan, and he wouldn't stop associating with Falon. Caroline had told him, long before he would admit it to himself, that Brad Falon was an emotional cripple, that Falon had no conscience. Morgan hadn't believed her, then, but of course she'd been right. Whatever it was inside a normal person that made them care about others, whatever it was that made them separate right from wrong, was missing in Brad Falon. Whatever made Morgan love Becky and Sammie so much he would die for them in an instant, had no meaning at all for Falon, love was a word without context, Falon could only pretend to love, just as he pretended to separate right from evil.

Caroline finished her pie and sat looking at Morgan, and he knew exactly what she was thinking. She didn't believe he would go back with Falon, yet she was sick with fear that he might. She was thinking, *Don't start again. Please don't let it start*, and Morgan was ashamed that even now, even after all these years, Caroline had to assess him all over again.

"What you're thinking hurts," he said. "But I guess I have it coming." He squeezed her hand. "I'll send him packing, you know I won't hurt Becky and Sammie. I don't want Falon around here, any more than you do." But even as he said it, embarrassment twisted his gut almost as if he were sixteen again trying to con Caroline, and he felt his face burning.

When Brad Falon flew out of L.A., escaping before the law fingered him on a land scam, he was nicely set up to put into motion events that would destroy Morgan Blake and his family. Pleased with this scenario, already planning the moves, he had no notion that he would, as well, entrap in his web a second enemy, that he would find himself in the perfect position to bring down Lee Fontana. As far as Falon knew, Fontana wasn't anywhere near Georgia or the East Coast, he knew no reason for Fontana to be there. After boarding a DC–4 in L.A., in his roomy seat Falon was soon enjoying the champagne and carefully prepared snacks including smoked salmon from Seattle and shrimp from Mexico. As he ate and drank, accepting seconds from the stewardess, he entertained himself by mentally undressing and imaginatively using the tall blonde in a variety of creative ways.

The stewardess didn't like his looks. Even when her back was turned, tending to other passengers, she could feel him watching her. He was a wiry, sour man who looked as if he'd never been young, there was no hint anywhere in that grim countenance of the shadow of a happy youth, his muddy eyes were set too close together, his face unnaturally narrow, everything about him seemed somehow wrong, she didn't like waiting on him, she drew back her hand when he touched her.

He had boarded the flight wearing Levi's, in a day when Levi's were worn only by cattlemen and horsemen, men easy in their wrinkled jeans and jackets that were softened by work and age. She was a Montana girl, she knew the difference, Falon's stiff new Levi's jacket still smelled of sizing, still sported the store creases. His snakeskin boots with red and blue flowers had never seen, or ever would see, honest cow or horse manure.

Falon watched the stewardess, wondering what she was thinking with that closed expression when she glanced at him; but then he put the hussy aside and he turned his thoughts to the action ahead, to his long-overdue homecoming. He intended, when home in Georgia again, to take care of the Blake family once and for all, in a way that would not only make Morgan suffer but would provide a lifetime of bitter payback for Becky's disdain of him, as she well deserved.

He hadn't seen Morgan since Blake went in the navy. But he'd seen Becky, all right. He'd see her again, and this time he'd make her glad to see him, real glad. Even if Morgan *was* home, Becky would need some excitement, Morgan was dull as mud, what could he offer a woman? By the time the plane touched ground at Chattanooga, the cabin was stifling hot. When the boarding door opened Falon pushed on through to the head of the line, he was the first to step out onto the rolling metal stair—into waves of heat radiating up from the steel grid and from the black macadam below. He'd forgotten how heavily the Southern heat pressed down on a person. Even a summer in L.A. could not be this oppressive, and it was still only spring. Ignoring the passengers crowding impatiently behind him, he stood looking down at the hot black tarmac and beyond at the three-story concrete terminal building, its outlines quivering with heat. Did those behind him have to fidget and grumble? What was their hurry? Some broad started carping about making a hurried connection, so it was all he could do not to turn and swing at her. He stood trying to get used to the heat, so damn hot he couldn't tolerate the fidgeting and nagging. Another woman was going on about her family waiting for her in the hot sun. He didn't move until the stewardess slipped by her passengers out onto the landing and put a gentle hand on his shoulder. He turned, scowling, then licked his lips at her. Anger blazed in her eyes, but she said nothing. He turned away again and descended the hot metal steps, frowning back at the passengers pushing close behind him, then he crossed the tarmac and into the cooler terminal.

The stewardess watched Falon turn to survey the passengers crowding down behind him, an amused smile lifting the corner of his mouth. She was deeply relieved to see the last of the sour, thin man. There was something unhealthy and cold about him, she couldn't really understand the fear he instilled in her. She turned back into the cabin feeling as violated as if he had physically assaulted her; she hoped he never flew with her again.

Falon carried his only piece of luggage, the leather valise containing an extra shirt, two pairs of shorts, two pairs of socks and a razor, stuffed in on top of ten packets of hundred-dollar bills, money he'd stashed long before the feds ever got on his tail, money they didn't know he had. The afternoon time was 3:35 by the airport clock. Chattanooga temperature was ninety-seven degrees, the humidity 91 percent. As he crossed the hot paving, his hair felt sticky, his shirt and Levi's were already clinging to him. He moved quickly through the terminal and out to the front sidewalk. He took the first cab in line, stepping in front of three old women dragging their bulky luggage. Pushing one of their suitcases out of the way, he stepped into the backseat, directed the driver to the center of town where the car lots would be lined up like Vegas gambling joints waiting for the suckers.

He left the cab, tipping exactly 5 percent, and wandered among the shiny vehicles, checking them out, moving from one car to the next, looking them over, then moving on up to the next lot. In the Ford lot he found a 1945 black sports car that suited him just fine. He paid cash, peeling off twenties and fifties from a roll that he drew from his pocket. He filled out the registration certificate under the name of Lemuel Simms. When he had completed the deal he laid his suitcase in the passenger seat, drove six blocks to a gun shop he'd spotted from the taxi. He bought a Colt .45 automatic with an extra clip and eight boxes of ammunition. In the car, loading the clips, he shoved one into the gun. Dropping gun and extra clip in his pocket, he pushed the boxes of ammo under the seat, and drove three blocks to the Merchant's Bank.

Removing a fourth of the cash from the valise, he deposited half under the name of James Halyer, opened a safe deposit box and put the rest in there. He repeated this operation at three more banks, using a different name for each, supplying the required identification for each. He finished with a thousand dollars on him. He hid the bankbooks in the double lining of his valise. As he headed the Ford for the main highway that ran south toward Rome and his parents' place, he knew he would do well with what he planned, as he always did when under pressure. He didn't mean to stay in Rome long, just until he pulled this job and got what he wanted. Growing up in that hick town had been a downer, he'd thought he'd never get out of there. Nothing to do but boost hubcaps, steal auto parts and batteries. No bars, no liquor, no dance halls, and most of the girls were straight as nuns, only a couple that would give out, and they were used by most of the male population in high school. Morgan Blake was his only buddy, though Morgan left the girls alone. Morgan had eyes only for Becky Tanner, the snotty little bitch, too good for anyone but Morgan.

He had to laugh remembering when he was in eighth grade, remembering the white dog, even if he had been sent to reform school for that little bit of fun. He'd been walking down the empty hall while school was in session, passing the front door of the second-grade room and then glancing through the half glass of the back door, looking up to the front watching the little kids at their show-and-tell, some brat standing in front of the class holding up his pet hamster.

Just inside the back door stood a line of cardboard boxes and a wire mesh animal carrier awaiting their turn. He could see movement in the carrier, something white and fluffy, and he'd heard a beseeching whine. He had stood a moment feeling excited and hard, his hunger intense. Then he spun away, around the corner past the boys' restroom to the tool room where the custodian kept his cleaning and repair equipment.

The room was usually unlocked, he had often prowled in there, and among the hanging tools was a large pair of hedge clippers, he'd watched the janitor use them on the box hedges that surrounded the school yard. Lifting them down, he'd released the catch letting the blades spring open sharp and gleaming in the glaring light from the hall.

Returning to the second-grade room, he'd slipped the back door open and pulled out the carrier with the fluffy white puppy inside. The class was so intent on a big dog doing simple tricks that no one noticed when he slid the cage to him. The puppy whined and licked his fingers through the wire, so touching. Kneeling, he opened the latch and let the puppy charge out licking and wriggling. He was rolling the pup over, rubbing its stomach to keep it still, holding its one leg up and holding the clippers ready when hands grabbed him from behind, jerked the clippers away and flung him backward. The man forced him to the floor, he looked up at the brawny school custodian, the big man's face contorted with rage. Falon had laughed at him, had kept laughing when the guy hit him, laughing, thinking about what he might have done, what he'd wanted to do, what that bastard had stopped him from doing.

Even when he was sent away to reform school, the first kid in his class to go there, that hadn't impressed Becky. The last time he saw her she'd scowled and turned away, hadn't even spoken to him. All through school, all those years, all she cared about was Morgan, she never would give him, Falon, a tumble—and a tumble was all he thought about. Lord, he could have used her. But he knew if he ever touched her, Morgan would beat the hell out of him, could be furious enough to kill him. He might have wanted Becky real bad, but he valued his own neck more.

After he left Rome, headed for California, he'd pulled a couple of nice heists; and he'd stayed in touch with his mother now and then, getting all the dull town news. She told him when Morgan married Becky and settled down in a rented house, and the next year they had a baby. Some years later when the war heated up, Morgan the patriot joined the navy and went off to fight, all that crappy flag waving. About that time, he, Falon, headed back to Rome. The army didn't want him, flat feet and a bad heart, they told him. What a crock, but that was fine with him. With Blake gone, he could hardly wait to claim what he wanted, he'd thought he'd have Becky then, easy. But the little bitch, even with Morgan gone she wouldn't let him near her, wouldn't speak to him on the street. Well, she'd talk to him now. He knew Morgan was home, but he'd soon take care of that. Morgan would be out of the picture soon enough and this time for good. Brad Falon wasn't one to give up, to turn away from the wrongs that were done to him, not without a payback.

19

ON THE NIGHT of Becky and Morgan's tenth anniversary, their little girl experienced a nightmare so violent yet so very real, a shocking prediction of a change in their lives that was beyond comprehension. If such a vision were to come true, nothing for the Blake family would ever again be the same, their very lives would be shattered.

It was heavy dusk when Sammie and her parents returned Home with their empty picnic basket after a day in the woods celebrating "their" anniversary. Morgan and Becky were laughing, holding hands, Sammie running ahead in the darkening evening past their neighbors' lighted windows, beneath the reaching arms of the maple and oak trees that shadowed the sidewalks of the small Georgia town.

Arriving home, they gave Sammie a quick bath and a bowl of soup and tucked her into bed, then Morgan put some records on: Glenn Miller and Artie Shaw, the music that had been theirs when they were courting. They rolled back the hooked rug, danced to the music that had made Becky so lonely during the war when Morgan was at sea. But now the war was history, the world was at peace or nearly so. Morgan had done his time, now there was nothing to part them. They danced with their arms around each other, held in a nest of security and love. He had come home safe, they had Sammie and were hoping for more children; the business he had built from nothing was growing; they were a solid family now and would not be parted again. It was near to midnight, they were dancing slowly, touching each other, mellowing into rising passion when Sammie's scream tore them apart, racing for her room, scream after scream, shock waves of terror.

Afraid to wake her suddenly, to jerk her from sleep, Becky flicked on the hall light, leaving Sammie's room in the half dark. The little girl was sound asleep but kneeling on her bed in a tangle of covers, hitting and fighting at the air, screaming, "No! No! Leave my daddy alone! Let my daddy go!" Fists clenched, she jerked and pulled at the empty air. "No! You can't take my daddy! No!" Her high, terrified cries shook her small body. Hugging her between them, they spoke softly to her.

"It's all right," Morgan whispered. "I'm here, I'm all right, I'm right here beside you, I'm not going anywhere. It's all right, baby, I'm right here with you."

They had no comprehension of what she was seeing, or of where such nightmares came from. No one on either side of the family had ever had anything remotely like Sammie's visions, which so often turned out to be true, and there was nothing in their family life to create this kind of disturbance, no fighting, no cruelty, not even any overly frightening stories read to her. Long after the child woke, Morgan continued to hold her. "It's all right, honey. No one has hurt Daddy, no one is going to hurt your daddy."

"Those men *wanted* to hurt you, they *tried* to hurt you."

Puzzled and deeply uneasy, Morgan held her and talked and sang to her, trying to make her understand that he was safe, that they were all three safe, but Sammie couldn't stop shivering. Her pajamas were soaked with sweat, her long pale hair clung damply to her cheeks and forehead. She burrowed into his shoulder, her face white, and when he tilted her chin up, looking into her brown eyes that were so like Becky's eyes, they were nearly black with terror.

"Policemen," she whispered, pressing harder against him. "Policemen we know, pushing you into a cage. Don't go there, Daddy. Don't ever go there again to the police station, don't let them put you in the cage. Fight them, Daddy, and don't go there!"

"Not policemen? Not Jimson? Not Trevis or Leonard?"

Silently, she nodded.

"Sammie, I went to school with those guys, I've known them all my life. What kind of cage, honey?" Neither Becky nor Morgan made light of Sammie's dreams, but this one was beyond understanding. "What kind of cage did you dream?"

"Bars. A room with bars." She pulled away, looking helplessly up at him, then clutched him again, digging her fingers into his shoulders, holding on to him as if he would vanish.

It took Morgan and Becky nearly two hours to calm her sufficiently to get her back to sleep. When Sammie wouldn't let go of her daddy, they took her into bed with them, and Becky brought her Ovaltine and half an aspirin. But even in the double bed cuddled between them, the child remained rigid, unable to escape her fear. She slept only when she was totally exhausted, Becky and Morgan holding hands across her, remembering too sharply her previous dreams that had, in real life, turned out to be accurate and powerful predictions.

Morgan slept at last, still cuddling Sammie and holding Becky's hand, but Becky couldn't sleep. What *had* Sammie seen, tonight, what terrible threat? What were these visions, where did they come from? She couldn't understand the dreams' source, she had ceased long ago to wonder how their little girl could see a future that no one should be able to know. She only knew that Sammie saw truly, her earlier dreams had proven that.

Becky and Morgan hadn't made too much of Sammie's visions in front of the child, but the dreams terrified them both. They had hoped that as Sammie grew older, the crippling experiences would fade and disappear, that she would outgrow them. Yet it seemed, recently, that just the opposite was happening. Becky had to believe there was more in the world than they could know. Sammie had proven that, somehow their daughter was able to touch an element of the future that was hidden to most people. She lay hugging Sammie and holding Morgan's hand, believing their child's prediction, and terrified for Morgan. He woke once, whispered, "Probably in her dream I was going into the jail to see about fixing Jimson's old Ford. It's always breaking down. You can see the cell bars from the office."

Becky didn't say, *Then who was shoving you behind the*

bars? Who was forcing you into a cell? She couldn't rid herself of the vision, it burned in her mind as clearly as if *she* had seen it happen, she lay awake all night trying to think of logical explanations and finding none at all, she lay holding on to her husband and their child, on to the life they shared, and though she was strong on faith and love and prayed that would keep them steady, she was equally certain that soon their life would be cruelly torn apart.

In the days that followed, Becky tried to counteract the dream and to reassure Sammie, she spent more time with Sammie after school, she invented fun things to do in the evenings, she cooked special meals. She told herself it was stupid to think this nightmare would come true, to keep dwelling on that barred room, to keep hearing Sammie's screams.

But what about the courthouse steeple struck by lightning, the bricks falling exactly as Sammie had seen? What about the kittens? The broken car?

She knew no way to shelter Sammie. She wanted Sammie to live her life with vigor, not in fear. When Sammie got that preoccupied, worried look, Becky tried to think of a new adventure to divert her, and some afternoons after school she would send Sammie off the two blocks to the shop, to be with her daddy. This afternoon, Becky hugged Sammie and watched her run down the steps hurrying toward town to the shop, wearing old, frayed jeans and carrying her small cotton work gloves and her cap. Sammie had only one side street to cross and she was a careful child. In a little over two hours Morgan would close up shop and bring her home again, a hungry little girl tired and dirty and deeply satisfied.

SAMMIE GLANCED BACK once at Mama then hurried on pretending to watch the birds and trees but thinking about her daddy and still afraid for him. No matter what else she dreamed, her thoughts always returned to the barred cage, to Daddy being pushed in there, and the men pushing him were policemen. But she had dreamed of another man too, the one who tried to hurt Mama, and who killed Misto. Now as she stepped over the sidewalk cracks and into the deepest shade, the shop was half a block ahead. Her gaze was fixed on its white roof shining in the sunlight when a black car came around the corner and slowed beside her.

Mama said to stay away from strange cars so she ran into a backyard but she would have run anyway when she saw the man driving, that same man with the close-together eyes. She stayed behind the tall gray house in the bushes until she heard the car drive away, then she ran as fast as she could all the way to the shop, and when Daddy picked her up she hugged him so hard he looked surprised, then hugged her back, harder.

"You all right? Something frightened you?"

"Fine," she said. "A dog . . . The Lewises' dog barked at me."

Morgan looked hard at her. "Is that all?" He looked like he didn't believe her.

"That's all," she lied, and grinned at him, then slipped down out of his arms and got to work beside him, handing him his tools from the black bag, and after a while the fear went away, as she worked close to her daddy, and she felt better.

20

THE FIRST TIME Lee left the ranch, first time he set foot off Delgado property since he arrived, was the day his parole officer showed up unannounced, as was the way of the U.S. Federal Probation and Parole system. George Raygor was waiting for him when he got in from the fields at noon with a truckload of melons and his noisy crew. Even in the hundred-and-ten-degree heat, Raygor wore a dark gray business suit, a red necktie closing the stiff collar of his starched white shirt. He was a young man, maybe thirty, his reined-in look as ungiving as that of any cop. Crisp brown hair cut short, rangy body, a deep tan, he looked as if maybe he played basketball. He stood on the porch of the mess hall as Lee headed there from the truck. Lee knew at once who he was, and from the way he looked Lee over, Lee guessed he was going to miss the noon meal.

Raygor introduced himself, gave Lee hell for not getting off the train at San Bernardino, and accompanied him over to his cabin where Lee toweled off the sweat and changed his shirt. As Lee bent over to wipe off his dusty boots, Raygor said, "Sit down a minute, Fontana. We're going into town on an errand, but first I want to read you your parole instructions. Here's a copy, and here are the forms you're to fill out and send in, the first day of every month." All business, stiff and cold and full of authority. These guys didn't warm up until they got some years of experience on them; even then, some of them never did. Raygor sat in the straight-backed wooden chair, watching Lee button his shirt, patronizing and impatient.

The last PO he'd had looked more like a lumberman, they'd got along just fine, even shared a swallow of moonshine now and again. But this one—Lee would like to punch him out, shake him up a little.

Well, hell, he'd felt cranky all morning, the pickers too loud, their hot tempers getting on his nerves, and twice the truck had broke down and he had to get Tony to fix it. Tony said it needed a new fuel pump, and Raygor had to pick today to come down on him. Hell, he'd done his time, or most of it. Parole board had no right to send some snotty-nosed kid still wet behind the ears to hassle and annoy him, kid probably just out of school with his fancy paper degree, thought he was big stuff driving back and forth across the desert hassling his federal caseload, pretending to help guys who didn't want his help. PO living fat off a good salary, looking forward to a secure retirement twenty years down the line, a nice nest egg for the rest of their worthless lives, courtesy the U.S. taxpayer.

Raygor, sighing patiently, began to read to him from the printed instruction form: "Your travel is restricted, you're not to leave Riverside County. You are not to change your job, or your address, without notifying me and getting permission. You are not to violate any law. You are not to own or possess a firearm of any kind. You are to fill out one of these reports each month, have it to me by the fifth, listing your present address, where you are working at that time, and what kind of work you're doing."

"Even if I'm still here at Delgado Farms, doing the same job?"

"Same job, same address. Fill it all in, no matter where you are or what you're doing. Besides the monthly report, I'll be seeing you once a month, every month. In your report, you are to give me a detailed account of all monies you have received, and all monies you have spent."

"I buy a candy bar, I have to write it down?"

Raygor nodded. "Right now, we're going into town where you'll put your prison earnings in the bank. Every week you'll deposit your earnings into the account. Mr. Ellson will see you get into town or will do it for you."

"What the hell do I want with a bank, I don't trust banks. Why is it your business where I keep my money?"

"It's my business because you're on parole. You can keep out a little for spending money but make sure you account for it."

Lee said no more, he swallowed back what he'd like to say. Silently he took off his boot, removed and unfolded the brown paper fitted along the inside, removed his prison-earned money and stuffed it in his shirt pocket. He didn't reveal to Raygor the seven hundred dollars he'd had when he entered McNeil, it was in his other boot.

Raygor stared at Lee's makeshift safe. "That'll be a

nice start on a savings account, with your wages to build it up. I talked with your boss. Mr. Ellson's going into town later, on business. He'll pick you up, bring you back to the ranch. You can have a look around Blythe, Fontana, but stay out of trouble. You were inside for ten years, this is your first time on your own except for the train trip down here. Take it easy, watch your step, you don't want to end up behind bars, locked up on the island again."

Lee stared at him coldly. "What the hell do you think I'm going to do in Blythe, hold up some mom-and-pop candy store in the middle of the day, rip off some old couple for forty, fifty bucks?"

Raygor looked back at him, and said nothing, his lean tanned face drawn into long, sour lines. Lee knew he was being unreasonable. The guy was just doing his job, doing what the authorities told him to do—but did he have to be so officious about it? His urge to pound Raygor didn't cool down until they were on the road, until he had slipped into the hot seat of Raygor's dusty Plymouth and they were headed away from the ranch, up the dirt road toward Blythe, bumping along between fanning rows of melons and string beans. Looking away over the rich green carpets of crops to the dry desert beyond where the sand stretched pale and virgin, Lee told himself that his anger at Raygor was a stupid waste of time, but he knew that what he'd felt back there wasn't all his own rage, that some of it came from the dark haunt like a residue of grease rubbed off on his hands and staining deep.

THE CAT, SITTING on the paddock fence, had watched Lee and Raygor leave the ranch in the officer's tan Plymouth, the four-door vehicle so thick with dirt it could have just been dug out of a nearby sand hill. As they drove away, and Misto felt Lee's anger at Raygor, he knew it was magnified by the heavy spirit that still sought to manipulate Lee; but the cat had to smile, too. Lee's eagerness to look Blythe over, with thoughts to an alternate plan, greatly pleased the tomcat; and as the Plymouth disappeared in a rising cloud of dust, as Misto watched it turn onto the highway heading for Blythe, he lashed his tail once, disappeared from the fencepost, and joined the two men, stretching out unseen on the mohair seat between them.

Lee glanced down, aware of the faintest breeze and then of the cat's warmth, and he smiled just a little. The cat, settling in for the ride, pressed his head against Lee's leg. Lee's Levi's smelled of cantaloupes and mud. But it was Lee's thoughts that held the tomcat, the various businesses he wanted to look over as he sought a plan that would not touch Jake, that would direct Lee's thieving onto a new path not so severely damning to Lee, as well. In this world of men, certain crimes stink of evil. Other crimes, though not strictly moral, do not burn so caustically into the fabric of the human soul.

HAVE TO MAKE your savings deposit at the post office," Raygor said. "Bank had a fire just a few weeks back. Moved their operation next door until they can rebuild."

"In the *post office*? You're asking me to give all my money, all I have in the world to some post office clerk for safekeeping?"

Raygor gave him a patronizing smile. "They have the

biggest safe in town, big old walk-in number, walls a foot thick. No one's going to pry your few hundred dollars out of there, Fontana."

As Raygor pulled up in front of the post office, Lee eyed the burned-out bank building next door, its windows shattered, smoke-blackened glass swept into a heap on the sidewalk mixed with dead crickets. Two of the burned walls had already been torn away, and a tractor and bucket sat beside the gaping hole. Big Dumpster was parked behind that, half full of blackened wood and debris. The stink of burned, water-soaked wood rivaled the smell of white poison and dead crickets. "How'd the fire start?"

"Electrical," Raygor said. "Fire marshal said it was a short in the lighting, sparks started a box of papers burning." Lee could see blackened file cabinets inside, their drawers pulled open, nothing but ashes within.

"Burned a lot of their paperwork," Raygor said, "and some hundred thousand in cash."

Lee stared at the man. "And now they're camping out in the back room of a post office. They can't keep their papers or money from burning, and you want me to put everything I own in there."

"All the deposits and remaining records are in the safe. Bank is negotiating with the post office to buy the building and the safe, underwrite new quarters for them."

Sounded dicey to Lee. What made those bank people think they could do business timely with the federal government? That transaction would probably take a decade to complete. How could you depend on bankers who were that gullible and trusting, themselves? Getting out of the car, he moved inside the one-story adobe building beside

Raygor. A half-dozen wanted posters hung on the wall to his left, surly, vicious-looking men, and Lee stopped to study them; he always took a good look to see who was roaming loose out there, you never knew when a heads-up might be useful.

Knowing none of them, he committed their faces to memory, then took a good look at the layout of the post office. The activity at the postal counter made his pulse quicken. As a pudgy bank officer met them and led them past the counter, Lee saw that the clerks were not only selling stamps, they were counting out stacks of money, big money.

The clerk, broad of girth in his dark suit, his hair thinning on top and combed to the side above his protruding ears, ushered them into a back room, a combination storeroom and office. Raygor made sure to come in with Lee, to see that he opened the account all proper, that he filled out all the papers. The two of them sat crowded at a small desk beside the pudgy banker, jammed in among rows of metal file cabinets, bookshelves stacked with black binders, and a narrow cot pushed in between with a pillow and rumpled blankets.

"Night man," the banker said, seeing Lee's interest. "Because of maybe another fire, you know," he said, gesturing vaguely, "because, it's just a post office building and all." Lee looked at the man as if bored, his heart lifting with another surge of interest. Beyond the bunk and bookshelves, a safe occupied the rest of the wall, a big iron walk-in door that must lead into an iron-clad room nearly as big as the office itself. Big old combination lock that, Lee thought, would take a skilled craftsman to finesse open, if you didn't have the combination handy.

Behind the desk was a back door maybe to the alley, set between two barred windows. It had a simple spring lock, but below that a heavy hasp with a big padlock that hung open now, during business hours. The inner door through which they'd entered was solid-looking, too. It stood open, and he could see the counter and the line of waiting customers; his interest settled on two men standing just outside, each carrying a zippered canvas cash bag, both bags bulging invitingly. Glancing in at Lee and Raygor, they seemed to be waiting for their turn with the lone banker.

Lee, focused on them, hardly heard Raygor ramble on about how much interest Lee would earn on his prison-earned money. Some piddly sum that would make a goat laugh. In the end, all he got for his cash was a dinky little savings book filled out by the flabby-faced clerk—Lee's prison money and ranch wages gone as completely as if sucked up by the desert wind, commingled with everyone else's cash, sucked into a mass of bookkeeping that, with a few strokes of the pen, could be lost forever. As they left the office, moving out through the post office lobby, the two waiting men had been joined by five more, each in possession of a fat canvas money bag. Lee looked them over good, then glanced at Raygor, scowled, and pretended to study his new bank book.

Outside again, standing on the sidewalk, Raygor gave him a dozen more instructions that Lee didn't listen to and then at last, having fulfilled his federal duty, he departed, leaving Lee on his own with a final admonition to stay out of trouble. Lee watched him pull away in his dirty Plymouth to head back across the empty desert, to harass some other unfortunate parolee. He'd been surprised when Raygor allowed him to keep part of his prison earnings. Lee had told him he needed to buy clothes, which the officer seemed to understand.

Now, alone at last, he wandered up the main street looking in the shop windows but his thoughts remained on the post office as the new job began to take shape. Yet at the same time, dark misgivings pushed at him, a fear of failure that wasn't his doing, a dark and unrelenting message that this was not the right path to take. Angrily he shook away the invasive thoughts. Walking the wide main street, he passed a small grocery, an ice cream parlor, a drugstore, the broad windows of a dime store. He finally located a shoe repair shop about as wide as a tie stall. In the dim interior, he took a seat on the shoeshine chair. He removed his boots, sat in his stocking feet reading the local paper as the thin, bearded old cobbler put on new heels. He read about the 4H winners at the local fair, studied the picture of a pair of dark-haired sisters with their two fine, chunky Hereford steers. He read about the latest episode in the eternal battle over water rights, with statements by the mayors of four nearby towns, which Lee skipped. A local man had been assaulted by his wife, shot in the foot after he beat their two children. The local sheriff had made him move out and issued a restraining order. The wife was not charged.

He watched the cobbler polish his boots, then pulled them on and paid him, asking for directions to the saddlery. He found it two blocks down, the storefront set back behind thick adobe pillars, the sidewalk in front piled with heaps of dead crickets. Stepping carefully to avoid staining his clean boots, he moved on inside.

The dim interior seemed almost cool, and smelled pleasantly of leather. Wandering toward the back, he found a table of Levi's, found a pair that fit him. He picked out two cotton frontier shirts, and bought some shorts and socks. Elbowing among the saddles and harness, he picked out a good, wide-brimmed straw Stetson. The saddles, and the headstalls hanging behind them, smelled so sweetly of good leather they made him homesick. He looked with speculation at a couple of used saddles, their wool saddle blankets matted with horsehair and smelling comfortably of sweat. He looked, but didn't buy. Not here in town, where he might be remembered later.

Leaving the saddlery, he had a good Mexican lunch at the same little café where he and Jake had eaten when he first arrived in Blythe, enchiladas rancheros, beans, tortillas, an ice-cold beer in a frosted glass. Then, with the afternoon to kill, he strolled the town letting his plan ease slowly together. Working out the details, he didn't sense the cat padding along behind him.

Trotting invisibly up the sidewalk, the cat flicked his ears, lashed his tail, and kept his attention focused on Lee as the old convict thought about the post office, smiling at his foolproof getaway that would leave no possible trail. The cat had no notion whether this plan would work, but to try to prevent Lee from any future criminal activity at all would be futile. The cat, silent and unseen, was caught up with keen curiosity in Lee's subsequent moves as the old convict put this one together.

Soon the faded storefronts gave way to small wooden cottages set on the bare sand as forlorn as empty packing crates. Some of the sand yards were picked out by low wooden or wire fences. The metal box of a swamp cooler was attached to each house, chugging asthmatically, their ever-dripping water cutting little rivers through the sand. In one small yard two husky little Mexican boys were hollering and jumping up and down throwing each other off a tattered mattress attached to rusted springs. A little girl, younger than the two boys, looked up from where she was playing in the dirt and caught Lee's eye. She pushed herself up and toddled toward him, gray powder dust falling from her hair and torn dress. She stopped just short of the sagging picket fence that separated them, stared up at him, screamed, squatted, and urinated a little puddle in the dirt. Lee's eyes flicked from the child to the porch where a black-haired woman sat on the steps holding a naked baby to her hanging breast. Her huge belly stretched her polka dot dress. Their eyes caught, she gave him a tired smile, then he moved on.

Beyond the houses rose the white wooden steeple of the Catholic church. The small sand cemetery next to it was, for the most part, raked and cared for, the individual plots cleared of weeds and debris, and decorated with pots of fading artificial flowers. A few graves were neglected, hidden by dry tumbleweeds and tall dead grass. A low, wrought-iron fence surrounded these, its curlicues woven with dry weeds. Five graves inside, the lettering on the stone markers worn nearly flat by age and by the desert wind. Lee stood at the rusty iron gate glancing around, looking toward the white Catholic church to be sure no one stood at a window looking back at him. When he was sure he was alone he swung open the squeaking gate and stepped on in, stood looking at the headstones choked with weeds, the neglected graves with, it seemed, no one to remember or claim them or to care. He studied the headstone of a child, and of a young man whose epitaph said he had left this world too soon. He paused at a grave marked James Dawson.

Dawson had been born September 10, 1871, the same year Lee was born. He died on November 3, 1945, nearly a year and a half ago. The lettering on this marker was sharp and clear, but from the looks of the grave, it had had no attention since Dawson was laid to rest. Maybe there was no one left, at least in this part of the country, to care or maybe even to remember him. Lee stepped close to the granite headstone, speaking softly.

"It won't be long, Mr. Dawson, and it'll be your birthday. You can't really celebrate it anymore, can you? What did you do with your life? What places did you see?" Lee smiled. "Would you like to come out of there, leave your grave and live a little while longer?"

Lee pulled a weed from the mounded earth. "Would you like to step out now, and live part of your life over again? How would you like, Mr. Dawson, to walk around in my shoes for a while?"

Fishing the field tally pad from his pocket, he found the stub of pencil and copied the dates of Dawson's birth and death. Slipping the pad back in his pocket, he stood a few minutes thinking, then he turned away, leaving the company of the dead man.

The cat watched him from atop a cluster of angels that guarded a family plot, his striped yellow tail hanging down over a stone wing, twitching impatiently. When Lee headed back for the center of town, again Misto followed trotting invisibly behind him, but once in town he gravitated to the roofs above and became clearly seen, stretched out in full view on the flat rooftop of the Surplus Department Store as he waited for Lee. Just another town cat taking his ease, letting the hot desert sun cook into his fur as cats so like to do. He watched Lee stop along the sidewalk beneath a spindly palm tree where he approached a pedestrian, a thin woman in a white dress, and asked for directions. She nodded and pointed, and Lee turned away smiling.

LEE FOUND THE library two blocks over, and pushed into its dim interior, the smell of the chugging swamp cooler wet and sour. Despite the damp air, the woman at the desk looked dried out, wrinkled from the desert sun. Her flowered cotton dress was limp with the breath of the cooler and with too many washings. When he asked for back issues of the local newspaper, she brushed her gray hair away from her glasses and gave him a tired stare. "What date you looking for?"

"November fourth or fifth, 1945."

When she found the oversized, bound volume for him, he carried the heavy book to a table and sat down in the hard wooden chair. Opening it out, he turned the yellowed pages with care until he had the dates he wanted. He checked carefully through the obituaries until he found James Dawson, complete with his most recent address.

Dawson had been a retired mining engineer, he died on a Tuesday night of sudden, massive heart failure. His father, Neal Dawson, had been a prominent lawyer in San Francisco. His mother, Claire Dawson, née Patterson, had been well known in San Francisco for her civic work for crippled children. Both were long dead. James Dawson, born in San Diego, California, had one surviving relative, a son, Robert Dawson, a practicing lawyer in New York. Lee jotted down the particulars, returned the book to the desk, and asked for two more sets of newspapers. "I didn't find what I wanted, I guess I wasn't so sure of the year."

He dawdled over the other two volumes for some time before he returned them and headed for the door. Before he pushed out into the hot street he turned back to thank the librarian. She smiled at him as if grateful for his courtesy. "Is there anything else I can help you with?"

"There is one other thing, I almost forgot. Somewhere I've lost my birth certificate. Would you know how to go about getting it replaced?"

"Where were you born? What county?

"I was born in San Diego."

"That would be San Diego County." She fetched a directory from the shelf above her, thumbed through and copied down an address. "Send your name and date of birth to this address, along with your father's name and your mother's maiden name. You'll need to send one dollar, and include a stamped, self-addressed envelope." She studied him with more interest than Lee liked. Maybe the old doll was lonely. Reaching into her desk drawer, she handed him a clean sheet of paper. "Post office will have stamped envelopes."

He thanked her in a way that brought a flush to her sallow cheeks, and sat down at a nearby table. He wrote out his request and information, folded a dollar bill inside, and placed it carefully into his pants pocket. He gave her a big smile, thanked her again, bringing another blush, and quickly left the library. Stepping out into the late afternoon heat he headed fast for the post office. He opened a post office box in Dawson's name, using Dawson's last address, thanking his good luck they were busy as hell and that was all the information they wanted. He bought two stamped envelopes, addressed one to the new post office box. He put that and his birth certificate application in the other envelope, addressed and mailed it, then headed for the train station to meet Jake. Scanning the street ahead, he didn't see Jake's truck—but he saw the yellow cat standing in plain sight on the roof of the train station, the big yellow tom looking down at him as if he could see clear through him, see Lee's every thought and intention.

Though Lee knew the nature of the cat, though they talked together when Misto felt the need, the cat's sudden appearances where Lee didn't expect him could still unnerve him. Lee was standing on the sidewalk looking up at the cat when a little girl raced by laughing at a flock of kids behind her. She didn't see Lee, she ran into his leg and half fell. He grabbed her shoulder lightly to help her right herself. Pausing, she looked up into his eyes still laughing—then stopped laughing, and turned pale.

She saw something in Lee's eyes that made her go white and still. Then she spun around and ran, her face frightened and grim. Lee stood looking until she disappeared. Pedestrians moved around him, glancing back at him puzzled and then moving on.

What had the child seen? Something of his own nature? Or had she seen that other presence, seen a hint of the dark spirit looking back at her?

But it was the child herself that unnerved him. She

looked so familiar, almost like the picture he carried of Mae. She had dimples, long blond hair, so like his little sister. Except this child's eyes were light blue, not dark, not like Mae's eyes in the faded photograph that he had carried all these years and didn't know why, only knew he couldn't throw it away. Only knew, or thought he knew, that somewhere down the road he'd know why he kept it. But this child, she had seen something in his face that had scared her and, as tough as the old cowboy was, or thought he was, that hurt him. Whatever had frightened her had upset Lee, too, made him turn away uncertain in himself, badly shaken.

21

OUTSIDE MORGAN BLAKE'S automotive shop the Georgia sun beat on the pavement, glaring up into the work bay where Morgan was replacing the fuel pump in a 1932 Chevy. It was just noon. He had pulled the Chevy onto one of the two lifts, but the lift was not raised. He was bent over the engine, his sandy hair tucked under a black cotton baseball cap, his lean, tanned face smeared with grease. He was priming the carburetor with gas when, from the other side of the upright hood, a man laughed. There was a long pause, as Morgan rose up. He stood unmoving, at the man's unwelcome voice.

"Hey there, Morgy. Long time no see, Morgy boy."

He hadn't heard Brad Falon come in, that was Falon's way, walking silently on soft shoes so you didn't know he was there. At the first sound of his voice, Morgan's whole being went wary. Falon used to practice that silent walk when they were kids, slipping up on him—or slipping up on

Becky, which neither she nor Morgan had liked. Even when they were only little kids, that had given him the creeps. He looked across the Chevy engine at Falon. There was no smile on the man's narrow face or in his close-set eyes. Across in the other bay, the farther one from the office, the new mechanic kept on working, paying no attention to the visitor, the tall, rail-lean, towheaded young man cleaning the plugs of a Ford truck, as oblivious of Falon as if he'd been invisible.

"What do you want?" Morgan said. "I heard you were in town, that you were out of prison again." He stood silently looking the man over. Everything about Falon stirred up a part of Morgan's life that he wanted only to forget. "I don't want you around here, Brad. What do you want?" he repeated.

Falon's narrow smile was no more than a grimace. His voice was hoarse, thin, and rough as he tried to make it jovial. "Hey, Morgy boy! Don't say you're not glad to see me, that's not good Southern manners! It's me! Falon, your old buddy!" He moved around the Chevy and slapped Morgan on the shoulder, his grin no more than an animal sneer. Morgan stepped back away from him, turned back to the engine, and set the last mixture screw onto the carburetor.

"Hey, I just got out of bed, Morgy. Couldn't get my car started, had to leave it at my girlfriend's." He yawned hugely, and pushed back his ruffled hair. "Car sounds like something broke off, loose and clattering. I'm afraid to try it again, it sounds like hell."

Morgan said nothing.

"You know I don't know anything about motors. I had to walk the seven blocks over here, and this humidity's got me, I'm not used to this weather anymore, I feel like a ton of lead weighing me down. Can you run me back over there, and have a look? I know you can fix it. I ain't even had breakfast yet. Come on, Morgy, I'll buy you breakfast. Or lunch, we'll go out to Sparky's for ribs, we can do that before you fix my car."

"I don't leave the shop at noon, Falon. Albert can run over there, Weiss is a better mechanic than I am." He looked across to Albert. Albert straightened up then, laid down his tools, and pulled off his canvas apron.

But Falon shook his head and took Morgan by the arm. "Come on, Morgy. Everyone has to take a lunch break. We'll just run out to Sparky's, be back in half an hour. Your car parked close, here?"

"Can't do it, Falon. If you want your car fixed, Albert will take a look at it. No one can eat at Sparky's in half an hour."

"Maybe you're right," Falon said agreeably. "Well, then, just run me over to get my car, I haven't seen you in a long time. I don't know Albert Weiss, here, but I know you're tops with a Ford. Just for old times' sake?"

"Sorry," Morgan said, and turned away. When, in high school, he'd finally distanced himself from Falon, much of the reason was that Falon kept coming on to Becky. Becky hated him. She had kept away from him then, and while Morgan was overseas. According to Becky, Falon had made no trouble for her, while he was gone, but still Morgan's distrust of Falon ran deep.

"Come on," Falon repeated. "For old times. I've got something to tell you, Morgy. Something I think you'll want to hear."

"I'm done with that crap," Morgan said, and began

wiping off his tools, slipping each into its slot in their black cloth case.

"This isn't anything like that," Falon said. "This is . . ." He was silent until Morgan turned to look at him. "This is about Becky," Falon said. "About Becky and that property outside of town that Becky's mother owns and maybe about your little girl."

Morgan began cleaning his hands with paper towels. "You're giving me a bunch of crap."

"That land next to Grant's farm?" Falon said. "Along beside the Dixie Highway?"

"What has that to do with Becky? What are you trying to pull?"

"Not a thing," Falon said easily. "Just a bit of information I thought might interest you. I was in the courthouse yesterday looking up the old deeds on my parents' house. I ran across a piece of information I thought you'd like to know about."

"So, what is it?"

"Come take a look at my car, and I'll explain it."

Morgan stared at Falon. "Have you *seen* Becky, or called her?" But then he wished he hadn't said that, hadn't let Falon know that it would even concern him. Not long before Falon was sent to prison, he came on to Becky real strong. She blew him off, told him to leave her alone, but that had hardly fazed Falon. Now, Falon glanced toward Albert as if he didn't want Albert to overhear.

"Whatever you have to say, Albert's welcome to listen," Morgan said.

Falon just looked at him, his stare pinched and stubborn. "What I have to tell you is about Becky and Sammie."

"So?"

"It's private."

Despite how Falon lied, his words stirred a cold chill in Morgan. Uneasily, and knowing better, he fished his car keys from his pocket. "I'll take a quick look. Then maybe I'll send Albert over, he might have to tow it in."

Falon turned, slid some change into the Coke machine, and fished out two bottles of Coke. Opening them, he handed one to Morgan and then headed out through the big shop doors.

Morgan's '38 Dodge was parked half a block down, under a shade tree where it wouldn't take up space in the shop's small parking area. He had bought it pretty badly wrecked, had done the body work himself, had put in a new block, had had it painted and upholstered in exchange for automotive work. Now it was almost like new, and it ran like new. He hoped no one saw him with Falon, after all the trouble they'd been in together in high school and then Falon's subsequent arrests. In a small town, everyone knew your business. If anyone saw him with Falon, they'd be sure to pass the word.

But what could just a few minutes hurt? Drive a few blocks, look at a stalled car right out in public? Auto repair was what he did for a living. And who knew, maybe what Falon had to tell him would be worth hearing, maybe something he'd be glad later to know about. Falon had worked in real estate for a while, years back, somewhere south of Atlanta. He knew Becky's mother bought and sold land from time to time, always with a little profit. Caroline had bought that property out on the Dixie Highway some four years ago, with an eye to rising land prices. She had leased the land to John Truet, who farmed it and the adjoining ten acres. Caroline's will left the land to Morgan and Becky, or in a trust for Sammie if they were gone.

Morgan didn't know what papers Falon might have seen in the courthouse, but there were stories in town of land swindles where tax records had been falsified and land bought out from under the legal owners. He had heard rumors, as well, about some kind of land development along the Dixie Highway, stories that had stirred idle talk around town. He supposed he could go on over to the courthouse himself, or Becky could, and find out what Falon was getting at. But it might take a lot of searching to come up with what Falon already knew, if there was any truth in his words. If there *was* something afoot about that property, Caroline needed to know.

But still he was edgy, his common sense telling him to take care.

Morgan's Dodge was burning hot inside, even under the shade of the oak and with the windows down. He let Falon talk him into a quick sandwich, just a few blocks up the street. But they'd barely pulled away from the curb when Falon, reaching down to straighten his cuffs, spilled his Coke all over Morgan's new upholstery.

Morgan shoved his own Coke at Falon to hold, grabbed a towel from the backseat, and began wiping up the spill. He scrubbed the stain as best he could, swearing to himself. He drove on quickly to the next gas station to rinse out the towel and scrub the seat better, and dried it with paper towels.

When he got back in the driver's seat, hot and angry, Falon handed him his Coke, and he drained it. "Skip the sandwich, Falon. Let's look at your car, I have to get back. What's this information you're so eager to tell me?"

"Tell you after we look at the car," Falon said. Of course he didn't apologize about the Coke. He was quiet as Morgan turned down Laurel, heading for the Graystone Apartments where Falon said his car was parked.

They were several blocks from the Graystone when Morgan began to feel uncertain of distances. Puzzled, he eased off the gas and went on more slowly, driving with care. The spaces around him seemed out of kilter, the distance from one corner to the next seemed all wrong. What was the matter with him? Other cars on the street appeared foggy, they were too near to him and then unnaturally far away. He nearly sideswiped an oncoming truck, and the driver blasted his horn angrily. When driving became too difficult, he pulled over, was surprised to see he was pulling up in front of the Graystone. He felt sick and dizzy, he was so confused he couldn't remember how to turn off the engine. He managed at last, clinging to the steering wheel.

"That's it," Falon said, watching him, "that black Ford."

Morgan looked blearily across the street at the uncertain line of cars. Light shimmered off them as if from giant heat waves. He guessed one of them was black, and maybe it was a Ford. He wasn't sure he had killed his engine, but when he looked down at the key, trying to figure it out, trying to hear if the engine was running, the dashboard heaved up at him, blackness swept him, and he knew no more.

Days later, trying to reconstruct those moments, Morgan would not be able to remember arriving at the apartments, would not be able to bring back anything after pulling away from the curb near the automotive shop and then Falon spilling his Coke. Everything after that was a dizzy blurr. But later, sitting on his cot in the jail cell as slowly his mind cleared, he would remember Sammie's nightmare, of him being shoved behind bars by men he knew and trusted, and he knew Sammie would suffer the most. He worried far more over his little girl than over what would happen to him, even if, as the cops said, he could go to prison for the rest of his life. He had no idea what had occurred to put him here. None of it made sense, and no one would tell him anything more. What he didn't understand was why Sammie had been sucked into this pain. What kind of fate was this, after they had been parted so long during his years in the Pacific, what fate so cruel it would seek to destroy them now?

22

LEE WAS BACK in Blythe four days later, another welcome break from the long hours in the fields, the dust choking him so he coughed up phlegm every night. Riding in the pickup beside Jake, he knew Jake's pocket bulged with cash, money to buy a drilling rig, a pretty expensive proposition. Ramon Delgado had heard there were a few jerry-built rigs for sale and they were headed for the farm auction, ready to buy if Jake found what Ramon wanted. Looking out at the green fields and the harsh glare of the desert beyond, Lee thought about the information he'd already picked up on some of the local businesses, and what more he meant to accomplish today. He felt good, things were coming together. The way the plan was shaping up, he wouldn't head for Mexico right away. He meant to lay a circuitous path that would put him back in the slammer for a short time before he moved on across the border. The degree of risk hinged on how

dependable Mark Triple would be, in getting him out of Blythe when he needed to disappear. But the robbery itself was still nebulous, his mark still uncertain, and even as he considered the possibilities, still the dark shadow whispered to him that this wasn't the smart way. That whatever alternate plan he chose would surely fail and he'd be back behind bars for more years than Lee could count. The relentless prodding stirred in Lee a deep anger at the devil's persistent invasion of his free will, he wished to hell Russell Dobbs had found *some* way, that half century ago, to keep from dragging his future descendants into his unholy bargain. Stubbornly Lee willed the shadow away, while beside him on the seat of the truck the cat rolled over, silently purring, his unseen smile heartened by his friend's growing resolve. Lee, sensing Misto's pleasure, hid a grin.

The truck rode like an edgy bronc, bucking through each dry wash, through the deep gullies that, though the sky might be clear overhead, could flood suddenly from a fast, heavy runoff pouring down from the far mountains. Sudden walls of frothing water boiling down faster than a horse could run, racing so hard across the desert and roads that it would roll a truck over and sweep it away. Lee, well aware of the danger, looked up toward the mountains where heavy clouds were gathering, where rain must surely fall soon. But Jake drove relaxed and unconcerned, listening to the softly tuned weather report on the radio. "If it starts to rain," Jake said, "we'll stay over in town, wait until the gullies dry up again."

Lee nodded. "You think you'll find the rig you want, that Delgado wants?"

Jake shrugged. "They're all home-built jobs, but with luck we'll find a good one. Ramon has planned this for a long time, drill some wells of his own, step out of the battle over water. The water table's high all over Blythe." Lee had always thought it strange that, even with water so close to the surface, the cotton and alfalfa and vegetable farms had to run irrigation canals from Blythe's complicated aqueduct system.

"Water table so high," Jake said, "that, come winter, the whole land will flood, destroy a man's crops, wash away tons of good topsoil. But then in dry weather we still need the aqueducts—or wells," he said, "to bring the water up."

According to Jake, back in the twenties before the weir and aqueducts were built, Delgado was one of only a handful of men who dreamed of making the dry, barren desert produce any food crops at all. Most people said they were crazy, but the men had stuck with what they believed, and Lee had to admire that.

He looked at Jake, thinking about the complications of his job, envying what Jake had made of his life, his and Lucita's lives. Lee knew he couldn't have given her this much, that he would have ended up running off, following the only life that seemed to suit him. He thought about this noon, how she had reached to touch his hand as she'd brought fresh towels and linens over to his cabin. He had just been changing his shirt, discarding his ripe work shirt, ready to head for Jake's truck, leaving Tony to handle the men, hoping the kid would act like a man and not like a snotty-nosed boy. He was buckling his belt when Lucita appeared at the half-open door, calling out to him.

She stood on the porch, but made no move to enter. Taking a step closer, she handed him a stack of clean sheets and towels. When he asked her in, she shook her head, but her eyes said something different. As she handed him the linens her hand brushed his and remained there, still and warm, for a long moment, her eyes on his generating a shock of desire.

Then she shoved the linens at him and was gone, down the steps again heading for the ranch house. He had stood looking after her, his pulse beating too fast, and then feeling let down and angry.

Turning back inside, he'd dropped the linens on the dresser, stripped his bed, wadded the sheets and used towels into the clean lard bucket she left in the room for laundry, pulled on his jacket and headed out to Jake's truck. But there had been one other incident, two evenings before, that had left Lee even more shaken.

The horses had been spooky ever since their panic when the dark spirit lurked in their paddock—for what exact purpose the wraith had come there, Lee wasn't sure. Simply to frighten Lee himself, to show his power? Some kind of promise of what he *might* do, what he was capable of doing? Whatever the devil's purpose, the horses hadn't really settled down, even days later. Lucita rode her mare every morning, to try to get her over her nervousness. The Appaloosa was pretty good in the daytime, but Jake said that on their evening rides both horses were spooky as hell. Having to be gone overnight up to Hemet where Delgado wanted him to look at some land, Jake had asked Lee to ride with her. He wanted to keep the horses on a steady schedule, wanted to keep working them, and he didn't want Lucita riding alone.

Lee was wary of being alone that long with Lucita. And he was eager as hell for the opportunity. When he headed on over to the stable, he found she'd already saddled both horses, and had strapped on scabbards. She handed Lee a loaded rifle, stowed her own rifle, and mounted matter-of-factly. She moved on ahead of him out of the ranch yard, the mare always liking to lead, and the good-natured gelding giving in to her. As the evening light softened around them, both horses were steady, nothing bothered them. Moving up the northbound trail between the verdant fields, Lucita didn't talk, she gave him no heated glances, they rode in a comfortable silence between the green crops and then, before the evening darkened, they gave the horses a gallop on a hard, narrow path in between the dry desert hills, where the trail was less apt to offer chuckholes. Lee wanted to stop there among the hills, out of sight of the ranch, and let the horses rest. He wanted to swing down out of the saddle and hold her close, wanted this night to lead where he dreamed it should lead. He wanted not to turn home again discouraged, knowing this was never going to happen. But that was how they did turn back, with nothing else between them, both paying attention to their horses and to the trail ahead as the evening darkened around them. He knew she felt what he felt, her little movements, her small glances; but he knew just as clearly that she would do nothing about it, that she belonged to Jake, that he was Jake's friend, and that that was how their lives would remain, no matter how his hunger for her stayed with him.

IT WAS TWO-THIRTY when Lee and Jake pulled into Blythe. The thermometer on Jake's dashboard said a hundred and fifteen, and that was with the windows open and a middling breeze blowing in. They'd passed a few trucks on the narrow desert road, all headed for the sale, same as they were, some with empty trailers rattling along and most likely those drivers carrying a wad of cash, too. They'd passed a number of trucks already coming back pulling loaded trailers. When Jake parked in the auction yard, Lee left him to wander the grounds.

The loud staccato of the auctioneer's voice followed him, its hammering rhythm soon making his head ache, the fast gibberish pounding unrelieved, mixed with the voices and laughter of crowds of people pushing and jostling around him. He walked through the lines of trucks for sale and then stepped into the barns where it was quieter. The narrow pens were nearly empty, only a few motley farm horses and half a dozen saddle horses left unsold. The morning auction had been livestock, the afternoon sales had begun with small vehicles and would work up to the big trucks and the heavy machinery that Jake was waiting for. Lee lingered over the saddle horses, speaking quietly, smoothing a rump, watching their ears swivel around at him. None of the horses impressed him much; but hell, for what he wanted, most any crowbait would do. Fellow could pick up one of these leftover nags real cheap.

But he wasn't ready to make a purchase. He stood looking, and then left the auction area, heading for the center of town, the rattle of the auctioneer following him a long way, only slowly fading. In the center of Blythe he crossed the wide main street, its baking heat reflecting up at him like an open oven, and he moved off in the direction of the post office.

Along the curb, cars were angled in solid, not a parking space to be seen. Auction was a big day in town. The little grocery was crowded, women and children carrying out wooden boxes loaded with staples, cornmeal, sugar, salt, and lard. An occasional horseman threaded through the street traffic; two farm horses stood hitched to an open wagon in front of the drugstore, heads down, sweat drying on their necks and shoulders. He could smell heat-softened tar from the roofs above him, the flat roofs of the one-story build-ings that had to be retarred every few years to keep from leaking. The tall, spindly palm trees that had been planted here and there in front of the stores looked like oversized, upside-down floor mops stuck in the sidewalks and streets, their drooping fronds ragged from the desert winds.

The crickets were mostly gone, at least the live ones, not crawling up every wall, but piles of dead crickets were still heaped in the gutters, their dark rotting bodies not yet shoveled up into some refuse truck, their stink so sour he could taste it as he approached the burned bank next to the post office. Heavy equipment was still at work there, a backhoe with a bucket, cleaning up the last of the black, sodden refuse.

Moving on to the post office, he'd meant to check his P.O. box; though there was no way they could have his new birth certificate to him yet, he burned to have a look. But the line snaking out the front door made him draw back, paus-ing in a shadowed doorway. Standing in the entrance to a small sandwich shop, he watched the long post office queue that trailed away down the sidewalk. Men in work clothes, a few men in suits, a few women, all in housedresses, half a dozen cowmen in faded Levi's and worn Western boots. His gaze paused on two men carrying heavy money bags, the canvas bulging beneath their zippers. Lee, his pulse beating quick with interest, tailed onto the line trying to look bored and patient.

Most of the patrons were buying money orders. As he edged nearer, then was finally inside the door, he watched amazed the amount of money passing across the counter.

Stacks of fifty- and hundred-dollar bills being counted out, some bundles handed across to the patrons, some put over into the care of the two postal clerks. Behind the clerks on a long oak table stood tall piles of greenbacks that, he supposed, had all come out of the safe. That made him smile, guessing that the meager wad of his creased tens and twenties from prison was mingled in with all that wealth. Shyly Lee glanced at the man behind him. "I thought it would only take me a minute. Is there always such a crowd?"

The soft, florid man hooked his thumbs in his suspenders, laughing. "You're a newcomer, all right. There's no bank in town, since the bank next door burned. Otherwise, you'd see these lines over there. Since the bank burned they do their business here. But even so, the post office is always busy, a lot of us pay our bills and make catalog purchases with money orders."

This was better than Lee had guessed, there was more money here than he'd ever dreamed. If he could bring off a heist like this, he'd be set real nice for wherever he wanted to travel.

"Won't be this crowded for long," the pudgy man was saying, "just until the new building's up." He shifted his weight as if his feet hurt. "Right now, you'd have to drive across into Arizona for the nearest bank. Not far, just to Parker. But it's easier to do business this way."

The line edged forward and they moved with it, Lee trying not to show his excitement. "That's a bummer, you have to go into Arizona to cash your paycheck."

"Oh, no. Folk here don't get paychecks. The pay, everything we do in this town, is pretty much on a cash basis. Most of the farmworkers are paid with cash. Same with the mining company. Payroll comes in by mail on the last train. Fridays, this place is like Fort Knox. They shut the front doors but the small operators come in that way. Foremen from the big outfits, most of them come around the back, from ranches and mines from all over, to pick up their cash so they can pay their men the next morning." The man seemed innocent enough in imparting the information. And why not, it was obviously common knowledge. Lee watched man after man, likely local businessmen and independent ranchers, approach the counter pulling out fat rolls of bills. The man ahead of him, dark hair slicked back, peeled off three one-hundred-dollar bills and two fifties as casually as Lee would flip out a quarter for a beer. When it was Lee's turn at the counter, he had to grin as he asked for four more stamped envelopes, thinking that in some way he might need them—and giving him time for a closer look at the stacks of money behind the counter, money he coveted.

Leaving the post office, he strolled along the outside of the building, looking more closely at the layout. The burned-out bank was on his left, facing the street. Beyond that was a vacant lot, then a cheap two-story apartment house. On the other side of the post office, a small hardware store, boxed in by adjoining stores, dry goods, a dime store, used furniture. When he walked around behind the solid row of buildings he found a narrow dirt alley running their length, with access to half a dozen back doors, including the heavy post office door with its barred window on each side. Just the simple snap lock on the outside, giving no indication of the big padlock concealed within. Across the alley stood an old wooden building that he thought might be storage for the hardware store, a stack of empty wooden nail boxes was piled by the back step. Behind that were more vacant lots, then a line of willows, then the empty desert stretching away.

He returned to the main street thinking about the moves it would take to bring off a robbery here, and about Mark Triple and his duster plane. He had seen Mark again on Saturday, loading up to dust another run of melon fields, and Mark had kidded him about trying a flight. The young pilot was flying up to L.A. in a few days, before he headed for the East Coast, he said he needed to get some work done on the prop. He had invited Lee to go along, and Lee, with the same flash of certainty that had led him to James Dawson, had eagerly accepted. Strange how things fell into place. Seemed like all his life, he'd fallen into situations which, most of the time, turned to his benefit, fitting right in with the plans he'd already started putting together.

Thinking of his possible moves in L.A., he paced the length of Blythe again. Even here in the center of town the desert wind brought the stink of the big cattle-feeding yards that lay outside of Blythe, with their modern feed mills and storage tanks. Thinking about that wealth, the wealth he knew lay in the big farms, and the cash he had seen in the post office, he stopped in a small grocery for a pack of gum, stood unwrapping a piece of Doublemint, smiling at the white-haired old man behind the counter. Old, Lee thought. Older than me but still working all day every day for a two-bit living.

"Someone told me there was some kind of airstrip here, just outside town. Not the commercial airport, some little dirt landing strip, they thought. Said they saw a little plane land somewhere on the other side of town," he said, pointing. "I thought that was kind of strange."

The old man laughed. "Could of seen a plane, all right.

There's an emergency airstrip some eighteen miles east of town. Lies just where the road runs in from Jamesfarm. Sometimes a rancher or the gypsum mining company use it." He jerked a thumb to the east. "Out on Furnace Road. Old, fallen-down barn near it, migrants camp there some."

Lee made small talk for a few minutes, then touched the brim of his hat and left. Walking back out to the auction site, he felt almost good enough to do a jig. His scenario was shaping up real well. The sun was settling low, casting the mountains' shadows long across the bare desert. The temperature, though evening was nearing, had dropped maybe all of two degrees.

He found Jake looking at the tires of a big drilling truck. From his grin, Lee figured he'd bought it. "They threw in a bunch of drilling rods," Jake said, "and I didn't have to bid as much as I thought. Come on, I'm dry as dust."

They headed for the same small Mexican restaurant, the jukebox playing loud and brassy, the tables crowded with groups of men talking and arguing, drinking cold beer and tying into their early suppers. Lee and Jake wedged into the last table, in the far corner, soon easing the heat with icy beer as they ordered a good hot Mexican dinner. Outside the windows the light continued to soften; but the noisy din in the small room, the loud conversations, half Spanish, half English, mixed with the loud Mexican brass from a record player, soon began to pound in their heads. They didn't talk much, they could only half hear each other, and they were glad at last to be out on the street again ready to head home. At the red pickup, Lee eased into the driver's seat, watching Jake step into the drilling rig. He followed Jake's taillights at a good distance as they headed away up the narrow, bumpy road.

23

It was the same afternoon that Brad Falon came to Morgan's shop asking him to look at his stalled Ford, that Sammie became sick at school. She grew lethargic and cranky in class, and when she started falling asleep at her desk, the school nurse called Becky. When Becky picked her up, Sammie crawled into the car yawning and dull. Becky felt her face for fever but Sammie was ice-cold, her skin pale and clammy. "Does your head hurt?"

"No," Sammie said drowsily.

"Do you hurt anywhere?"

"No." Sammie sighed and snuggled closer. By the time they got home she was sound asleep. Becky managed to wake her, and half carried her inside. She got her settled on the couch, pulled off Sammie's skirt and blouse, and examined her carefully all over for spider bites or bee or wasp stings. She could find no blemish. She parted Sammie's hair with her fingers, searching for a bite there, feeling for any painful area. Sammie complained of the cold, her whole body was chilled through, though the day was hot. When Becky took her temperature, it was lower than it had been at school, a full degree below normal. She covered Sammie with a warm blanket, thinking she'd wait just a little while before calling the doctor, to see what developed. The nurse had said they had five children out with the flu. She made a glass of hot lemonade, and went to fetch the aspirin. When she returned, Sammie was asleep again.

But it seemed to be a normal sleep, she was breathing easily. Becky set the glass on the coffee table, stood watching Sammie for a few minutes and then, straightening the cover over her, she left her sleeping. She stayed near to Sammie, working at the dining table on the dry-goods books, looking up often at Sammie, and rising to feel her face. The child slept deeply; Becky woke her at suppertime but she wasn't hungry or thirsty. She didn't want to eat, didn't want the thermometer in her mouth again but Becky managed to persuade her. Her temperature was lower, 96.4. Sammie was still so groggy she turned away from Becky's hug and was asleep again. It was then, turning away to the phone, that Becky called the doctor. When she gave Dr. Bates Sammie's symptoms and temperature, he said it sounded like the bug that was going around. He said to keep her warm, not to give her any more aspirin, to get plenty of liquids down her, and to call him back in an hour.

In less than an hour she woke Sammie. She had to cajole her to hold the thermometer between closed lips.

The minute she removed the little glass vial, Sammie was asleep again. The gauge read 96.0. When she finally reached Dr. Bates he was at the hospital with an urgent stroke case, he said he'd be there as soon as he could.

James Bates had been their family physician for three generations, he still took care of Becky's mother, took care of all of them. He listened again to Sammie's symptoms, said again that there was some kind of summer flu going around, said if Sammie got worse, to bring her to him at the hospital.

Looking at the clock, Becky realized it was way past time for Morgan to be home. Usually he called when he was late, so she figured he'd be along soon. She set the chicken and rice casserole on the back of the stove, and examined Sammie again for insect bites, even more carefully this time. The child didn't want to wake, didn't want to be bothered. When she did speak, her voice was so blurred it was nearly incoherent. The time was past seven, and still Morgan wasn't home.

Morgan did sometimes work late when a customer was in a hurry for his car, but he always called to let her know. Sharply concerned now, she phoned the shop. The phone rang eight times, ten, but no answer. Ten minutes later she called again, in between pacing with worry. Again, no answer. When it was fully dark and Morgan still wasn't home, she phoned again, let it ring and ring and then she borrowed her neighbors' car, bundled Sammie up, called Dr. Bates to tell him where she'd be. Sammie was only half conscious as she carried her to the car, covered her well, and drove first to the shop.

The office and bays were dark, the bay doors closed and locked tight, the parking area dark and empty, both Morgan and Albert Weiss, the new mechanic, were gone. She cruised a ten-block area looking for Morgan's car. When she didn't find it she drove home again but Morgan wasn't there. She carried Sammie inside, tucked her up on the couch again, and looked in the phone book for Albert's number.

There was no Albert Weiss listed. She called the operator, told her it was an emergency, but she had no listing for him, either. Becky sat at the dining table, her hands trembling. She phoned her neighbors. They said they wouldn't need the car until morning, that she could keep it all night if she needed to. The Parkers were an elderly couple, both in ill health, and she couldn't ask them to keep Sammie. She bundled Sammie back in the car and headed for her mother's, she meant to leave Sammie with Caroline, the doctor could see her there. Or if Sammie got worse, Caroline would take her to the hospital. Both Becky and Caroline preferred to keep her at home, both were a little wary of hospitals, though for no particular reason. Once Sammie was settled, Becky intended to go look for Morgan, to drive every street in Rome and every surrounding farm road until she found his car. She didn't imagine that he was out drinking or with another woman, she knew him better than that. Something had happened to him, and when she thought about Brad Falon newly back in town, a sick, almost prophetic fear touched her.

Approaching her mother's sprawling white house, she was eased by Caroline's welcoming lights. Maybe Morgan was here, maybe he had stopped by for something. Her own birthday was only a few weeks away, maybe they were planning a surprise and had lost track of the time.

But Morgan's car wasn't there. She parked in the drive,

got out, carried Sammie across the lawn and up the front steps. When Caroline answered the bell and saw Becky's face, she took Sammie from her. Settling the child on the couch, she sat close beside her easing Sammie onto her lap as Becky described Sammie's sleepiness, her low temperature, and then her worry over Morgan. Caroline took charge as she always did, and soon Becky was out the door again, shaky with concern for Sammie, and frightened for Morgan, driving the dark streets of the small town looking for him, looking for their old blue Dodge.

LEE, ALONE IN the pickup following the drilling truck, was pleased by the silence after the noisy, busy day. The sun was gone behind the western hills, the glaring desert softened, now, into deeper shades, the dry gulches and low mountains catching streaks of gold in the last light. He spotted a coyote slipping along a wash, just its ears, a flash of its back, and the tip of its tail, maybe hunting alone, or maybe not. In the quiet he thought about James Dawson, and smiled. Both Lee and Dawson born the same year, Dawson with no one nearby to tend his grave or to care about him, maybe no one to know he was dead, a lonely old man lying in that little cemetery just waiting for someone to come along and take notice of him, to revive and resurrect him.

When, ahead, he saw Ellson's truck buck into low gear for a long incline, Lee slowed to keep the distance, noting the gravel road that led off to the right following the slope of the rock-strewn mountain, marked with a faded wooden sign that read JAMESFARM. Somewhere down that road, not too far, should be the airstrip. Beyond a scraggly patch of tamarisk trees, he glimpsed an old barn, lopsided and about ready to collapse; but maybe it would hold up for a while longer.

He was going to need a car or truck and, as he scanned the upper slopes of the mountain, he knew he'd need a horse; that meant a trailer, too. And he sure as hell needed a gun. Easing his foot on the pedal, he swallowed back a tickle in his chest. He'd better not screw up this time or they'd lock the door on him for good. He followed Ellson's taillights, heated with the growing excitement that a new job always stirred.

As evening settled in around them, Jake's headlights came on and Lee switched on his own lights, their beams driving the last desert shadows into falling night, then soon into blackness. And, in the shadowed cab of the truck, Lee knew suddenly that he was not alone, he felt a cold presence nothing like the comforting nearness of the ghost cat. In the dark cab he turned to look at the seat beside him, and his hands tensed on the wheel. A woman sat beside him, her full, dark skirt swirled around silk-clad ankles, her black hair blending into the shadows, her face unseen. For an instant he thought it was Lucita, then knew that it was not. This was a thin-faced woman, a hard and lethal beauty. Watching her, Lee swerved the truck so badly that he had to fight frantically to right it, jerking the wheel, trying to keep his eyes on the road.

"Relax, Fontana," she said softly, "I did not mean to frighten you."

"What the hell did you think you'd do?" The timbre of that voice, even in the tones of a woman, resonated with the cold chill Lee knew too well. "Why would you appear as a woman? How do you do that, turn yourself into a woman?" If the dark spirit had to torment him he'd rather it did so as a man, or what would pass for a man.

She smiled. "You have a new project, Fontana, and that is good. Very good."

"What the hell do you want? Get out and leave me alone."

When she touched his arm, he shivered. "But in choosing this new plan, Lee, you have abandoned the Delgado undertaking." She waited, watching him. "Think about this. Why not take on both challenges? That would be a real triumph."

"Get the hell out of here, go haunt someone else."

"You could do that, Lee, you could lift both the post office money and the Delgado payroll. Think of what they'd add up to. A real fortune, a success that would make you famous across the country, you'd be in more history books than your grandpappy."

"Why the hell would I want to be famous, and have every cop in the U.S. after me?" The truck went into a rut again, too near the edge, and he gave his attention to his driving.

"It would be so easy, Lee," she said, rubbing his thigh with an elegant, thin hand. "So easy to pull off both jobs, to make a really big splash in the world."

But then as she spoke, suddenly he knew the cat was there, he could feel Misto rubbing against his neck, winding back and forth along the back of his seat, could hear him hissing softly. When Lee looked for the ghost cat in his rearview mirror he saw only the black empty glass of the back window, there was no moving reflection, nothing visible—but the woman was visible enough, her pale, long face cold and evil. And the wraith knew the cat was there and she drew back.

Lee said, "What do you want from me?"

She laughed. "I want the same thing from you, Fontana, that I wanted from Russell Dobbs." She reached out her slim hand and began again to stroke his thigh. When he knocked her hand away, she laughed. "I admire the way you go about your work, Fontana. You never have to build yourself up to a job as some men do. You lay it all out, you are all courage and you do what is needed."

Well, that was a lot of bull.

"You're quick, Fontana, and efficient—most of the time. But now—I don't like to see you turn fearful, as you have with the Delgado payroll, I expected better of you."

He said nothing.

"You could take down the payroll and then double back for the post office money, you're famous for your timing. You could pull off a smart, sophisticated operation that would totally confuse the feds." Again she laid her hand on his leg, again he brushed it away, gripping the wheel tighter.

"Why go to all the trouble of two jobs," he said, "when one haul is enough. I only have so many years to spend the damn money."

"For the fame, Lee, for the prestige. For the challenge," she said softly. "The biggest job you ever accomplished, bigger than anything Russell ever pulled off."

Lee wondered what would happen if he stopped the truck, opened her door, and shoved her out of there, wondered if he *could* do that. But of course she would only vanish, turn to smoke in his hands, disappear laughing at him.

"Your time on earth is so fleeting, Lee, you should really plan further than that, you should plan not just for this short mortal life. In a few more moments, as *I* measure time, all of this world that you see around you now will be dust and forgotten, and you will be forgotten, too—unless," she said softly, "unless you grasp the eternity I offer you. Unless you're bold enough to let yourself live forever.

"It would be so easy," she said, "to go on forever creating new . . . enterprises with your special talent, so easy to work with me, to step into eternity beside me carrying out plans bigger and more rewarding than any you can even imagine."

Lee stared ahead at Jake's twin taillights.

"This is your last job on earth, Lee, it should be the wildest and most audacious, the biggest haul you've ever made, should leave behind you fame and admiration."

Behind him the cat had begun to growl. The woman didn't turn, she made no sign. "I can guarantee the success of both jobs, the entire farming and mining payrolls of this whole area, all the cash in the post office on that particular evening, *and* the full Delgado payroll. Enough cash to buy you a whole state in Mexico, to buy you the most beautiful women, the finest home, the most elegant horses."

"And what the hell do you get out of that?" But he knew what she'd get, she'd own his soul, and he wanted no part of it.

"Under my guidance, Lee, when you die at a venerable age you will possess powers you never dreamed of, you will know eternal life, eternal adventure, you will never be bored or sick or old again, your every moment will be an even more . . . prurient and visceral challenge than you have ever yet known."

He wanted to stop the truck and haul her ass out of there.

"My proposition appeals to you," she said softly. She ran her hand too close between his legs, then reached to touch his cheek, drew her finger across his lips. He flinched at her touch, let the truck hit a rut that sent it skidding sideways toward the soft desert sand, he spun the wheel, got it straightened out just before it hit the sucking dunes. Screeching the brakes, he pulled over.

"Get out! Get the hell out! If I burn in hell for what I do, I'll get there on my own, not because of you."

But already she had vanished, the seat beside him was empty.

Shaken, he jammed his foot hard on the accelerator, racing to catch up with Jake. He wished he was up there riding beside Jake and not alone on the dark, empty road. Even the cat seemed to be gone, he spoke to it and felt around the seat and behind him but could feel nothing. Had the cat helped drive her off, with its snarling anger? But then where had he gone, where was Misto now?

Could the devil have hurt the cat?

But that couldn't happen—something in Lee believed in the power of that good spirit, even more than he believed in Satan's evil force. Maybe he and the cat together had driven away the dark wraith, maybe their combined rage had liberated them both for the moment—and even as that thought brought a smile to Lee, Misto appeared beside him, smiling, too. Sitting tall beside him, twitching the tip of his yellow tail, laying a big, possessive paw on Lee's arm, Misto smiled up at him highly amused at their combined power against the eternal and destructive forces, against the despair that roamed, like slavering beasts, the vast and endless universe.

24

MORGAN WOKE DIZZY and sick, jammed in a dark, cramped space, his face pushed up against something rough that, when he felt it with his unsteady hand, he thought was automotive upholstery, rough fabric almost like the mohair with which he'd upholstered the Dodge. Even moving his hand that few inches sent a sharp pain through his head, a shock so severe that his stomach went sick and he thought he was going to throw up. He remained still for some time, then gingerly he tried to ease out of his confinement, to straighten his legs, but when he tried to sit up, the effort made his head pound and throb. Gingerly he fingered his forehead expecting to find blood, but he could find no wound. Moving slowly, he eased onto his side, the pain jabbing through his skull. The back of a car seat rose in front of him, the map pocket with a familiar silver flashlight sticking up, and under the driver's seat a child's blue jacket wadded up, Sammie's jacket with the bunny on the pocket that had gone missing weeks ago. He was in his own car, lying doubled up on the floor of the backseat, his legs bent under him twisted and stiff. Slowly he rose up clutching at the back of the seat, pulling himself painfully off the floor until he was able at last to kneel and could see out the window.

Low sun shot between a tangle of trees, its rays blinding him. How could the sun be setting? He thought, when he could think at all, that it should be around noon, he had a hazy memory of someone coming into the shop at lunchtime, of someone in the car with him.

Falon? Brad Falon? Wanting him to go somewhere? Why would he go anywhere with Falon, he had nothing to do with him anymore.

The low sun was so harsh that when he closed his eyes, the red afterimage of overhanging tree branches swam painfully. He realized he was parked in a dense woods, he had to be somewhere outside of town. Why would he be hunched down in the backseat of his car, alone, parked somewhere in the woods? Shielding his eyes, he could make nothing of the location, there were woods all around Rome. And if the sun was setting, how could he have slept all afternoon? He felt so heavy, thick limbed, even his tongue felt thick and the taste in his mouth was sour. If he had gotten sick suddenly, why hadn't he gone home? Why would he have come out here, into the woods, alone?

And when he looked at the sun again it had lifted higher. That wasn't right. He squinted at it, puzzled. The sun wasn't setting, it was rising. How could that be? It wasn't evening, it was morning. Slowly he reached for the window handle. With effort, he rolled down the glass. Cool, fresh air caressed his face. Morning air, not the stifling heat of a Georgia dusk.

Trying to clear his head, trying to think back, he was sure he'd left the shop around noon. Yes, he had left with Brad Falon, something about Falon's car breaking down. He couldn't remember where they had gone, but he was sure it was lunchtime. So how could it be morning, now? If he'd gotten sick, he would have left Falon and driven home, not come out here into the country. When he tried to get up and shift onto the seat, the pain in his head brought tears, and again his stomach heaved, dry heaves that sent pain shocking through him.

Had he gone somewhere with Falon and there'd been an accident? And Falon slipped away from impending trouble, leaving him alone? That would be like Falon. Through the open window the sun rose slowly higher between the trees. He didn't have his watch. He thought it might be around seven o'clock. He didn't wear his watch working, it got beat up too bad. A little breeze blew in, stirring a sour smell within the car, the same as the sour taste in his mouth, a taste and stink that it took him a while to recognize.

Whiskey, he thought. The sour smell of bootleg whiskey, same as when a few of the boys got together with a half-gallon jug out in the woods or at someone's house, you could smell it on them four hours afterward. Why would whiskey be in his car? You couldn't just walk into a store and buy liquor, even beer, this was a dry county. And neither he nor Becky bought bootleg, neither of them drank. With unsteady fingers he searched again for a head wound, feeling for blood, knowing he had done this just moments before. His mouth tasted like he'd swallowed something dead. The inability to remember, to know why he was here or how he had gotten here, struck fear through him. He had turned away from the blinding sun, pressing his face into his hands trying to think, trying to remember, when behind him the door was jerked open. He was pulled out onto the ground stumbling and falling. Trying to get his balance he spun around hitting out at his assailant, scraping his knee painfully on the metal doorsill.

Strong hands forced him upright, he struck at the man, still trying to get his footing, and then he saw the uniform. Cop's uniform. Morgan dropped his fists, stared into the round face of Richard Jimson, the youngest member of the Rome police force. Light brown hair, the cowlick that wanted to hang over his forehead pushed back beneath his cap, light brown eyes that usually were smiling. Jimson wasn't smiling now. What was this, why the anger? He and Jimson had gone through grammar school together, were on the baseball team, went squirrel hunting together when they were kids, had always been easy with each other, even in high school when Morgan was still running with Falon. Jimson watched him coldly, the officer tense with rage. Jimson was a stranger, now. His eyes hard on Morgan, he slipped the handcuffs from his belt, pulled Morgan's hands behind him, and snapped them on, the metal chill around his wrists.

"Move it, Morgan." Jimson's round face was hard with anger. He forced Morgan across the narrow dirt road toward his patrol unit. Morgan could see, beyond the police car, a white farmhouse with a red barn. The old Crawford place, the narrow dirt road leading back to it lined with sourwoods and maples. Jimson opened the back door of the black-and-white, silent and remote. He put his hand on Morgan's head so he wouldn't bump it, getting in. Pushed him into the backseat behind the wire barrier and slammed the car door. Morgan didn't fight him, he didn't resist. Sitting handcuffed in the backseat, knowing he was locked in and feeling dizzy and sick, he realized that the stink of whiskey wasn't just inside his own car, it was coming from his clothes, his shirt and jeans.

He looked out through the side window toward his car. It was pulled so deep in the woods that from the road it was hardly visible. He could see just beyond it the twisted oak that marked lovers' hollow; he guessed every small town had such a hideaway, a tree-sheltered clearing scattered with empty bottles, Coke bottles, unmarked bootleg bottles. He hadn't been out here since high school when he and Becky used to come out and park.

Jimson stood by the open driver's door, the radio in his hand, calling for assistance. Why would he need assistance? Morgan couldn't see enough of his own car to tell if it had been wrecked. At the thought of a wreck, fear iced along his back, brought him up alert. "Becky and Sammie," he shouted at Jimson, "was there a wreck, are they hurt? Where are Becky and Sammie?" He couldn't remember them being in the car, couldn't remember bringing them out here. Pressing his face into the wire barrier, he shouted crazily at Jimson. "Where's Becky? Where's my little girl? Were we in an accident? Are they hurt? Are they all right?"

"They're all right," Jimson said dryly. "As right as they can be."

"What does that mean? Are they hurt? Tell me."

Jimson was silent, staring in the mirror at him.

"Was there an accident?" Morgan repeated. "Is that why my car—why I'm out here? Where are they?" Becky's face filled his vision, her brown eyes steady on him, Sammie's elfin face so close to him he thought he had only to reach out and touch her soft cheek, reach out and hug her. "Where are they?" he repeated. "What's this about? *Was there an accident?*"

"They're at home," Jimson said. "You *know* there was no *accident*." Why was he so enraged? Morgan started to press him, to ask what he meant, when another patrol car came barreling down the road and pulled up beside Jimson's unit.

Sergeant Leonard stepped out. Morgan had known the brindle-haired police veteran since he was a kid, had an easy friendship with the older man, but now Leonard was as hard-faced and angry as Jimson. Morgan watched a young trainee get out the other side, a blond-haired young college type who, Morgan had heard, was good at cataloging evidence. Leonard stood looking into the backseat at Morgan. "Give me your car keys."

Handcuffed, Morgan dug clumsily in his pocket for the keys and handed them over. Jimson slipped in behind the wheel of the black-and-white, as Leonard moved away toward Morgan's car. Jimson started the engine, spun a U-turn on the narrow, empty road. Morgan hunched down in the moving car aching and sick, trying to figure out what was happening, what *had* happened, trying to put the scattered pieces together—and worrying about Sammie and Becky, still terrified for them. And ashamed, because somehow he had failed them, because he had suddenly and inexplicably lost control of his life, had failed the two people in the world who *were* his life.

"What was it, Jimson? What did I do, what happened?" He didn't expect an answer, as closemouthed as Jimson had been. The woods swept by, the familiar farms, the long, stinking rows of metal chicken houses. As they neared town and turned onto Main Street, Jimson glanced in the mirror again at Morgan, his brown eyes flickering between rage and puzzlement; for an instant a touch of their friendship showed through, conflicted and uncertain.

And now, nearing the jail, all Morgan could think of was Sammie's nightmare where he was locked behind bars, her terrified screaming that his friends were locking him in a cage. He wanted to fight his way out of the squad car and get home, find Sammie, tell her everything was all right, he wanted to hold her safe and tell her Daddy was all right.

But he wasn't all right: he was coming more awake now, and as Jimson circled the block to park behind the police station, slowly Morgan began, with effort, to put events together. He had gotten into the car at noon, he was certain of that. Falon *had* come into the shop, urging him real pushy as was Falon's way. He remembered he'd been working on John Graham's Chevy, replacing the fuel pump, remembered hearing Falon's voice, looking up to see Falon there on the other side of the raised hood. He was sure, now, that he'd left the shop with Falon. They'd gone to look at Falon's car? He thought Falon had wanted to tell him something, but he couldn't remember what.

But that had to be yesterday, he'd apparently spent the afternoon and night in the car, and he could remember nothing of those hours. A whole afternoon and night wiped from his memory. He knew he hadn't been drinking, no matter how he smelled or what he tasted. Had he been drugged with something worse than bootleg? And then left there in the woods alone, passed out cold, abandoned by Falon?

He remembered wiping up Falon's spilled Coke, but didn't remember much at all, after that. He looked into the rearview mirror at Jimson, wanting to ask if this was Friday, wanting to know if it had been just yesterday that he and Falon had gotten in his car, wanting to ask Jimson why he couldn't remember anything after pulling away from the curb where he'd parked, driving just a few blocks, and then growing so dizzy and confused. He thought there was something about the Graystone Apartments. Was that where they were headed? He couldn't remember arriving there.

"Jimson, I have to call Becky." When he hadn't been home all night, she'd be frantic. What had happened after Falon spilled the Coke? Those hours between yesterday and this morning had been taken from him as if they never existed, the whole night had been stolen from him. What had he done during those lost hours, those vanished and terrifying hours?

Jimson pulled around behind the impressive stone courthouse to the basement area below at the back, the entrance to the jail. Morgan watched his own car pull in behind them, to a fenced, locked area. He supposed the car would be held as evidence. Morgan knew, from walking through the lockup area, that the cells were small and dirty and they stank. Jimson parked the patrol car just at the back door of the jail, killed the engine, and got out. He opened the back door and motioned Morgan out, Morgan awkward with his hands cuffed behind him. Morgan stumbled up the steps ahead of the officer, herded along by the man who should be his friend, who now was as cold as if they'd never met. Jimson opened the big steel door, pushed him inside, forced him along the hall, on past the cells and up to the front, to the booking desk.

Morgan was booked into Rome City Jail at ten-fifteen that morning. Reeking of whiskey, he drew sharp, surprised looks from the staff and the other officers. At the front desk, Jimson fingerprinted him and filled out the forms, asking Morgan coldly for the answer to every printed question though he already knew the answers, he knew Morgan's personal history as well as Morgan himself did. It was the charges that Jimson wrote down, that left him shocked.

Bank robbery? *Murder?* He looked at Jimson, feeling sick, looked at what Jimson had written. That couldn't be right, not murder. He couldn't have killed anyone. Nothing that could have happened to him, a hit on the head, some kind of drug, could make him kill someone. Nothing would allow him to *forget killing someone.* It was hard enough to forget what he had done during the war. Now, he wanted an explanation, he wanted to shout at Jimson and shake him until he found out what this was about.

But to make a fuss now might only make the situation worse. When Jimson finished filling in the report, he marched Morgan down the hall, shoved him in through a cell door so brutally that he fell sprawling across the concrete.

"Jimson?"

The officer turned, watched him as he struggled up.

He tried to talk to Jimson, tried to tell him he thought he'd been drugged, tried to reconstruct what little he *could* remember: Falon showing up at the shop, his leaving with Falon, Falon spilling the Coke, Morgan turning to wipe it up.

Jimson said, "There was no Coke, no Coke bottles, no bottles of any kind except the empty moonshine bottle."

"I didn't have any moonshine. You know I don't drink—no matter how I smell," he said sheepishly. "You *searched* the car, and found nothing else? There were two Cokes, Falon bought them at the shop, from the machine. Ask Albert, he was there, working at the other lift."

Jimson's face softened, but just a little. "There was something sticky spilled on the seat." He shrugged. "It might be Coke. We'll look into it."

Morgan looked back at him, deflated. What could a detective find in a stain of spilled Coke? Maybe a trace of some drug? Or maybe nothing. And Falon could have ditched the bottles anywhere. Easy to toss them back in the woods in lovers' hollow, two more empty bottles rolled in dirt and buried among years of collected trash.

He watched Jimson lock his barred door, drop the key into his uniform pocket, watched his retreating back, watched the heavy outer door close. He was locked in a cell by himself—at least for that he was grateful, thankful for the privacy. Maybe Jimson had taken pity on him. Or maybe Jimson thought Morgan had turned too dangerous to share space with the town's three drunks. All he knew was, this wasn't happening, couldn't be happening. There was no way he could have killed someone, and no way he could have forgotten such a horrible act as if it had never happened.

When Jimson had gone, Morgan sat down on the stained bunk. The cell wasn't as big as their small bathroom at home, but this cubicle wasn't blue and white and sweet smelling, it was scarred with the filth of generations, that the janitor had tried repeatedly to scrub away, he could see the paler but still visible scour marks. Walls scarred with the shadows of old graffiti, newer smears of dirt, and stains of urine behind the toilet. He read the scribbled messages that were still legible, repeated the four-letter words to himself as if they might help him hang on to his sanity. Two inscriptions begged God's mercy, penned by someone lying on the iron cot writing at a forty-five-degree angle. The cot's striped mattress was grimy along the edges and sported three long brown smears. A threadbare blanket and a worn sheet were folded at the foot of the cot beside a grimy pillow. The washbasin was streaked brown with years of iron-rich water. Above the basin hung a ragged, torn towel. Across the corridor a drunk was singing dirty words to "Down in the Valley." He used the toilet, washed his hands and face with the tepid water but avoided the towel. He smoothed his hair with his wet hands, cupped water in his hands, rinsed his mouth again and again but couldn't get rid of the dead taste. What had Falon put in his Coke? This had to be something stronger, even, than moonshine. There was no other explanation for the way he felt and for his loss of memory. Whiskey wouldn't do that, and how could Falon have forced that much whiskey down him? No, the liquor was soaked into his clothes; even his boots, when he pulled them off, smelled of booze, and the leather was still faintly damp.

But as he sat there in the cell alone, his sense of innocence began to fade. What *might* have happened during those long hours he couldn't remember? What *might* Falon have made him do, what would he have been *willing* to do, drugged, that he wouldn't do while sober?

He spread the sheet over the cot and lay down. The corridor light in his face made his head throb. From the moment Jimson had jerked him out of his car, scenes from yesterday and detached snatches of conversation had swum through his head in a muddle, none of it making sense, Falon's voice urging him to leave the shop, Falon trying to get him to go somewhere . . . He remembered telling Falon he never left the shop for lunch. Well, it was too late now to change whatever had happened. What he didn't understand was why? Falon was mean, had always been mean, but why this horror just now, when he and Becky and Sammie were finally together again?

But that would be exactly Falon's way: hit them when they were happiest—out of sadism, out of a hunger for Becky that she had never encouraged and that, for all these years, could have festered, could have left Falon waiting for just the right moment, the cruelest moment. But was fate—certainly not the good Lord himself—so cruel that Falon's evil would at last be allowed to destroy them?

25

T**HE PLANE BURST** out of the clouds with a buzzing roar banking directly over Lee, it dropped straight at him, its shadow swallowed him, then the dark silhouette swept on by, raking the field below the lowering plane; at the far end of the rough, unplowed land the yellow Stearman touched down. Wheels kicking up dust, it swung around and circled back toward him, its propeller ticking over slowly as the plane taxied. Lee stepped aside as it rolled up to him. The front cockpit was empty. In the rear cockpit, young Mark Triple pushed back his goggles, but didn't kill the engine. "Hop in, Fontana."

Reaching for the struts, Lee made the long step up onto the wingwalk. Pausing, he looked down into the open metal hopper where Mark had bolted in a makeshift seat for him. Not much to hold him in there, only that little leather strap screwed into the sides of the plane. He glanced back at Mark.

"Climb on in, it's safe as a baby carriage." Leaning forward, Mark handed him a pair of goggles. "They'll keep the bugs out of your eyes. Make sure your seat belt's fastened."

Warily Lee stepped in, groping for the seat belt. He got the ends together, pulled the belt so tight he nearly cut himself in half. He wasn't half settled when the engine roared again and they were moving, Lee gripping the sides of the hopper hard, the ground racing by in a brown blur. He was lifted, weightless, as the tail came up, then a belly-grabbing leap, forcing him to hang on tighter than he had ever clung to a bucking cayuse. Ahead, a flock of birds exploded away in panic. Looking gingerly over the side, he hung on with both hands as the plane banked, tipping sideways. They swept low over the rusty tin roofs of the packing sheds, not a soul stirring in the ranch yard. In the paddock, Lucita's spotted mare crowded nervously against the rail fence, staring up at the rising plane. In Lucita and Jake's yard Lee glimpsed a tiny flash of white, Lucita's little Madonna. Then they were out over the green fields, the melons and vegetables, the cotton and alfalfa broken by irrigation ditches thin as snakes, then the sharp line where the green stopped and the pale desert stretched away to the low Chuckawalla Mountains, brown and barren and wind carved. He'd feel more secure if he were riding behind Mark instead of up here in front where he felt like he should have control but didn't—but hell, if this bird took a dive he wouldn't know what to do anyway.

Forcing himself to settle back, he concentrated on the panorama below, so different than what you could ever see from the ground. He told himself this was a good feeling, floating high above the earth with nothing to hold him up there, and he tried to set his mind on the job ahead, patting the traveler's check folder in his shirt pocket, making sure it was safe. He'd never pulled a scam like this one. The excitement of it made his stomach twitch, but also made him smile. Yesterday he'd skipped lunch, borrowed Jake's pickup and headed for town, first for his post office box—and his birth certificate was there waiting for him. Smiling, he'd headed for the Department of Motor Vehicles where he applied for a driver's license in the name of James Dawson, hoping to hell the clerk hadn't known Dawson. Hoping the DMV wouldn't check past the P.O. address, wouldn't start digging around in the birth certificates. There must be a lot of Dawsons in the world, but he had to have some kind of ID. He told the clerk he was a mining consultant moving down from San Francisco, would be doing some work for Placer Mining Company. Said he hadn't had a driver's license in years because the last company he worked for furnished a driver, he said that when he was in the city he preferred to take the cable car or walk. He'd had to take a driver's test, a piece of cake on the open desert roads, and he had aced the written test.

Fifteen minutes after he received his temporary license he had returned to the post office, parking around on the next street out of sight. Entering the lobby, standing in line before the window with the temporary cardboard sign reading BANKING BUSINESS, he was encouraged by the long line. A busy teller, hurrying through her transactions, was just what he wanted. A teller making quick decisions wouldn't want to linger over unnecessary questions. When his turn came he gave the young redhead a grandfatherly smile, asked her for seven hundred dollars in traveler's checks, in hundred-dollar denominations. He had stood admiring the young smooth look of her as she recorded the check numbers in the customer's transaction folder, which was printed with the logo of the bank. He told her conversationally that he was on his way to San Francisco. She said she loved San Francisco, that the fee would be two dollars, and she had counted out the traveler's checks to put into the folder. As he reached to his hip pocket, he picked up the folder. He dug convincingly in his pocket for his billfold, then looked surprised, looked up at her, frowning. "Oh, shaw. I'm sorry, miss. I left my wallet in the car."

She smiled at him understandingly, and paper-clipped the checks together, glancing past him at the long line of customers. "That's all right, sir. I'll hold them until you get back. Just come to the window, you needn't stand in that long line again."

The customer behind him pushed impatiently closer as Lee slipped away pocketing the folder, leaving the young clerk cashing a paycheck.

Outside the post office, moving away around the corner out of sight of the post office windows, he swung into the truck and left, heading back for the ranch, the empty folder safe in his Levi's pocket. That had been yesterday. Now he was on his way to complete the rest of the transaction.

His stomach dropped as the plane lifted higher yet, to clear the rising mountains, and he tried to ease more comfortably into the sense of flight, into the sudden lift, the speed, the throb of the engines. The wind scoured his face, sharp and cold. Below him the deep, dry washes dropping down from the mountains and across the desert floor looked ancient. Washes that during a heavy rain would belch out enough water to flood the whole desert, flood the highway deep and fast enough to overturn a car and drown an unwary driver. Maybe, Lee thought, every place in the world had its own kind of downside, unexpected and treacherous. Soon they were over San Bernardino, sailing smoothly over miles of orange and avocado groves, the lines of trees as straight as if drawn by a ruler. A few small farms, fenced pastures where horses and cattle grazed, a few small towns surrounded by green hills—and then the square grids of L.A. streets, neighborhoods of little boxy houses, and the main thoroughfares choked with traffic. Blue ocean beyond to his left, rivulets of white waves rolling in, and to his right the Hollywood Hills rose up, their pelt of green trees broken by the occasional glimpse of a mansion roof or the blue square of a swimming pool. This was the moneyed Neverland he'd read about, a place he'd never have reason to visit. Beyond the Hollywood Hills, forested mountains towered up, wild enough, by their look, to lose a man back among their rough ridges and gullies, wild enough to hide a man where the feds might never find him.

Lee eased down in his seat as Mark banked and circled, approaching the L.A. airport, the mountains swinging so close to Lee he caught his breath and clutched the seat hard again, staring straight out at what he thought was his last sight of this earth before they crashed into a thrusting peak, and died.

The ghost cat wasn't frightened, he rode effortlessly on the wing above Lee, needing no support, watching

Lee, amused, entertained by Lee's fear, laughing as only a cat can laugh—though he felt sympathy for the old cowboy, too. If he had been a mortal cat, at that moment, riding in the little plane, he'd be crouched on the floor scared as hell, wild-eyed and out of control.

When Mark had first landed the plane back at Delgado Ranch and Lee stepped aboard, the cat had leaped lightly to the lower wing and then drifted up to the high wing, unseen. He had ridden there weightless as the plane took off, the wind tugging at his invisible fur, flattening his unseen ears without annoying the cat at all. Riding the yellow Stearman filled Misto with feline clownishness, caught him in a delirium of delight that perhaps no other creature *but* a ghost cat could know as vividly. The yellow tom didn't often give himself to this degree of madness, he was for the most part a serious cat, but now he wanted to laugh out loud; sailing aboard the little manmade craft was more delicious than any binge of catnip, he rode the Stearman balanced without effort, he was one with the wind, he was a wind dancer, so giddy he wanted to yowl with pleasure. He let himself blow away free on the wind and then flipped over to land on the plane again, cavorting and delirious; he played and gamboled until Mark dropped the little craft smoothly down, to the landing strip in L.A., settling to earth once more. There the cat stretched out on the upper wing, lounging and watching to see what would happen next.

Taxiing, Mark quickly moved her off the runway, moved on past the terminal where passengers were boarding a big commercial plane, and headed slowly for the small hangars beyond and a metal building, its tin roof

peeling paint. DUKE'S AIR SERVICE. REPAIR. CHARTERS. FLY-
ING LESSONS. There, he cut the engine.

In the cockpit, Lee sat a moment, reorienting himself.
At last he dropped his goggles on the seat, undid the seat
belt, eased himself out of the hopper and climbed down.

But when he stood again on the ground he felt so small,
and the earth felt unsteady beneath him, his balance so
changed that for a moment he couldn't get his footing. He
watched Mark greet the mechanic, jerking a thumb at the
prop. "It surges in high pitch," Mark said. "Surges real bad."

Lee moved closer to get Mark's attention. "You going
to be a while? I'd like to go into town if there's time."

Mark laughed. "See the big city. Sure, this will take . . .
maybe three hours or better. You can catch a bus over there
in front of the terminal. I'll stay here and swap lies."

The bus was nearly empty. When Lee chose a window
seat close to the rear door, when he sat down laying his
jacket across the other seat, he sensed the cat next to him,
and that cheered him. In the plane, where the hell had the
cat ridden? Had he needed to hang on for dear life, or had
he been free to do as he pleased? Had he been afraid during that bouncing ride, or was such an experience nothing
at all to a freewheeling ghost cat?

It was a half-hour ride into downtown L.A. The instant they passed the first bank, Lee rose and pulled the
cord. He expected the ghost cat would tag along, but he
didn't sense him near. He had ceased to worry about the
little cat, a ghost wasn't mortal, nothing of this world
could harm him, and how secure and amazing was that?
Only something otherworldly could touch Misto, and so
far as Lee could tell, he had taken care of himself just fine.

Walking back to the bank from the bus stop, he ran his finger into his shirt pocket, again making sure the paper with its record of the traveler's checks was safe. He was feeling nervous, beginning to wonder if that young inmate, young Randy Sanderford, had given him the straight scoop about this scam.

The bank lobby was crowded, the lines long, and that was good. He picked a young, gentle-looking teller, and tailed onto the end of the line. The nameplate beside her window said Kay Miller. He fidgeted in line and tried to look worried, and as he stepped up for his turn he let his face twist into despair. Leaning into the window clutching the grill, he encouraged his voice to tremble. "Excuse me, ma'am—Miss Miller—I'm just worried sick and my missus is out in the car just crying her eyes out."

The young woman's clear green eyes searched his face, she leaned toward him over the counter, the gold heart on her necklace swinging. "What is it, sir? What's wrong?"

"I've lost my traveler's checks, every one of them, all the money we have. My wife said the money would be safer in traveler's checks, we're headed up to Oregon, I have a job there, and now—lost. Just—they're gone. I don't know where I could have dropped them . . ."

Lee clutched his bandana to wipe his eyes. He could feel the stares of people behind him. The teller started to reach out through the cage as though she would take his hand, then drew her hand back, but her face showed real concern. Maybe she had a forgetful father, Lee thought, some gentle, addled old duffer who too often stirred her pity. She said, "Do you have something to identify the lost checks, sir?"

"Not much, I'm afraid." He pulled the little slip of recorded numbers, in their transaction folder, out of his shirt pocket. "Just this."

Her gentle green eyes brightened when she saw the folder. She took it from him carefully, looking at the name of the issuing bank. "May I see your driver's license, sir?"

He handed over the temporary license. "Just had it renewed." He let his unsteady voice carry softly. "It's my wife's sister, she—we're having to move up to Oregon to look after her, we don't think she has very long, and with the money so short . . . I just don't know how I could have lost them. They were so loose in the folder, one came out accidentally. My wife said they'd be safer in the glove compartment, and I thought I put them there. But then I couldn't find them. I thought maybe I put them in my pocket when we stopped to get gas, but I paid for the gas with cash and . . ." He shook his head, clenching his hands together like a little old lady, trying to look shrunken and pitiful. "I could give you our address in Oregon, if there's any way you could help us?"

Her eyes widened as she glanced at the line behind him, he knew everyone was listening, and she let her soft voice carry. "Mr. Dawson, we like to give our customers personal service. But, you see, our bank manager's out today."

Lee swallowed.

"But Miss Lester is here. If you'll excuse me, I'll get her." She smiled at the line of waiting customers, and left the window. When Lee turned to look, most of the faces behind him were soft with sympathy. Only two men were scowling, impatient to take care of their business. Lee glanced down shyly, ducking his head, smiling sheepishly; most of the folks smiled back, nodding encouragement. He could see, at a desk at the back of the bank, Miss Miller speaking with a dark-haired older woman. The woman looked up, studying Lee. As the two women talked, the tension behind Lee in the line was like electricity, sympathy and impatience mixed, and Lee's own nerves were strung tight. He was shaking with anxiety for real; by the time the pretty young teller returned to the cage, he was so nervous he could feel a cough coming. He did his best to swallow it back, but the cough racked him so hard he doubled over. He swallowed back phlegm, at last got himself under control. As he straightened up, another fit of coughing almost took him when he saw the sheaf of traveler's checks in the young teller's hand.

"I can reissue the checks, Mr. Dawson," she said, smiling. Lee heard a pleased murmur of voices behind him. As he let out a breath, shaken and weak, he felt the cat brush against his boot, pressing hard, as if to say, *See, everything went just fine.* Lee watched Miss Miller count out seven one-hundred-dollar traveler's checks. She showed Lee where to sign them, recorded the numbers, and clamped them securely into a new folder for him. Lee started to cough again, trying to thank her.

"We're glad we could help," she said softly. "Please be careful with them, now. You and Mrs. Dawson have a safe trip up to Oregon, and I hope her sister's better soon."

Collecting the folder, he thanked her again, reached through the grid to pat her hand, and then turned away moving slowly, almost feebly out of the bank.

On the street again, pretending to hurry to rejoin his

weeping wife, James Dawson picked up his speed and, once he'd rounded the corner, he was moving fast and grinning with smug success. Not a damn thing wrong with that scam.

It took him more than an hour to cash five of the traveler's checks, walking long distances between stores, buying a few items in each, half a dozen pairs of shorts, a shirt, some work gloves and, in a hardware store a small trenching tool. He saved the last two checks for the pawnshop. And as he moved around the town, every now and then he could feel the cat pressing against his leg, could feel it now as he pushed in through the barred pawnshop door. Why was the cat so interested? Just plain nosiness? Or was the ghost cat bringing him luck? Helping him along, tweaking the sympathy of young Miss Miller and her superior, maybe even weaving a sense of honesty around Lee as he dealt with each clerk and shopkeeper. Could the ghost cat do that? More power to him, then, Lee thought as he pushed in among the crowded counters of the pawnshop.

There were no other customers. Every surface was stacked with binoculars, cameras, musical instruments, jewelry, guns and ammo, all of it familiar and comforting. A pawnshop was always his destination soon after parole or release, a pawnshop was a source of sustenance where he could gather together the supplies to feel whole again, the equipment he needed to feel capable again and master of his own fate. Even the square-faced shopkeeper behind the counter seemed comfortable and familiar, the way he peered up over his horn-rimmed glasses, the way his veined hands stayed very still on the newspaper he had been reading, waiting to see if Lee wanted to sell, or buy, or try to rob him, his hands poised where he could reach, in an instant, the loaded weapon he'd have ready just beneath the counter. The man gave Lee a shopkeeper's all-purpose smile. "Help you?"

Lee eased down a row of showcases, looking through the glass tops. "Like to see what you have in the way of revolvers."

"Something for protection?"

"You might say that. Some critter is getting my calves—got home from a trip up north, my wife was pretty upset. I've watched for two nights—I don't know what's after them but I mean to find out."

The man slid open a glass door. "Here's a nice little snub-nose I can let go at a reasonable price."

Lee looked down at the cheap little handgun. "I don't want a toy. I want a gun." He moved on down the showcase. "There. Let me see that one."

He accepted the heavy revolver, opened and spun the cylinder, and eased it closed. He saw how the bluing had worn off from riding in its holster. He looked down the length of the six-inch barrel, examined the scars on the wooden grips. A forty-five-caliber, double-action no-nonsense handgun designed on the lines of the Paterson Colt. Not so fine or rare a weapon, but it would do for what he wanted. "How much?"

"Hundred dollars. Hundred and thirty with the holster."

"I'll take both, and a box of ammunition."

But when Lee pulled out the traveler's checks, the man did a double take. He looked at Lee hard for a minute.

"These are the last two. Always carry them when I

travel. Hope you don't mind. Won't be needing them now, for a while."

At last, under Lee's innocent gaze, the clerk cashed the checks. Lee bought a wide roll of gray tape that the shop used for packing; he paid for that, too, and, knowing the guy was wondering if he'd been taken, he mosied on out, paused to look again in the shop window, then walked casually away to the bus stop. Moving on around the corner out of sight, he leaned against the brick building letting his rapid heart slow, waiting for the next bus bound to the airport. The twenty-minute delay made him real nervous before the bus finally appeared, before he was safely aboard and away from the watchful owner of the pawnshop.

Getting off at the air terminal, double-timing across the long stretch of tarmac, he arrived back at the hangar just as the mechanic was pushing his wheeled tool chest away from the yellow biplane. Reaching into the plane, Lee stashed his packages under the makeshift seat, then stood watching Mark approach from the office, where he had gone to pay the bill. As they pushed the plane out away from the hangar, Lee couldn't help wondering where the cat was now, but knowing that wherever he lingered at the moment was exactly where he wanted to be.

"You heading out next week," Lee asked. "Headed for Vegas?"

Mark nodded. "Vegas, and then on to Wichita."

"Don't know if it would fit in with your plans," Lee said, "but I'd sure like to see Vegas, play the tables for a day or two."

Mark grinned. "You getting to like this flying?"

Lee nodded, grinning at him.

"Might arrange it, if you can get the time off."

"I can get the time off. I'll be in town next Thursday on some business, I can get a lift in. Don't suppose you could pick me up there, on your way? I'd pay for your gas to Vegas. Fellow told me there was an emergency landing strip just outside of town, at the junction to Jamesfarm."

Mark scratched his head. "I was going to leave Wednesday, but what the hell, for the price of gas, I'm flexible. Sure, hell yes, I'll pick you up, say Thursday evening? Smoother ride over the mountains when the air's cool. I know the strip, I had a leaky oil line coming back from Vegas one time. That strip saved me from burning up the engine. How will you get back from Vegas?"

"I'll hop a bus. How about six-thirty or seven, Thursday night?"

"Make it eight-thirty, I'll have some things to clear up, that night. Take us an hour and a half to Vegas. My girlfriend doesn't get off until nine." He grinned at Lee. "This thing burns thirty gallons an hour."

Laughing, Lee crawled up into his seat. "I can make that much in an hour or two at the blackjack table." He snapped on the goggles, buckled his seat belt, tucked the brown paper packages securely between his legs, patting the forty-five. Wherever the ghost cat was, he wondered if he was in for the ride to Vegas as well, if he'd be with him for the rest of this gig, for the bad time Lee expected to endure before he headed for the border, rich and living free.

26

Two hours after Brad Falon had slipped into Morgan's blue Dodge, and Morgan pulled away from the tree-shaded curb near the automotive shop, Falon himself sat in the driver's seat, with Morgan sprawled in the back, passed out cold. Leaving the Graystone, in front of which he had parked, and driving sedately through town, Falon returned to park behind the apartment. Making sure Morgan was still deep under, and seeing that the windows were down partway so the comatose man wouldn't suffocate, Falon left the car. Walking across the few feet of tarmac, he entered the apartment building through the back door. He didn't go upstairs to his girlfriend's place where he'd been living, he'd fill Natalie in later. She'd go along with whatever he said, whatever he told her to say. Crossing the small lobby to the front door, the afternoon sun glittering in through its carved glass panes, he left the building and crossed the street to the little neighborhood market where he liked to buy magazines and sweets. He purchased a pack of gum and a candy bar, and talked idly with the owner, remarking on the time, which was just two-thirty, and setting his watch by the store clock. Leaving the market, he entered the lobby through the front door again as if he were going on up to their apartment. Instead he continued out the back, where he slid into Morgan's car. He had left his own black convertible in plain view parked in front of the building.

In the backseat of the Dodge, Morgan hadn't moved, he was still deep under. Smiling, Falon drove the few blocks to the elementary school and parked in the alley behind the gym. Getting out, he dropped a small metal box into one of the refuse cans, and eased his hand in to pull a tangle of brown, wadded paper towels over it. Getting back in the car, he drove the nine blocks to Shorter Street, its maple trees shading the entries to several small businesses, the barber shop, a sandwich shop, a women's clothing store, a bank, a dry goods and a five-and-dime, stores supplying most of the necessities of the small town except for livestock feed, lumber, and gardening supplies, which could be acquired just a few blocks over. Parking beneath a large live oak half a block from Rome Southern Bank, again he left the windows cracked open to the hot afternoon. Pocketing his loaded .38, he tossed a light windbreaker over Morgan so he wouldn't be easily noticed from the sidewalk, and he left the engine running.

Rome Southern wasn't the biggest bank in town but it was on the quietest street. Paradoxically, it was just two blocks from Morgan Blake's house. Falon had driven by there just a couple of days ago, had seen the little Blake girl coming down the street, no mistaking her dark eyes, exactly like

Becky's. When he slowed, she'd looked up at him, startled. Becky's eyes, yes, and even as she ran from his car behind the nearest house, something had twisted in his belly.

All during high school Becky had refused to go out with him—she was Becky Tanner then—using the poor excuse that she was dating Morgan. He told her she could be going with them both, that he'd show her a real good time, better than Morgan ever could, but she'd had a snotty, stuck-up attitude. She wouldn't date him, wouldn't give him a tumble—when a tumble was all he wanted. He hadn't forgotten or forgiven that.

He left Morgan's car at exactly two forty-five, and approached the bank. He had already changed shirts with Morgan and put on Morgan's greasy work boots. To make his hands look like Morgan's he had rubbed black watercolor paint from the child's paint box into the creases between his fingers and around his nails and the cuticles, wiping off the excess. He had wiped his prints off the tin paint box, and smeared the colors all together in a wet mess. Who would think anything about a ruined paint box that some kid threw away? Earlier, getting Morgan settled in the backseat, he had pulled half a dozen hairs from Morgan's head and placed them in an envelope, which was now safe in his jacket pocket.

Approaching the bank, he took from his other pocket a blue wool stocking cap, the kind you'd wear in winter, and pulled it on. The street and sidewalk were empty except for three small children bouncing a ball against a storefront a block away, paying no attention to him. Just out of sight of the bank's glass doors, he pulled the cap down over his face, lining up the two eyeholes he had cut in the front. Then, with his hand on the revolver in his pocket, the hammer cocked, he shoved in through the bank's front door.

THE PORTLY, UNIFORMED security guard had been looking up at the wall clock checking it against his pocket watch. Adjusting the watch, which was five minutes slow, satisfied it was time to close up, he started across the tile lobby to lock the door and pull the shades. He glanced across to the teller's window, where Betty Holmes was placing paper collars around packs of tens, putting away the last of her change. She, too, was eager to lock up for the evening. She smiled at the elderly guard, flipping her long, pale hair over her shoulder. She liked Harry Grogan, he had been at this job ever since he retired from the police force fifteen years before, long before she came to work here. She knew he could feel the years weighing on him, just as her father complained about the aches and discomforts of increasing age. She knew Harry meant to quit soon and help his wife, Esther, at home where Esther still took in sewing. Grogan planned to put in a bigger garden and try canning some beans and homemade vegetable soup which was, in every household with a garden, a favorite winter staple. Harry said Esther never had time for canning and she'd sure be glad of the help. Betty watched Grogan ease the heaviness of his service revolver, lifting his belt away from his body as he moved toward the bank's front door—then everything happened fast, the sudden thrust inward of the heavy glass door, the masked figure exploding in jamming a revolver into Harry's belly as Harry reached for his gun.

Two shots exploded. Harry's gun never cleared the holster, the shots dropped him in a dance jig, he fell twisting and lay still. The gunman lunged past him straight at her window and before she could react he grabbed her hair, jerked her into the wrought-iron barrier. Pain exploded in her belly as her ribs cracked against the counter bending her double. He jerked her harder into the metal teller's cage and rammed the gun in her face, the gun and the navy blue mask filled her vision, and his cold expressionless eyes.

FALON WAS PRETTY sure the guard was dead. As he rammed the muzzle of the .38 into the teller's face, two women appeared from the back. They stopped, frozen, their faces going pale and dumb.

"Get the money," he shouted. "In the drawers, in the vault. I want all of it. Do it *now*, or she's dead." The two women remained still with shock. Falon gestured the cocked gun toward a pile of empty canvas bags that lay folded on the back counter. "*Move!* Put the money in the bags. *Now*, or I blow the broad's head off."

They moved, scuttled like frightened rats to do as they were told. His new voice amused him, he had practiced for a long time to perfect Morgan's deeper voice, his lower tones. The two tellers were unlocking and jerking open drawers, grabbing out money and dropping it into the bags. The younger, dark-haired one moved quickly but the old, skinny broad was slow and shaking. He'd started to yell at her again when a man, a bank officer, appeared from an inner office down at the end of the lobby. Looking surprised, taking it all in, he lunged for a phone.

"Back off. You touch it, they're all dead!" Stepping around the end of the counter, Falon stood over the blonde. She was still conscious, holding herself and moaning.

"Get over here," Falon shouted at the bank officer. "Get over here now behind the counter with the rest of them!" But when he grabbed the limp girl and jerked her up she came to life under his hands, clawing at him trying to jerk the mask off his face, her own face white with rage.

He jerked her off him, pulled her long hair, bending her backward, her face cut by the bars. The other two women had backed away from the cash drawers, they stood dumb and shaking again but the blonde still fought him, kicking at his shins, her fear wild and so exciting he laughed, fear had always thrilled him, as far back as he could remember, other kids' fear of him, a helpless animal's fear. Remembering grammar school, the puppy's white silky hair filling his fist, he twisted the girl's hair, jerking her up against him, contorting her body so violently that he felt her urine drench his leg. Enraged that she'd do that, he slapped her with the butt of the .38. She swung around, jammed her knee in his crotch. He doubled over. She scratched his arm deep and then went for his face. Hunched with pain, he threw her to the floor and screamed at the two tellers, "Get the rest of the money in the bag or I'll kill her, kill all of you." When the girl at his feet tried to get up he kicked her in the face, then in the ribs. "Get the money," he snarled, "all three of you, all of the money. *All* of it!" He felt high and he felt good, he was filled with power.

When he had the two loaded money bags, he locked the bank officer and the women in the vault and spun the dial. Before he left the bank carrying the two canvas bags he dropped the hairs from the envelope into the blood on the marble floor. When he hit the door he had already pulled off the stocking cap and shoved it into one of the bags. Quickly he slid into the Dodge, pushed the bags under the seat. He was ten blocks away when he heard sirens; he never had heard a bank alarm, maybe it only sounded at the station and that didn't seem fair.

The sirens grew louder but he eased on at a leisurely pace, heading north to the outskirts of Rome. He parked Morgan's car in a patch of woods next to the red pickup he had "borrowed" earlier from a man that he knew would be out of town all week. He crammed the money all into one bag and dropped it into the cab of the pickup, left the other bag with a few scattered bills under the passenger seat of Morgan's car. He changed shirts and boots with Morgan, hard to do, manipulating a limp body. He emptied the bottle of bootleg whiskey over Morgan's clothes, smeared some in his mouth, the rest on the driver's seat. He wiped his prints off the bottle, forced Morgan's prints onto it in several handholds. Holding the bottle with his handkerchief, he shoved it under the seat with the canvas bag.

Pulling the red pickup out onto the narrow macadam road, he got out and picked up the four wide boards on which he had parked to prevent tire tracks in the raw earth of the shoulder. He scuffed leaves over the indentations the boards had made, threw the boards in the bed of the pickup, and headed around the outskirts of Rome, up toward Turkey Mountain Ridge. The way he figured, taking his time to hide the money in the one place where no one would ever look, he'd have the truck back in his friend's driveway well before midnight, would be back in Natalie's apartment in perfect innocence, fondling her in her warm bed. He had no thought for the dead guard or the girl he had hurt, he had no idea of the extent of her suffering nor did he care, his thoughts were on the damage he had done to Morgan Blake, for taking Becky from him, and on Becky for turning her back on him. Soon now Morgan would be hurting bad, as would Becky, and that was only right, that was as it should be, those who crossed him were meant to pay, and he was making it happen.

IN BLYTHE, THE ghost cat, as he accompanied Lee in the careful laying of his plans, was aware as well of Falon's brutal robbery even as the iron door to the vault was slammed and the manager and tellers locked inside. Misto hurt for those who had been beaten, for the guard who had been killed and for his poor wife newly widowed. He hurt for Morgan, who would suffer long and hard, too, for Falon's cruelty, and he hurt for Becky and Sammie. But at this juncture there was little he could have done. A momentum was building that was beyond the ghost cat's frantic powers; this shifting of fate was now far too strong for one small and angry feline.

But he knew this: the lust of Brad Falon against the Blakes was inexorably drawing Lee in. Lee would soon become a part of the scenario, as surely as pressures could build beneath the earth toward an explosive cataclysm. The paths of Morgan, and Brad Falon, of Sammie and Lee were tangling ever closer; and the ultimate outcome, the final choice, would be Lee's to make. Uneasily the cat watched and waited, often giving Lee a gentle nudge, rubbing warm against him, his purring rumble meant to remind the old convict where survival lay: Lee's ultimate afterlife lay with those who could give of their love, never with that which destroys love and joy. Never with that which would leave nothing of Lee but dust, scattered and gone, swept to nothing by the winds of time.

27

PAUSING ON THE porch of the mess hall, Lee stamped dust from his boots, startling a flock of chickens that flapped up squawking, kicking sand in his face. Beside the tool house the trucks stood idle, and the packing-shed doors were shut tight. Looking in through the wide screens, he could see that the mess hall was empty; but the smell of cooking breakfasts lingered. On Sunday mornings, the men fixed their own meals. Moving on inside the screened room and back between the long tables, he stepped into the kitchen and set about making his breakfast.

The big wire basket on the counter was full of rinsed dishes left to drain and several burners of the oversized commercial stove were still warm. The stove was familiar to Lee, from working in a number of prison kitchens. He found bowls of eggs in the refrigerator alongside rolls of chorizo, and there were packages of tortillas on the counter and a couple of loaves of bread. The big commercial coffeepot was warm but nearly empty and was of a kind he didn't know. He found a saucepan instead, and made boiled coffee. He fired up the stove's big gas grill, started the chorizo, and when it was brown he broke three eggs beside it. He dropped two slices of bread in the big commercial toaster, buttered them from a gallon crock, and carried his steaming plate and coffee mug to a table beside the long, east-facing screen, where the edge of the rising sun was just appearing over the sand hills and above the scraggly willows.

The cash from the traveler's check scam was in his hip pocket. He'd left his new gun and the ammo hidden inside his mattress, had ripped the stitching just enough to slide them in. Not very original, but they wouldn't be there long. His cabin didn't offer a lot of options, not even a cupboard under the sink. But no one seemed to have been in there since he'd moved in, his few personal possessions, his clean clothes, Mae's picture on the dresser, never seemed disturbed.

He had dreamed of Mae again last night. He didn't dream of her often but when he did the scene was shockingly real. Again she had been in a strange place, lying half asleep on a flowered couch, a blanket tucked around her, and her face very pale. She woke and looked up at him, looked right at him. "Cowboy," she said, reaching up to him, her thin little hands cold in his hands. She was telling him that he had to come and help her, when Lee woke.

It must have been around midnight, though in his dream it seemed to be morning. Outside his window the moon had already moved up out of sight above the cabin roof. He lay wakeful a long time staring into the dark, seeing Mae so vividly, hearing her voice so clearly—Mae's voice, and yet not quite her voice. There was something different in the way she spoke, an accent of some kind. Dreams could be so deceiving; but something in her voice left him uncertain and puzzled. The child had to be Mae, but something was different not only in the way she spoke, but something in her searching look that wasn't quite like Mae, something that teased and puzzled him so that when he slept again he worried restlessly. Even as he stirred and tossed in his dreams, part of him knew that Mae would be an old woman now, if she was still alive. Maybe he had dreamed of a time long past, when Mae needed him and he wasn't there for her?

But he didn't think so. This child belonged to the present, this child so like his small sister, this little girl was real and alive, now, today, this child reaching out to him, badly needing him.

Trying to settle his puzzled uncertainty, he told himself he'd let last night's dreams run away with him, that he needed to calm himself, not indulge in crazy fancies. Forking up the last of his eggs, looking out through the screen to the bunkhouses, he watched half a dozen pickers lolling on the long, roofed porches, and he could hear the murmur of Spanish radio stations clashing together in a senseless tangle. In the yard, a ball game had started, loud and energetic, lots of shouting and swearing in Spanish. He watched four young pickers leave their bunkhouse all dressed up in clean shirts, clean jeans, and polished boots, laughing and joking. They piled into an old blue Packard and took off, heading for town. He hoped that wasn't the last car to go. The next step in his plan depended on a ride into Blythe—but he could still see Tony polishing his car, and that was what he was counting on. Smearing jam on the last of his toast, he crammed it in his mouth, washed it down with the last swallow of coffee. He got up, picking up his plate, thinking about the day ahead.

He hadn't had much time to get himself organized but so far the moves had been smooth. It was the dreams that unsettled him. When he dreamed of Mae, the devil's urgings had backed off. But then, when he least expected it, the dark presence would return, pressing him to center his attention on the Delgado payroll, to set Jake up for a long prison term, and to move in on Lucita. He would wake from these encounters angry and fighting back.

No one but Lee himself, the cat, and the dark incubus knew the inner battles of Lee's sleepless nights, his dreams sometimes so conflicting that he began to think of himself as two people: his own natural self with the code he had known all his life, and the stranger whose hunger and viciousness didn't really belong to him. He didn't see Lucita much during the day. When he did, he knew she wouldn't play his game. But his hunger for her could still turn fierce, wanting her for himself—and too often the devil would reappear, urging Lee on to pursue her.

Last night the cat had waked him from such an encounter, had spoken so angrily that Lee had had to listen. Crouched on the foot of the bed, Misto had awakened Lee hissing and growling, kneading his claws so hard in the blanket, catching Lee's foot with a claw, that Lee rose up out of sleep staring at him, startled.

Why do you listen to him? the cat hissed. *You have grown older now, Lee, and you are wiser. But in your resolve, and in your body, you are weaker, while the devil is still strong. He will always be strong. Now, in your declining age, do you plan to let him beat you? Is Satan strong enough, now, to beat you?*

Now, leaving the table, still hearing the cat's words and angry at his own weakness, Lee returned to the kitchen, rinsed his dish and cup and set them to drain, then he headed out toward the bunkhouses.

Beyond the softball game two young Mexicans were tinkering with the engine of a cut-down Ford, the car's radio blaring its hot music. Near them Tony Valdez, stripped to the waist, was sloshing a last bucket of water over his two-door white Chevy coupe. The car was maybe fifteen years old, but looked in good shape. Lee went on over. "Nice car, Tony."

Tony grinned. "Haven't had it long." He picked up a rag and began to wipe down the roof and hood.

Lee ducked to look inside. A Saint Christopher medal dangled from the rearview mirror, but the interior was clean and uncluttered. "Don't suppose I could talk you into driving me into town?"

Tony gave the hood a final swipe. "Sure can." He wiped the rest of the car quickly and efficiently, then turned away from Lee, wringing out the rag. "I'm leaving, pronto. Five minutes." He grinned at Lee again. "She doesn't like me to be late." Turning, he headed for his bunkhouse.

Waiting for him, Lee stood watching two men playing with a thin, mangy black dog, shaking a stick for it to grab. The radios were still dueling, metallic music against what sounded like a Spanish church service. When Tony emerged from his bunkhouse he was as clean and polished as his white car, a fresh white shirt with cuffs turned up once, open at his chest to show the silver cross against his brown skin, a pair of freshly creased blue slacks that made Lee guess the men must have an ironing board in the bunkhouse. Tony walked gingerly through the dust, trying to save the polish on his black boots. Easing into the clean Chevy he held out each foot and wiped off the dust with a rag.

Getting into the clean car, Lee held out his boots and brushed them with his hand, hiding a smile. "You better be careful, Tony. She'll have you before the altar."

"That's okay by me. Maybe Delgado would give us one of the cabins, that would sure beat living in the bunkhouse." He backed the Chevy around real slow so not to raise any dust, pulled out of the yard heading for the road into Blythe. Not until they were on the harder dirt road did he give it the gas, the car coming to life like a spurred bronco. They were rolling through the crossroads burg called Ripley when Lee spotted a FOR SALE sign on a rusty truck parked beside the gas station. "I'll get out here," he said quietly. "Something I need to do—catch a ride later."

Tony pulled over, glancing at Lee with curiosity. "You sure?"

"I'm sure," Lee said, swinging out. Tony sat a moment looking around the bare little crossroads, then put the car in gear. "See you tomorrow, then," he said, easing away, looking at the gas station and the old truck with interest. When his car had disappeared, Lee walked back up the dusty road to the filling station.

He circled the old pickup. There was a rusted hole in

its bed, covered by a piece of plywood. The tires had little tread left. Years of use had worn the ridges on the running boards smooth and concave. Lee opened the driver's door, studied the worn pedals and cracked leather seat. A few rusted tools, a hammer, a length of cotton rope, and a trenching tool were stuffed into the narrow space behind the seat. He got in, stepped on the clutch, moved the shift through the gears. They seemed all right. He stepped out, walked around the truck again. It had a spare tire, and it had a trailer hitch but no ball. As he turned toward the office a fat man in bib overalls came out through the screened door. "Like to hear it run?"

Lee nodded, and opened the hood. The man slid in, easing his belly under the steering wheel. He cranked the truck without any trouble. The straight six-cylinder engine idled smoothly, with a soft clatter. Lee reached in under the hood close to the carburetor and pushed the throttle forward. The racing engine sounded smooth, and when he released the rod it dropped back to a soft clattering idle. The man killed the engine and stepped out.

"It's been a good old truck for me. I was just able to buy a newer model."

"Are there any tools, in case of a flat?"

Grunting, the fat man lifted the seat cushion to show Lee a tire iron, a heavy lug wrench, and a screw jack.

"How much?"

He dropped the seat, stuck his thumbs under the straps of his overalls. "Two hundred and fifty dollars."

"I'll give you two hundred cash."

"Two and a quarter and it's yours."

Lee pulled the money from his back pocket, counted it

out. The owner reached into his bib pocket for the pink slip, signed the back of it, and handed it over. "Fill out the rest and mail it to Sacramento, you'll get a new one in your name."

Lee dropped the pink slip in his shirt pocket. "Know anyone who has a horse trailer for sale?"

"Not personally. I did see an ad in this morning's paper. Let me get it." He turned, heading for the office. Lee stepped into the truck, eased it around close to the screened door. The fat man returned, handed the folded paper through the truck window. "Keep the paper, I've read it. River Road Ranch is about five miles south out of Blythe, next road to your right, you'll see the sign."

Lee found River Road with no trouble. About a quarter mile down, through dry desert, he turned up a long drive to an adobe ranch house. It was low and sprawling, but not too large. Pole construction supported the wide overhang of the roof, sheltering the long porch against the desert sun. A man sat on a rocker in its deep shade, his boot heels propped on a wooden box. Lee parked, watched him come down the steps: a thin man with sparse hair, his Levi's and boots well worn. His walk was that of a horseman, a little stiff, a little bowlegged. From the truck, Lee said, "I saw your ad on the trailer."

"Kendall, Rod Kendall. I still have it, pull around the side of the barn," he said, stepping onto the running board.

"John Demons," Lee said, not wanting his name remembered. Easing the truck around to the back of the barn, he pulled up beside a narrow, one-horse trailer, a homemade job of wood and angle iron with a sheet-metal roof. The tires looked good, though, and it had a ball hitch hanging from the tongue. "How much?"

"It's yours for seventy-five dollars."

Lee was going to dicker, but then he saw several horses move into view from behind some tamarisk trees in the fenced pasture. "You wouldn't have a horse to put in it? Nothing special, just a good saddle horse."

The man grinned. "You ever know a rancher that doesn't have a horse or two to sell? Could let you have either one of those mares. The black's seven, the buckskin about nine."

This meant to Lee they were both fifteen or better. He was about to dicker for the black mare when a gray gelding followed the mares, ducking his head, edging them aside from the water trough. He moved well, and looked in good shape, a dark, steel gray. "What about the gelding?"

Kendall paused a moment, looking Lee over. As if maybe he cared more about the gelding, didn't want him used badly; but he must have decided Lee looked like an honest horseman. Leaving the truck he stepped to the barn door, shouted into the dim alleyway. "Harry! Harry, bring the gray in, will you?"

Lee watched a young boy, maybe twelve or so, halter the gelding, lead him across the field and out through the gate. No lameness, no quirks to his walk. Stepping out of the truck, Lee rubbed the gray's ears, slid his hand down his legs and lifted his feet. He seemed sound, and he was shod, his feet and shoes in good shape. Opening the gray's mouth, he looked at his teeth. The gelding was about twelve. Well, that was all right, they wouldn't be together for long.

He dickered for a saddle and saddlebags, a bridle with

a heavy spade bit, a halter, four bales of hay, and a sack of oats. He got that, the horse and trailer for two hundred dollars. He pulled out of Kendall's ranch with a balance of two hundred and forty dollars left in his pocket, and he hadn't touched his savings account, which would alert Raygor.

Conscious of the weight of the trailer on the old truck, he took his time driving back into Blythe. The gray pulled well, he didn't fuss. In Blythe there wasn't much traffic. Lee moved along in second gear until he recognized the side street he wanted. He parked along the curb near the post office.

The main section of the post office was closed on Sunday, but the lobby that housed the P.O. boxes was open. He filled out the title transfer section on the truck's pink slip, using the name James Dawson and the Furnace Creek Road address. Lee would never receive the pink slip, but it wasn't likely he'd need it. As he sealed the envelope he looked with some interest at the wanted posters hanging above the narrow counter. The newness of one caught his eye, and the word "Blythe."

"Luke Zigler. Age 33. Five feet, ten inches, 190 pounds. Swarthy complexion, muscular build. Under life sentence for armed robbery and murder. Escaped Terminal Island Federal Penitentiary, March 20, 1947. Zigler's hometown: Twentynine Palms, California. May attempt to contact friends there. Subject should be considered armed and extremely dangerous. Persons having any information are requested to contact the nearest office of the Federal Bureau of Investigation, or local law enforcement."

Blythe wasn't far from Twentynine Palms or from Palm Springs, the man could be anywhere in the area. Zigler's eyes, vacant under bushy brows, stared coldly at Lee from the grainy black-and-white photograph. Lee had seen enough of his kind, in prison and out. But still, that look disturbed him. Haunted, half-crazy bastards, stick you in a minute for no reason.

He gave the poster a last look, dropped his envelope in the mail slot, and left the lobby. But all the way back to the ranch, among other thoughts he kept getting flashes of Zigler's ugly face, and flashes of those he had known who were like Zigler, men he wouldn't want to meet again. Driving and preoccupied, he was unaware of the ghost cat riding with him and that the yellow tom was as unsettled by Zigler as Lee had been, that the cat might be even more riveted than Lee by the evil in Zigler's cold stare.

Lee drove onto the Delgado land by a narrow back road, keeping the tamarisk trees between him and the ranch yard, moving slowly to keep the dust down, turning at last onto a narrow trail he'd spotted days before, a track barely wide enough for the truck and trailer. The times he'd walked down here, he'd found no tire marks in the fine dust and no hoof prints as if Jake and Lucita might have ridden down this way. Usually they headed north, up between the planted fields. This trail led to the river, where mosquitoes could be bothersome.

Pulling in deep among the willows and tamarisk trees, he knew the truck and trailer were out of sight, tree limbs brushing the top of both, the strip of woods dim and sheltered until, farther in along the narrow track, he broke out into an open area of hard-packed earth some twenty feet across, the woods dense around it. He killed the engine and got out.

An overgrown footpath led down to the broad, turgid water of the Colorado. A circle of dead ashes shone dark in the clearing, tall weeds growing through the campfire of some forgotten hobo or migrant worker. Dropping the tailgate, he squeezed through to the gray's head, and backed him out.

He tied the gelding to the side of the trailer, brushed off his back, and settled the faded saddle blanket in place. The gray swiveled an ear when he swung the saddle up, and filled his belly with air. Lee bridled him, led him out a few steps then tightened the cinch again. The gray looked around at him knowingly. Swinging into the saddle, Lee walked him around the clearing then moved him out toward the river at a jog. He cantered him, stopped him short, backed him, spun him a couple of times, let him jog out slow, and he felt himself grinning. He rode for maybe half an hour up along the river. It had been a long time since he'd felt a good horse under him. "You'll do," he told the gray. "I guess we both will."

In the falling evening, as he unsaddled the gray and rubbed him down, his thoughts turned sharply back to the South Dakota prairie when he and Mae were kids, to the long summer days when, hurrying through his chores, they still had daylight to slip away while Ma and the girls were getting supper and his dad was maybe in town or busy with the cattle in a far field. He could see Mae's smile so clearly, her dark eyes, her dimples deep as she stepped up onto her small cowhorse.

Why had he dreamed of Mae last night? And why had that other little girl, in town that day, stared up at him shocked, bringing Mae so alive for a moment? Why was his little sister, from half a century gone, suddenly so clear and real in his thoughts? Riding up along the river, he'd felt for a moment almost as if she rode behind him, her small arms around his waist, her head resting against his back as she used to do; the feeling had been so strong that near dark when he returned to the clearing he felt he ought to help Mae down off the gray before he stepped down, himself.

Shaking his head at his own foolishness, he tied the gelding to the trailer again, and then secured two five-gallon buckets to the side, one filled with water from the river, the other with a quart of oats. He heaved the hay from the pickup into the trailer, broke open one bale, pulled off two flakes of good oat hay, and dropped them on the ground where the gelding could reach them. He shut the tailgate so the gelding couldn't get in at the rest. Leaving the quiet saddle horse with the truck and trailer, leaving him to sleep standing, he set out through the falling night on the two-mile hike back to his cabin, keeping his mind, now, on the job ahead.

28

HALF AN HOUR after Morgan was booked into the Rome jail, Jimson returned, moving in through the heavy outer door, looking in through the bars at Morgan. "Becky's on her way. I couldn't get her at home, she was at Caroline's." Morgan was surprised Jimson had bothered to call her. But he knew that wasn't fair, Jimson was only doing his job, and when Morgan looked up at him now, some of the old warmth had returned.

"She's been out all night looking for you," Jimson said, "looking for your car. She started to cry when she knew you were all right, that you weren't lying dead somewhere." The officer paused, a frown touching his round, smooth face. "She said to tell you she wasn't bringing Sammie, said Sammie has a cold, she's left her with Caroline." The officer colored a little. "She said to tell you she loves you." Quickly he turned away again, locking the outer door behind him.

Morgan stared after him. Of course she wouldn't bring Sammie, not here to see him locked behind bars just as in her nightmare. What had Becky told Sammie when he hadn't come all night, when Sammie didn't hear him get up and shower this morning, when he didn't appear at the breakfast table?

What would she tell Sammie if he didn't come home at all, if this couldn't be straightened out, if he was kept in jail and was arraigned and even tried, a prisoner escorted back and forth to the courtroom? Thinking about what might lie ahead of him turned him shaky, cold and despondent again. How could he be charged with murder? He had killed no one. Not even if he'd been drugged would he kill a man—except in the war, he thought, bitterly.

There was only one explanation for his long lapse of memory, his long and debilitating sleep, and that was that Falon had given him some drug. Easy enough for Falon to get drugs, maybe some kind of prescription that was passed around among Falon's sleazy friends. Opium, maybe, that was easy enough to get, it was prescribed for colds and the flu. Dover's Powder, he thought it was called, something like that. He supposed, unless they found the Coke bottle, there was no way to tell. He doubted the Rome cops would go looking for Coke bottles, as surly as they'd been. And even then, could a chemist or pharmacist find such a thing?

Sitting on the sagging bunk, he put his face in his hands, sick and cold with fear. No matter what Becky told Sammie about why he wasn't home, at some point Sammie would have to learn the truth, and what would that do to her? They'd tried never to lie to Sammie, even when she was very small; only those few times that, because she was so young, the truth would have been inexplicable to her. Now, this morning, *would* Becky lie, so that Sammie wouldn't know so soon that her worst nightmare had come true? He couldn't bear to think of his little girl's terror. Or of Becky's own pain, when she heard the inexplicable charge of murder. What could he have done last night—what could Falon have done—to make this happen, to hurt the two people in the world whom Morgan loved more than life itself?

He and Becky had been sweethearts since before high school, they had married the week after they graduated, just a small wedding in her mother's garden. He lay thinking about their honeymoon at Carter Lake, how happy they had been, how perfect life had been then. They had stayed in a cabin borrowed from a friend of Becky's mother's, had spent most of that week in bed, a little of it walking the woods or in leisurely twilight swims. They didn't give a damn that they had little money and would have to live with Becky's mother at first, in the bedroom behind the bakery kitchen. He liked Caroline, had always liked her, though they had had their moments when, in high school, he still wouldn't stop running with Falon. That week on Carter Lake they would lie in bed spent from loving each other, planning how soon they could buy their own business and maybe even buy a house, planning how many children they would have, planning the beginning of their real lives as if they had only just been born.

The next week after their honeymoon he went to work as a mechanic at one of the three local gas stations, and Becky found a job with an accountant. When she'd learned enough, she left to start her own freelance accounts, to build her own new business. She had the same drive and stamina that had helped her mother succeed alone in the bakery business after Becky's father died.

Becky had taken only a little time out to have Sammie, balancing her customers' books while caring for the baby. When war was declared, he'd joined the navy rather than being drafted. During his absence, their need for each other, their passion had built intolerably. All the time he'd been gone his dreams had been only of Becky and of their baby girl, of the business they would build together and the large family they planned, of a rich, long life together.

When he got home, they had saved enough for a nice down payment on the old abandoned gas station. His mother would have scraped to send him to college but he'd never wanted that, he had no use for that kind of learning. He loved machines, he loved cars and trucks, anything mechanical, and he had gotten further education for that, for the learning he really wanted, in the navy.

All the time he was gone, Becky sent him pictures of Sammie. She had his pale Irish coloring, but Becky's dark eyes and turned-up nose, she was the spirit of their spirits, she was proof of the eternity of their union, her existence filled him with an even deeper love of being alive in God's world. At six years old Sammie had handled her bicycle like a pro, she knew how to make her own bed and how to mix and cut out cookies for her mother—but the minute he got home she became Daddy's helper, his gamin-faced grease monkey.

Becky had already taught her the names and uses of most of his automotive tools and where they belonged in the pocketed black cloth wrapper where he kept them, and Sammie soon loved working on cars. And why not? A little training in mechanics wouldn't hurt; when she grew older, she could do anything she wanted with her life. Becky kept her dressed in jeans and hoped, just as Morgan did, that the child would develop some other loves besides pretty clothes. Becky said frills would come soon enough without encouragement. Sammie made her mother laugh aloud when Morgan brought her home at night dirty faced, grease-stained clothes, dog tired, and so deeply happy with having helped her daddy.

Now, this morning, Sammie would be asking for him, she would want to know why he had left so early, even before he'd had breakfast. Maybe Becky would tell her he'd gotten home late and left early to work on a special car for one of his longtime customers. But Sammie was only a little girl. When she did at last learn the truth, how would she cope with this? How could she ever sleep again, knowing that any nightmare, any terrible dream, would be sure to come true?

He had turned away from the bars, was smearing tears away with the back of his hand, when the barred door clanged open behind him. Morgan turned, ashamed of crying, looking up at Jimson. The officer motioned Morgan out, walking behind him. "Becky's in the visiting room."

"She's alone?" Morgan asked.

"She's alone," Jimson said. Sergeant Trevis met them halfway down the hall and the tall, lean officer gestured Morgan toward the little visiting room, standing behind him as he entered.

Becky stood on the far side of the table that occupied

the center of the room, her knuckles white where she gripped its edge, her face drawn and pale. The room was hot and stuffy, the one small, barred window behind her was open but admitted only hot, humid air laced with gas fumes from the street, the traffic noise loud and distracting. Morgan approached the table, stopping at Trevis's direction. He and Becky stood looking across at each other, separated as if they were strangers.

"Did they tell *you* what happened?" Morgan said. "Do you know what the charges are about?"

Behind him, Trevis stepped on in and closed the door. When Morgan turned to look at him, Trevis looked politely away. Morgan wished they could be alone. He knew Trevis would record in memory their every stilted word. James Trevis, thin and rangy, had played basketball in high school two years ahead of Morgan, then had served a hitch in the marines, had returned home to continue with the law enforcement he had learned as a military policeman. Morgan glanced at him again, and moved on around the table. Trevis looked away, and didn't stop him. Morgan put his arms around Becky, they stood for a long time in silence, desperately holding each other.

When Becky spoke at last, her voice was muffled against him. "They told me nothing. Sergeant Trevis only told me the charges." She took a step back, her hands on his shoulders, looking up at him. He reached to gently touch the smudges under her eyes. The look in her dark eyes told him she knew more about what had happened than she wanted to say, that she didn't want to talk in front of Trevis. If a man *had* been killed last night, no matter what the circumstances, by now it would be all over town.

She said, "I called Mama's attorney. I know he's an estate attorney, that he doesn't do this kind of work, but he gave me a couple of names. I've made appointments with both.

"And they did tell me," she said, "that you were drunk. When Sergeant Trevis told me that," she said, glancing up, "I asked Dr. Bates if he would come and talk with you. *I* know you weren't drinking, I thought maybe some kind of drug. Has he been here yet?"

Morgan shook his head. As for an attorney, Morgan had never had need of one, and there were only a few lawyers in their small town, two with reputations that he and Becky didn't like. He couldn't think who would handle charges like this, someone they could trust. Becky's dark eyes hadn't left him, she looked at him a long time then pressed against him again, holding him tight. "Someone has to tell you what happened," she said. "It isn't fair for you not to know."

Trevis moved to the table beside them. "As soon as you're questioned, Morgan, we'll lay it out for you."

Morgan nodded. That made sense, so he couldn't make up some story to fit whatever had occurred. Trevis moved again, as if to separate them, but then he let them be.

"It's some kind of mix-up," Becky said. "We'll find out the truth." She looked up at Trevis. "The police will find out, they're our friends, Morgan, they'll find out, they'll make it all right again."

Morgan wished he could believe that. "You went looking for me last night, you borrowed a car, you and Sammie . . ."

"When you didn't come home, I went to the shop, before I took Sammie to Mama's, she wasn't feeling well. The shop was locked up tight, the new mechanic was gone. I didn't know where he lived, and the operator had no phone number for an Albert Weiss."

She held Morgan away, letting her anger center on the mechanic. "Yesterday when you left, when you weren't back by closing time, did he just go on working? Didn't he wonder where you were, didn't he worry when you weren't back to close out the cash register and lock up? Why didn't he call the house? At five o'clock he just locked up and went home? How ironic. You hired Albert because he was calm and didn't get ruffled, because he didn't fuss about things. He was calm, all right," she said bitterly. "He didn't wonder—because he didn't care."

Morgan could say nothing. She was right. That was Albert's way, he was a silent man, not the least interested in others' business, focused solely on the cars he repaired.

"Where did he think you'd gone! And then this morning he just—he just opened the shop and got to work?" she said incredulously. "He might be a good mechanic, but his brain stops there. He could have come over to the house last night to see if you were all right, see if you'd come home." Her voice broke, she took a minute to get control. "You could have died out there last night, died in the car, all alone."

"You just kept driving," he said, "driving around looking for me?"

"I drove all over Rome and then out around the farms, over on the Berry campus. At last I called the station, talked with Officer Regan. He told me the patrols would keep an eye out, he said he was sure you'd turn up, that it was too soon to file a missing report. I drove down every back road, some of them twice, but I didn't see the car. Later, when Jimson found you, he said it was parked way back among the trees, that it was easy to miss." The muscles in her jaw were clenched. "Parked out near lovers' hollow," she said, and it didn't occur to him until that moment that she might have thought, last night, that he was with another woman.

But Becky knew there wasn't anyone else, there was no woman in the world he'd look at except her. Holding her close to him, needing her steadiness, he tried to tell her what he could remember, tried to bring the fractured scenes from yesterday clearer, tried to make sense of them. Trevis stood intently listening. Morgan knew he would write it all down the moment Becky left, that Morgan's words would be compared with the formal questioning that he would soon face. The police had to know, early last night, about the robbery and murder, but of course it would be policy not to mention it to Becky. Morgan had no idea whether they thought, at that point, the two events might be connected. Both cases were police business, and the officers kept conjecture to themselves.

Morgan told Becky how Falon had wanted him to look at his car, that he hadn't wanted to go, told her what Falon had said about her mother's property out on the Dixie Highway. Slowly, talking it out, he was able to put those moments together more clearly—until the moment when everything went hazy and the afternoon fell apart into a wavering and senseless haze.

"When Falon spilled his Coke, I wiped up the spill and then pulled into Robert's gas station to get some wet paper towels. I came out, finished my Coke while I was cleaning the seat. I remember the Coke tasted kind of funny, but I didn't pay much attention. When I had the seat pretty clean, and dried off, we headed for the Graystone Apartments, I remember that. I'd driven a couple of blocks when the street started to look fuzzy, the cars and buildings blurred, the distances all warped. I remember pulling over, dizzy and sick. After that, nothing's very clear. Everything looked strange, twisted and unreal."

"You drank all your Coke?"

He nodded. "Falon handed it to me, I drank what was left in the bottle, tucked the bottle in the side pocket so it wouldn't drip on the floor. I drove until things began to reel, then I pulled over."

Becky looked up at Sergeant Trevis. "Have you picked up Brad Falon?"

Trevis's face went closed, his look ungiving. "We questioned him." Trevis searched Morgan's face, and turned to glance at the door. "I shouldn't tell you this much, until after you're interviewed."

Morgan waited. He didn't see what difference it could make, as long as *he* told the truth.

"Falon said he was with his girlfriend from one-thirty yesterday afternoon until this morning." Trevis looked more kindly, with perhaps a touch of regret. "We talked with her, she swore Falon was there in her apartment. At this point," he said, "we haven't enough to bring him in."

"What girlfriend?" Becky said.

"That's all I can say," Trevis said.

Neither Becky nor Morgan had heard anything about what women Falon might be seeing; they'd had no reason to know or to care. But now, from the look in Becky's eyes, Morgan knew she meant to find out. He wanted to say, *Be careful*. But she would do that, he let only his look warn her: *Take care, Falon can be vicious.* He said, "What did you tell Sammie?"

"That you worked late, got home late, had to get up real early to fix a special car."

He smiled. "Did she believe you?"

"She might not have, except she was so disoriented herself. She has a cold or the flu, something . . . Dr. Bates came out, to Mother's. He said the usual, keep Sammie warm, lots of liquids and rest, half an aspirin every four hours. She doesn't have a fever, and she isn't coughing, she's just very dull, so sleepy she can hardly stay awake."

"How long?" Morgan said. "How long has she been like that?"

"From around noon yesterday," Becky said. "So sleepy she couldn't stay awake. If I woke her, she'd just drift off again, she just wanted to lie there on the couch and sleep, she slept most of the afternoon." Her description struck a chill of fear through Morgan.

"Once when I woke her, she said she felt dizzy, that every time she went to sleep she dropped down, deep down into darkness. So dark, she said, falling down into darkness."

Morgan went ice-cold. "That . . . That's how I felt, when I woke in the car. As if I were trapped deep down in some heavy darkness. Even in the patrol car, and here in the cell, moments when I could hardly keep awake, so dull, wiped out."

They looked at each other, frightened. Filled with

Sammie's perceptions, with her sure and specific cognition. As if Sammie had experienced exactly what Morgan had felt, Morgan's confusion and dullness, her daddy's helpless lethargy. Becky shivered and clung to him, a coldness reaching deep inside her like an icy hand.

She said at last, "I called Dr. Bates again, though still Sammie had no fever, no pain. He wanted to put her in the hospital, but I didn't want that. I wanted her with Mother, I knew she'd take her to the hospital if she needed to. Once she was settled at Mother's and sound asleep, I went looking for you. I feel sick that I must have passed our car twice and never seen it. The last time, it was just getting light, I must have just missed the police.

"But then," she said, "the strangest thing. When I got back to Mama's, Sammie was awake, sitting up and more alert. Mama said she woke cranky, that Sammie complained that her head hurt. Mama gave her another aspirin and called the doctor again. She was ready to take her to the hospital when Sammie came awake, sat up, and looked around her, surprised she was at Mother's.

"Mama got her to drink some juice and eat a little hot cereal." Becky looked at him, frowning. "That was . . . That was when Jimson found you. Early this morning, just after sunup? That was when Sammie woke."

"The sun was in my eyes," Morgan said. "I thought it was sunset, but then figured out the sun was coming up, that I must have slept all night in the car, I was trying to figure that out when Jimson jerked the door open and dragged me out."

Becky glanced at Sergeant Trevis. She didn't like talking about Sammie in front of him, she had no notion what he would make of the conversation. Trevis let them stay close together, let them talk. He was more eager to listen, apparently, than to take Morgan back and separate them.

"By the time I got home to Mama's and sat down to eat some breakfast, Sammie was brighter, she came to the table and shared some scrambled eggs and toast with me. When the station called to tell me you were here, that you were in jail, it was all I could do not to panic. I asked if you were all right, I didn't want to say much in front of Sammie, but the minute I got my purse, ready to leave, she had pulled on her sweater and meant to go with me, she was so tense, fidgeting with impatience to be with you, so out of control, so determined and stubborn I had a hard time making her stay behind with Mama. She said she had to talk to you, she had to tell you what she'd dreamed while she was sick. You remember that old man she talked about when she was playing with the airplane she made? The man she called the cowboy."

"Yes, she's talked to me about him."

"She said she had to tell you about him. Somehow, in her mind that dream was connected to your being here. As little as I said, she figured out where you were, she figured out that the prison dream had come true." Becky looked at Morgan helplessly. "She said this dream of the cowboy was part of what was happening to you, said she had to tell you." She looked uncomfortably at Sergeant Trevis then turned away, muffling her face against Morgan's shoulder.

"When I left, she clung to me," Becky said, "she tried to come with me, she wept and wept, and all I could do was hold her." Becky was weeping, too. He held her as she had held their child, seeking to heal her, wondering if anything could ever heal her, or heal Sammie, if any power could heal the three of them.

Morgan was hardly aware when Trevis turned and nodded to him, letting him know he must go back to his cell. Becky stepped back, freeing Morgan, wiping at tears again. "Do you have our car keys?" But then she realized the booking officer would have taken everything from Morgan, everything in his pockets.

Trevis said, "We have them, we've impounded the car for evidence."

"Oh. Of course." She looked at Morgan. "I still have the Parkers' car. If it's very long, I'll use Mama's old Plymouth. I need to see the attorneys. I want to see Mama's attorney, too, before I see the others, I want advice from someone we trust."

"I didn't rob any bank, Becky. You know I didn't kill anyone."

"I know that. But even if the police want to believe you, they have to do it their way." She looked at Trevis. "I know you'll find out what happened. Did you find the Coke bottles?"

"No Coke bottles in the car," Trevis said. "McAffee's out searching the woods."

Morgan felt stupidly grateful that they would take the trouble. He'd felt so betrayed by the police, abandoned by the men who were supposed to be his friends. He knew that was foolish, that they had a job to do, but now those few kind words, knowing they were trying to help, lifted his spirits some. He prayed they'd find the bottles, both of them. Only one bottle would have a trace of drugs, if that was what had happened. He knew no other way to explain the yawning cavern of emptiness he'd experienced, that had left his whole being hollow.

"If you find the bottles," Becky said, "you'll finger-print them?"

Trevis nodded, looking put out that she would ask such a dumb question. He cleared his throat, turned, and opened the closed door. Becky hugged Morgan once more, kissed him and then turned away. As Trevis ushered Morgan back to his cell, she was met in the hall by another officer and escorted on out to the front. Morgan glanced back at her once, then was through the door of the lockup, through his barred cell door and locked in again. He lay down on the bunk, sick and grieving. He'd gotten himself into a mess, out of pure stupidity, had brought their lives shattering down around them. Had left Becky to fight, alone, a battle that terrified and perplexed him.

And Becky, outside the courthouse getting in the bor-rowed car, left the Rome jail wondering how she could keep Sammie from coming with her on her next visit. The child was so stubbornly determined. What would it do to their little girl to see her daddy in jail, after the terror of her nightmare? Yet she knew she couldn't keep Sammie away, not when she burned with such an urgent need to see Morgan, with what seemed, to Becky, might in fact be a critical part of the wall that fate had built around them.

29

On Lee's last night at Delgado Ranch he didn't stay in his cabin, he slept under the stars beneath the willows, near to the gray, his head on the saddle, the saddle blanket over him. He dreamed not of the robbery as he usually would, sorting out, in sleep, the last details; he dreamed of Lucita. He'd had dinner with her and Jake, a painful evening, only Lee knowing this was the last time they'd ever be together, the last time he'd be even this close to Lucita.

She had made chiles rellenos for dinner, she knew they were his favorite, and that, too, bothered him. Almost as if she knew he would be gone in the morning, though of course she couldn't know. Sitting at the table in their cozy dining room, feeling guilty in his longing for her, and feeling ashamed that he was running out on Jake after Jake had gone to the trouble to get him the job, he told himself that at least he hadn't turned on Jake—though even now, at this late hour, he felt a pang of greed for the fat Delgado payroll. All evening his conflicting emotions kept him on edge, his remorse, his painful, bittersweet farewell that only Lee himself was aware of—only Lee, and the big yellow tomcat.

The cat had made himself clearly visible tonight, had strolled in through the kitchen door before even Lee arrived. He lay stretched out now in the living room on the big leather couch, looking through to the dining room watching their last, sad gathering. He felt nearly as heavy with angst as Lee, at leaving the Ellsons'. He had come to like and respect Jake, and each day he was drawn more and more to gentle and beautiful Lucita, Lucita who baby-talked him and who stroked his neck and under his chin just the way he liked. As many lives as Misto had known over the centuries, and as many painful partings, tonight he seemed filled with the deepest pain of all, at leaving this gentle lady.

But leave her Misto did, looking regretfully back, following Lee not long after dinner. The last cup of coffee was finished, the bowls of flan had been scraped clean. Lee thanked Lucita for dinner, a casual hug, a casual good-night and he was through the door, down the steps, and out into the night before he might fumble something that should be left unsaid, before he tangled himself in his own emotions, his own embarrassed dismay at leaving them.

Returning to his cabin he finished packing his saddle-bags, made sure he had the roll of heavy tape handy in his pocket where he could reach it. He turned off his cabin lights as if he'd gone to bed, lay in the dark for nearly an hour, occasionally stepping to the window to look across at the bunkhouses and at the ranch house, watching until all the windows were dark. Still he didn't leave the cabin until Jake and Lucita's lights had been out for some time.

Carrying his saddlebags, silently he shut the door behind him and moved down the steps. Even the chickens slept, none woke to fuss at him as he crossed the ranch yard. Beneath the pale wash of stars he walked the two miles to the clearing and settled in for his last night at Delgado ranch, smiling as the gray nickered to him and then pawed at his hay, snorting softly.

Since he'd brought the gray here to the clearing, he had checked on him every day, had fed and watered him morning and night and brushed him down, all in the dark before breakfast or long after supper, walking across the black desert and among the willows and tamarisks that skirted the south field. He was surprised that Jake or one of the pickers hadn't come down this way, hadn't seen the truck and trailer here by the river and come to investigate. He was sure that hadn't happened, or Jake would have said something. And in the evenings when Jake and Lucita rode, they headed north away from the river, avoiding the seclusion where hobos or migrants sometimes liked to camp. Lee had been wary about strangers, but there was no sign anyone had been around disturbing his hidden retreat.

Now, bedded down beneath the cool night sky he lay thinking about Lucita, her brief glances at him sometimes, a quick look that had held a suppressed longing that both knew wouldn't go any further. Once when she was feeding her chickens and had knelt to examine a layer's hurt leg, cuddling the fluffy red hen close to calm her as she fingered the small wound, she had looked up at him, the spark clearly there for a moment; but then abruptly she put the hen down, rose, and turned away.

It had been a stupid dream to think she'd ever leave Jake for him. And now, the minute the robbery was known and Lee had vanished, though Jake might understand his drive and his need, Lee would have lost Lucita's respect forever, would have lost her as a friend as well as the lover she would never have been.

Twice during the previous week he had had supper with them, not a fancy meal like tonight, but more casual, tacos and beer one night, the other evening a bowl of green chili. Both times he had excused himself early, soon turned his cabin light off and waited for a while, then headed for the clearing, to quietly ride the gelding through the willows along the river, taking peace in the silent dark and in the companionship of the gray.

Lee's parole officer had shown up this morning, and that had put him off, had left him edgy. But it was good luck, too. This monthly visit meant Raygor wouldn't be around again for a while, it meant that he might not know, for some time, that Lee was gone. Jake would be obligated to tell him, to call the San Bernardino office, but Lee didn't think he would. He thought, when Raygor contacted Jake, he'd make up some excuse. Jake would know, by then, that Lee was on the run, and would buy him what time he could. Rolling over, looking up at the stars one last time, Lee felt the cat slip in under the blanket beside him and immediately he felt easier, stroking the tomcat, smiling at his rocking purr. Maybe Lee thought, his PO wouldn't approve of what he was about to undertake, but the ghost cat, purring and snuggling close, seemed fine with the plan.

THE GELDING WOKE Lee, pawing for breakfast. Lee gave him a quart of oats but they wouldn't have time to fool around with hay, it was starting to get light. He stood in the coolness of the new day stretching, scratching, then walked to the river to relieve himself. He packed the truck, tucked a flake of hay into the manger of the trailer, led the gray in and tied him, and closed and fastened the tailgate.

He opened the cylinder of the heavy revolver, checked that it was fuly loaded. He had slept with it under the saddle blanket that was his pillow. Closing the cylinder, he slid the gun into its worn holster and laid it on the truck seat. He opened a can of beans from his pack, ate that with a plastic spoon wishing he had something hot, thinking about sausage and pancakes from the mess hall. He could smell the good, warm scents of breakfast drifting down to him, where the men would be crowding in, swilling coffee and filling their bellies.

Stashing the empty can in a paper bag in the truck cab, he made one last walk around the clearing. He picked up the fold of baling wire from the bale of hay, and scuffed away the chaff where the gelding had been feeding. Returning to the truck, he dropped the wire in the paper bag, stuffed the gloves he had bought into his back pocket, and slid behind the wheel.

He cranked the engine, listened to its soft clatter, and moved on out through the hanging branches onto the dirt track. Easing along, he had one more moment of unease over what he had begun. Was this the smart thing to do?

Well, hell, he didn't know about smart, but he was on his way, he'd started something that had felt right at the time, and he meant to finish it. In the slowly lightening morning he pushed the intruding shadows out of his mind; driving along the narrow dirt path, at the main road to Blythe he shifted from low to second, felt the trailer balk and then come on as he turned north.

Once he had gained the outskirts of Blythe he pulled into a truck stop, filled the pickup with gas, checked the oil and filled the ten-gallon barrel with water. In the little twenty-four-hour café he ordered two ham-and-cheese sandwiches to go. At the cash register there was a cardboard display of pocket watches, shoved in under the glass counter between boxes of candy and gum. He bought a watch, set it by the restaurant clock, wound it and tucked it into the watch pocket of his jeans. He'd have a long wait, he didn't want to hit the post office too early, but he needed to be back at the remote airstrip no later than seven. He had all day to wait, but then at the last he'd have to hustle. It was a long pull from the post office up where he'd be headed. He hoped to hell he didn't have a flat, on either the truck or the trailer. All these tires had seen better days. He'd have to unload the gray to change a tire, and that would slow him down more than he liked.

He traveled north out of Blythe on the same road he and Ellson had taken. The old truck rolled right along, though he didn't push it, he let it go over thirty only on the gentle downgrades. He rode with both windows cranked down and the wind wings open. It was still cool but it wouldn't be for long. Twice he slowed the truck thinking of turning back and chucking the whole plan. Then, angry at himself, he pushed on again faster. It wasn't like him to have second thoughts so late in the game, that made him impatient with himself; and when he remembered suddenly that he'd forgotten to fill the radiator, that turned him hot with anger.

Well, hell, he guessed the gray wouldn't begrudge a quart or two from his water barrel. Lee told himself to settle down, he tried to bring back the old steady calm with which he always worked. His plan was to wait in or behind the old barn beyond the Jamesfarm cutoff, leave the gelding and the trailer there, go on into town in the truck late in the day, as evening settled in. Hit the back door of the post office late, when the ranch foremen started showing up for their money. He'd have a long wait, all through the middle of the day, and then a fast hustle. Thinking about the moves, and the last-minute timing, he began to sweat.

Maybe he shouldn't wait all day at the cutoff and risk being seen, maybe he should move on up into the dry hills and lay up there. Return to the cutoff in late afternoon, leave the gray and the trailer there. Hit the post office, return to the cutoff until it started to get dark, leave the truck and trailer with Dawson's ID and then, as he'd planned, head for the mountains on horseback. That was where the timing grew critical. If he took too long or was delayed, he'd miss the last, crucial move. Thinking about that, his gut began to twitch. He had to get up into the mountains, bury the money, and be back down at the airstrip in time to meet Mark.

Well, hell, he could do that. Mark had said eight-thirty. That gave him two to three hours. That was the plan, the rest, the getaway itself, was a piece of cake. There might be a few weak spots, but there was risk in everything. He pulled off his straw hat, flipped it onto the dashboard, and headed past the cutoff up into the hills.

Hidden among the sand hills, he had a little nap and so did the gelding, sleeping on his feet. At three o'clock Lee loaded the gelding up again and headed back down for the Jamesfarm cutoff. He was halfway there when the truck dropped, jerking the steering wheel, and he felt the dead thump of the tire on the sand road. Swearing, he let the truck bump to a stop, set the brake, and stepped out.

At least it was on the truck, not the trailer. Front tire, and he thought maybe he could change it without unloading the gray. He kicked the bastard tire hard, kicked it again, and knew he had to cool down. There was plenty of time, he'd planned it to give himself time.

He looked up and down the empty road. Not a car in sight, the desert so quiet he heard a lizard scramble off a rock into some cactus. But he reached into the cab for the revolver and laid it on the floorboards. Then he lifted the seat cushion, pulled out the jack, the tire iron, and lug wrench, and dropped them beside the flat tire. Before he got to work, he blocked the truck and trailer wheels with rocks. By the time he got the wheel changed he was sweating, and breathing hard, was so tired that it seemed a huge effort even to tighten the lug nuts. He couldn't get his lungs full of air, and there was a heaviness on his chest so he had to rest several times before he finished tightening the last lug. The emphysema hadn't been this bad in a long time, he knew it was the stress. He struggled to get the blown tire and wheel up into the pickup, wondering why the hell he was keeping them. Too tired to lift the seat cushion, he threw the jack and lug wrench on the seat. He removed the rocks from under the wheels, beat the dust and sand off his pants, and crawled into the driver's seat, sank behind the steering wheel feeling weak and old, swearing with anger at his weakness.

Cranking the engine, he eased on slowly so as not to jerk the trailer. He rolled on, cursing old age, until he saw the Jamesfarm sign, saw the old barn among the scrawny tamarisk trees. He pulled in among them, backed the gray out under the low, salty-smelling branches. He tied the gelding to a tree, then checked out the barn.

It leaned a bit to the right, and half the roof shingles were missing, but when he shook the supporting timbers, nothing wobbled, the barn stood steady. There were four fenced stalls inside, four tie stalls, and an open space for a truck or tractor. He unloaded the gray then, backed the trailer in there, out of sight of the road. Before he un-hitched it, he opened both truck doors to keep the cab cool, and unloaded the water barrel.

He led the gelding into one of the larger stalls, fed him, tied his water bucket to the rail. After filling that, he filled the truck's radiator, then washed the grime and sweat off his face and hands. He had moved the saddle from the pickup bed into the trailer, had turned back to get the bridle, which had fallen to the ground, when the gelding jerked his head up, and Lee tensed.

The gelding snorted, looking back toward the big door, and Lee heard a faint noise, a dry snap. He spun around, grabbing the bridle as a blurred image flickered across the truck window. A man filled his vision, a crazed look in his eyes, a knife flashing in his hand. As he charged,

Lee swung the bridle. The heavy bit hit him hard in the throat. He staggered but came at Lee again. Lee stumbled backward into the open truck, grabbed the lug wrench, and swung it at the man's face.

The heavy wrench connected hard, the man fell, twisting away. Lee backed against the truck, looking around to see if there was another one. The gelding was rearing and snorting, white eyed, blowing like a stallion. Lee reached for the gun on the seat, watching the shadows around him. The man lay on the ground unmoving. What had he wanted? The truck? The horse? Or was he just some nutcase, out to hurt anyone who looked weaker? Lee remained still, watchful and tense until the gelding began to settle. When the horse had calmed and turned away, when Lee was sure there was no one else, he rolled the man over with his boot, holding his gun on him.

The body was limp. The face was a pulp of blood from the blow of the lug wrench. There was a bloody hole where his nose had been, as if the bones had been driven deep. Lee felt his breath coming hard. He palmed his revolver, glancing at the gray to see if anything else alerted him, but the good, sensible gelding had put his head down again and started to eat.

Lee eased himself down on the running board, sucking air. Where the hell had the guy come from? Had he been in the barn all the time? Sleeping, camping out in the old barn? Lee thought he'd looked around good. He had seen no sign of anything to alarm him, nothing in there that he'd noticed but some old gunny sacks, twists of bailing wire, a rusty bucket.

Rising from the running board, Lee studied what he

could see of the dead man's face, what was left of it. Dark eyes beneath the blood, bushy brows soaked with blood. Despite the gray's quiet assurance, Lee still wasn't certain the man had been alone. Nervously he circled the barn and then eased away into the trees beyond, looking back watching the barn, and watching behind him; the light was beginning to soften, but so far, by his watch, his timing was okay. Some twenty yards into the trees he found a small clearing and a makeshift camp. One dirty blanket, a backpack with some canned goods, an empty cook pot. A single metal plate lay beside a miniature fire, near an unopened can of beans, a can opener, and a spoon. As he turned back toward the barn, he could see again the man's dark eyes under the bushy, bloodied brows. He stood over the body, looking more carefully. Despite the gaping wound he could see how close the eyes were together, the face long and thin. Zigler. Luke Zigler, peering out from the wanted poster hanging in the Blythe post office.

Zigler, serving life for murder and armed robbery, escaped from Terminal Island some two hundred miles to the north but born and raised in Twentynine Palms. If that was Zigler's home, maybe he'd been waiting here for someone he knew, maybe had camped here to join up with a partner, and that made Lee nervous. He sure didn't want to leave the gray here for some badass to find. But what other choice did he have? He sure couldn't leave Zigler, either, for someone to discover.

Double-timing back to the truck, he studied his watch, thought a minute, then dragged the body around the truck. He searched Zigler's pockets but found no identification, false or otherwise. A few dollars, chump change. Lifting Zigler by the shoulders, breathing hard, he managed with a lot of grunting and straining to heave him up into the passenger seat. He rolled up the window halfway, closed the door, and pulled Zigler snugly against the doorframe. He slipped his own straw Stetson from the dashboard, jammed it on Zigler, settled it down over his battered face.

Before getting in the truck he ground Zigler's blood into the dirt, scuffed it in good. He rubbed the gray behind the ears, talked to him a minute, gave him another flake of hay, and left him happily munching his early supper. If the gray grew alarmed, if some no-good approached and tried messing with him—or if Lee himself didn't return— Lee figured the gray would jump the four-foot rail easy enough, would take off out of the barn running free.

Inside the truck he rolled up Zigler's window, and settled the hat a little better. He pulled out with Zigler's body riding easy beside him. Driving, he lifted the revolver out of its holster and pushed it into his belt at the small of his back. He made sure the bandana around his neck was knotted loosely, as he wanted it. The sun was disappearing in the west and, as he moved out from the stand of salty trees, a cooler breeze eased in from the desert.

30

THE OLD TRUCK entered town looking like many another farm vehicle, rusted and dirty, a ranch hand half asleep in the passenger seat, leaning against the window with his straw hat pulled down, maybe a little drunk, this late in the day. Several times Lee had slowed the truck to make sure no blood had seeped through the straw hat, and to wipe away trickles of the blood that crept down Zigler's face, using a rag he'd found stuffed behind the seat. The blood had stopped now. As he drove carefully past the post office, a clerk inside was closing the venetian blinds, though lights still shone within as he locked up the front part for the night. Lee guessed the small business operators and the larger companies would pick up their cash from the back office. Two big pickups passed him and turned the corner heading around to the back, new vehicles marked with the names of two local ranches. He heard truck doors slam, heard a muffled knock and then voices, heard the back door open and close. He hoped to hell his timing was right. When he heard the men leave, when no other trucks showed up, he turned left between the post office and the burned bank, left again to the little dirt alley behind, and parked beside the wooden storage building.

He took his hat from Zigler and turned the man's body so his face was half hidden, propping Zigler's arm up over the seat back to hide his smashed nose. He wiped Zigler's blood off the hatband, jammed the hat on his own head, and made sure the red bandana around his neck was loose enough. He stepped out of the truck leaving the door ajar, moved quickly to the metal-sheathed door and thumped on it hard, feeling as edgy as if he trod on hot cinders.

"Yes? Who is it?"

Lee leaned close, speaking loudly but garbling the words. "Placer Mining," he slurred. This was the weakest point in his plan, that Placer hadn't already been here and gone, that he could get in and get out again before their legitimate messenger drove up.

"Placer?"

Lee grunted.

"You're early today."

Lee relaxed a little. He'd started to say something more when he heard the spring lock turn. He pulled the bandana up over his face and drew the revolver. The instant the door cracked open he hit it with all his weight jamming it hard in the face of the startled guard. The man staggered back snatching for his gun and grabbing at his glasses, but he was already staring into the barrel of Lee's cocked forty-five.

"If you want to live, do exactly what I tell you." Lee's blood surged with excitement at the thought of killing the man, a sensation that shocked him. This poor fellow wasn't Zigler, who had attacked him and who deserved to be taken out. This was just a soft young bank guard, probably hired at the last minute and obviously not well trained at the job. The frail man gaped at him, his glasses flashing in the overhead light as Lee backed him deeper inside, pulled the door shut behind them, and slid the padlock into the hasp. He had no reason to want the man dead, to envision him bloodied and dead. The sharp thought upset him, yet he found himself shoving the gun hard into the man's terrified face, taking pleasure in seeing the little man tremble and gasp. This wasn't Lee's mode of operation, his robberies were coolheaded and precise, he didn't set out to abuse the weak and frightened. This was not *his* thinking, that had turned his blood hot with malice, he didn't like where this was coming from. Angrily he eased off, pressed the barrel of the gun sideways instead, along the man's cheek. "Get that empty mail sack, there on the desk. Take it in the vault and fill it, stuff *all* the money into it. I'm right behind you, you make one dicey move and you're dead."

Standing in the door to the vault, Lee watched the frightened clerk retrieve bundle after bundle of big bills from a set of metal drawers, watched him stuff the contents down in the bag. Two more bags stood on the floor against the wall, one full, one empty. Lee watched him fill the empty one, fight it closed at last, and pull the drawstring. The bag that was left, already bulging, was marked PLACER MINING.

"Is that all of it?"

"Yes, sir. You can see there's nothing left."

"Set the bags by the door, then bring the desk chair in here."

Looking scared, the man did as he was told, wheeling the chair inside.

"Sit down, hands behind the back of the chair. Is the vault vented?"

"Yes, sir, but . . . The vent only works when the fan is on. That—that switch inside the vault door."

"If it's an alarm, you're dead."

"It's the fan, I swear."

Lee backed toward the door. He hesitated, watching the man. This was stupid, the damn thing had to be an alarm.

But a plain electric switch? Wouldn't an alarm look different? Some kind of metal plate and handle or metal button? When he looked up where the clerk was looking, he could see the fan, through a dust-coated grate in the ceiling just above them. He reached for the switch, paused a moment waving the gun threateningly at the guard.

"It's the fan switch, I swear. I've got a wife and two kids at home. Please . . ."

Lee flipped the switch. The fan started sluggishly, *thump*, *thump*, then took hold and began to whir. Lee backed out the door, eased to the desk while still holding the gun on his victim. He picked up a hole punch, returned to the vault fishing the roll of tape from his pants pocket. Working awkwardly, one-handed, he taped the clerk's arms and legs to the chair. Only when the man was secure, did he slide his gun back in his belt.

With the punch he made holes in a long piece of tape, pressed this against the man's mouth, wrapping it around to the back. That would smart when someone found him and pulled it off, but the little man looked relieved that he could breathe.

"You may be here for a spell," Lee said. "You want me to take your glasses off?"

He grunted and shook his head.

Lee dragged the mail sacks out of the vault, looked the man over once, shut the heavy door and spun the dial. Turning, he eased the back door open, stood to the side looking up and down the alley. Dusk was falling fast, the sky deepening into gray, but the alley, the buildings and truck and Lee himself were still visible. When he didn't hear another vehicle coming down the side street he moved on out. He carried the three bags to the truck, dropped them in back, and covered them with the saddle blanket.

Stepping into the cab, he pulled his bandana off and stuffed it in Zigler's pocket. He resettled Zigler's position a bit, took off the straw hat, put it back on Zigler, tilting it down again over the man's bloody face.

He started the truck, pulled out onto the hard dirt alley, which he followed for several blocks before cutting back to the main street. Car lights were on, the windows of the stores that were still open were brightly lit. Driving slowly out of town, he was just another farm worker, his truck dirty and nondescript. Opening the wind wing, he let the thin evening breeze cool him, he hadn't realized how bad he was sweating. But now, with Zigler beside him, he had to smile. The dead man made a nice change to his plans. Somehow, his dead companion made him feel steadier and more in control.

When he got back to the gray, everything was as it should be, the gray sleeping on his feet, not nervous or watchful as if anything had disturbed him. He saddled the gelding, fished a length of rope from the truck and tied the three canvas money bags on top of his saddlebags, tied the trenching tool across those. Putting on the gloves he'd brought, he wiped his prints off places on the trailer he'd touched. Lifting the tongue, he pushed the trailer deep inside the old barn, into the shadows. Last of all, he wiped any earlier fingerprints from the hitch.

He returned to the gelding, put him on a lead rope, and led him up close to the driver's door. Stepping into the truck, he slipped the rope in through his open window and started the engine. Pulling out slowly, leading the gray, he eased away from the barn and up the incline to the little turnoff that led up into the hills. The gray followed willingly, trusting Lee, moving along at an easy jog. Lee drove until he found a deep embankment that was steep enough for what he wanted, an ancient, dry waterway, sheer and far to the bottom.

Pulling onto the shoulder and getting out, he led the gelding across the road out of the way and secured his rope among a scattering of boulders. In the dusk, the pale desert floor held the last of the light. He could see the old barn far below, and the airstrip. Off beyond the strip by several miles lay a ranch, the thin lines of fences, a barn, a windmill, a cluster of trees, and a glint of white that would be the ranch house.

Returning to the truck, still wearing the gloves, he

got in and angled the truck facing the cliff. He set the hand brake, then wiped clean the steering wheel again for good measure, wiped the lug wrench, the jack, and the door handles. He slid Dawson's driver's license deep into the dead man's back pocket, then, opening the driver's door and stepping out, he pulled Zigler's body across the seat and arranged it behind the steering wheel. He wiped the revolver good, pressed the dead man's fingers to it, in the firing position, then laid it on the seat near Zigler's right leg. Reaching in, with the hand brake still set, he started the truck, the gear in neutral, and let the engine idle. Along the edge of the canyon, the wind blew sharply up at him. He cranked the steering wheel toward the edge. If he wasn't quick, he'd be as dead as Zigler. In one move he released the brake, forced the gearshift into low, and jumped clear, giving the truck a shove to get it moving.

It lurched over the bank and down the side with a hell of a rumble, kicking up rocks, plowing up dust that blew in his face. He listened to the truck fall bouncing against the cliff, sounded like it was turning over and over. He heard it hit a boulder and bounce, then a heavier sound, as if it had rolled. Warily he peered over but it was too dark to see down into the canyon, too black down there to see anything. He thought about climbing down and putting a match to the truck—if he could get down, in the dark, without breaking his neck. But what the hell? If the law found the truck, what did they have? An escaped convict gone over the cliff, false ID, a truck with false registration, and a dark revolver the bank teller might recognize with its six-inch barrel, wooden grip, and worn bluing.

Returning to the gray, he patted the canvas bags behind him as he stepped up into the saddle. He made sure the money rode steady and secure as he moved the gelding on up the western slope of the mountain. The gray moved out at a fast walk even climbing, but at last he tired at the uphill pull and wanted to slow. Lee let the willing mount take his own pace, he had enough time. His pocket watch said seven o'clock, straight up. He had an hour and a half, and that was plenty.

When the gray had rested, Lee urged him along again. They were high up on the northwestern slope at the base of a pinnacle rock when they stopped in the shadow of an overhang, and Lee stepped off. He untied one of the canvas bags, sat down against the bank with the bag between his knees and opened it. In the fading light, he counted roughly through the money, his heart pounding. Looked like, altogether, he might have around three to four hundred thousand. Hell, he could buy half of Mexico for that. The crisp green bills felt good in his hands. He managed to stuff two canvas bags in the saddlebags. Then, just below the cliff, he dug a deep hole in the dry desert. Even with the trenching tool, he was out of breath when he'd finished, and now time was getting close. Breathing raggedly, he dropped the saddlebags into the hole, laid the third bag between them, and covered them. He kept the trenching tool. Feeling pushed now, he stood for only a moment looking out over the valley, mentally marking his position. He could just see, down to his left, the airstrip like a small scratch next to the dirt road to Jamesfarm.

He let the gray pick his own way down the bare mountain, around boulders and across ravines. The land was dark now but the sky still silver. When they hit the road he pushed the gelding to a gallop. He could barely make out the emergency airstrip now, couldn't see the faded orange windsock drooping or filling in the gusting wind. Descending fast, thankful the gray was sure-footed, he began to worry that Mark had been early, hadn't seen him and had gone on, though he hadn't heard a plane. Or maybe Mark had changed his mind and had made other plans.

Pulling the gray up near the old barn, in among a small cluster of scrubby willows, he dug a second hole. It was harder digging among the roots and in the dark, but then he hit a patch where ground squirrels had made tunnels, and it went faster. When he had a saddle-sized hole he laid the blanket in and laid the saddle on top, the skirts and cinch and stirrups folded in, hoping the rodents would leave it alone, hoping he'd buried it high enough above the wash so the hole wouldn't flood. He didn't cover the hole, but waited quietly beside the gray, his chest heaving. The sky above was darkening now, too, the far mountains humping in heavy, deep blackness. Alone and wondering if Mark would come, he was getting fidgety when he heard the faint drone of the plane and saw its lights high above the mountains.

Only then did he remove the gray's bridle, point him in the direction of the ranch on beyond, and slap him on the rump. The good gelding snorted and took off at a gallop, glancing back once at Lee. Lee laid the bridle in the hole with the saddle and trenching tool. With his boots he scraped sand and dirt into the hole, covering them well, stamped them down, then scuffed leaves and dry grass over the bare scar of earth. As the Stearman's lights grew large and descended, he walked out, staying clear of the strip.

The plane bounced once on the wind and touched

down. He waved both arms over his head as it taxied toward him, though he guessed Mark could see him against the lighter sand. Near him the plane paused, idling.

Walking on out, Lee had to grin. He'd done it. A third of a million bucks, hidden, and all his. Maybe in due time the losers would be reimbursed for some of it by the U.S. government. He didn't know how this bank insurance worked, but as wasteful as Washington was, they wouldn't miss the money. Feeling good, he stepped up on the Stearman's wing walk and eased down into the hopper, where Mark had added a heavy blanket for his comfort. Lee fastened his seat belt, gave Mark a thumbs-up, and they were off, Mark heading clear across the country, for Wichita and then Florida, Lee choosing the shorter distance to establish his alibi. At the time the post office guard was first tied up and robbed, Lee would have had to be four hours or more away, hitching with an unknown trucker, heading for the roulette and blackjack tables of Vegas. And Mark, if anyone ever thought to make the connection, which wasn't likely, would have been much farther away, gassing up the Stearman at small, country airports where the young pilot always paid cash, an unrecorded flight not likely to ever be traced.

31

BECKY MANAGED A visit with Morgan the next day while Sammie was in school but when she picked the child up, Sammie guessed at once where she'd been; she was so agitated at being left out again, at not seeing her daddy, was so completely focused on telling Morgan something deeply important to her, that Becky gave in at last; she knew that stubborn determination wouldn't go away. When she looked into Sammie's dark and grieving eyes she was filled, herself, with Sammie's same driving need to tell him whatever was so urgent, so very meaningful to her. Sammie might be only nine, but she was not like other children; her perceptions awed and frightened Becky, and Becky had to listen to her.

But there was one thing that Becky made her promise not to tell Morgan. Her daddy knew nothing about Falon's break-in and his attack on them, he didn't know about any of the trouble they'd had with Falon. She had always thought, long before Morgan was arrested and put in jail, that if Morgan knew how Falon had behaved he'd be so enraged he might kill Falon. She had kept silent to protect Morgan and now, with Morgan locked up, what good would it do to tell him, it would only create more hurt, more desperate and helpless rage.

"Grandma made carrot cake today," Becky said. "We'll stop at her house for a little snack first, then we'll go to see Daddy. On one condition," she said, looking down at Sammie. "You remember to keep your promise not to tell Daddy about Falon coming to the house?"

Sammie looked up at her. "You mean, the last time?"

"I mean all the times, as we agreed. Clear back, long ago. Even that time when—"

"When he killed Misto," Sammie said.

Becky nodded. "You know I've never told him, it would be too upsetting."

"You were afraid of what Daddy would do."

Becky nodded. "And right now, Daddy has enough to worry him without hearing about that ugliness." She knew there'd be a police report from when Falon broke in the last time. She just hoped they hadn't told Morgan about that.

Sammie looked up at her a long time, but said nothing. She was still quiet when they pulled into Caroline's drive, she didn't say a word as they went inside. Sitting at the big kitchen table as Caroline cut a piece of carrot cake for her and poured a glass of milk, Sammie hadn't said a word.

"Can you promise that?" Becky said. "*Will* you promise—for Daddy's sake?"

Sammie ate some cake, took a sip of milk. "I promise," she said at last, but in a reluctant little voice. Becky looked sternly at her. Sammie blinked, and looked down. "I promise," she said more boldly. Caroline watched them in silence. "I promise," Sammie repeated, and then she tied into her milk and cake.

THE EVENING LIGHT was softening as they pulled into the courthouse parking lot. Sammie was still quiet as they went inside, the child walking very determined, very straight in her light summer jacket, her chin up, her eyes straight ahead. Whatever *was* on her mind, whatever she needed to tell Morgan, no matter how shaky Becky felt at the emotional disaster it might cause, this couldn't be avoided. Whatever Sammie had to say, Becky half expected a meltdown that would leave Sammie tearful and leave Morgan intolerably shaken.

Maybe her mind was filled with a dream she hadn't told Becky, a worse nightmare even than the last one where Morgan was thrown in jail—that trauma would stay with them for the rest of their lives, she couldn't imagine what would be worse than that prediction.

For a moment, she wondered if this had to do with Morgan being drugged, wondered if Sammie had seen something in a dream where Falon was giving him a drug as well as alcohol?

She had already talked with their doctor about that. Dr. Bates had visited Morgan in jail, had questioned him, had done what small, simple tests there were to do, had looked at Morgan's pupils, had checked his heart, even smelled Morgan's breath.

He said whatever Morgan had been given could have

been an overdose of some prescription medication. He said there wasn't much in the way of testing, if they didn't know what they were looking for, particularly this long after the dose had been given. Dr. Bates said that, because Morgan didn't drink, a sufficient amount of bootleg whiskey could have knocked him out overnight, could have left him uncertain and groggy, the way the police found him. But he didn't see how Morgan could have been forced to drink so much without trying to refuse, without remembering. He did say that some bootleg whiskey contained additives to make it more potent, but usually that was found in the bigger cities, not in moonshine from these small, backwoods stills.

At the jail, Sergeant Trevis ushered them into the same small, ugly visiting room, Sammie holding Becky's hand tight, her own hand cold and tense. Becky hardly noticed the scarred table and two metal chairs. The afternoon heat inside the small room was nearly intolerable, and the street noise added to their stress. Becky sat down with her back to the window. Sammie stood waiting near the door, tense and watchful, listening to footsteps coming down the hall.

Officer Jimson stood behind Morgan, and as her daddy entered, Sammie flew straight into his arms, clinging to him, pushing her face against his chest. Morgan pulled out the empty chair, sat down with Sammie on his lap. He kissed her cheek, buried his face in her pale, clean hair. At the other side of the table Becky sat quietly, trying not to send emotional vibes, wanting to let Sammie have her say without interference or distraction. Even Sergeant Trevis seemed tuned in to Sammie's urgency, he stood back against the wall, looking at the floor, remaining very still and disconnected as if his attention were miles away.

When at last Sammie pulled away from her daddy's hug, she took his face in her two small hands, looking deeply at him. Her words startled Becky, they were not what she'd expected. "I dreamed of the cowboy," Sammie said. "He's coming, Daddy."

Becky looked down, trying to hide her frown, her hands clenched out of sight under the table. What *was* this, what was this about the old man?

"He's coming now, Daddy, he's coming here to help you."

Morgan looked at her, puzzled.

"I knew he'd come," Sammie said sagely, looking deeply at him. "I dreamed before that he would, I dreamed about the airplane. That's part of how he's coming, he was so happy with escaping in the plane. He's coming, Daddy. But not right away. There will be jail for him, too. I dreamed of prison walls around him, but not here. Far away from here.

"Prison walls around you both," she said very low, glancing at Sergeant Trevis and then away. "But at first in different places." She put her arms around Morgan, pressed her forehead against his chest, speaking half muffled against him. "You'll be in prison, Daddy, a big prison right here near home. But then the cowboy will come there, you'll be together then. You'll both be there, inside that high wall. And then, Daddy—then the cowboy will help you."

She looked at Morgan hard. "You'll get away from there, Daddy. In the dark night the cowboy will help you get away. Only the cowboy can save you, he'll help you prove the truth, he will help you, Daddy."

Morgan looked at Sammie a long time, his expression stern and unchanging, but tears welled in his eyes. When he looked up at Becky, a long look over the child's head, his gaze was filled with fear, with disbelief, with dismay at the thought of prison.

"How do you know?" Morgan whispered. "How can you know this?" But then from somewhere deep inside, Becky saw his calm certainty rise. She watched Morgan's faith surface, his faith in Sammie, sure and trusting, his faith in a talent and knowledge that no ordinary human would possess. "How can you know?" he repeated.

"The cowboy," Sammie said, looking deeply at him. "My dream, *my* cowboy. My dream told me. The cowboy *belongs* to us. *He* doesn't know that, he doesn't know about us, not yet. It will be a long time," she said, "a long journey. I dreamed of snow and prisons and then he is sick, but then he will get better and he will come to us and he will help you."

Sergeant Trevis seemed to be paying no attention, looking blankly away as if his mind were on something far distant, as he took in Sammie's whispers.

Again Sammie took Morgan's face in her hands. "You mustn't lose hope, Daddy. You must take what comes, until the cowboy is here with us, until he comes to help us."

Across from them, all Becky could do was wipe away her own tears, rise from her chair, come around the table and put her arms around them, holding them close, holding the two of them close to her, wondering, frightened but strangely hopeful.

32

As the Stearman lifted higher into the night wind, Lee pulled the blanket over his legs, looking down over the lower wing where the pale desert caught the last gleam of light. For a second just below them he saw the gray jogging free, the good gelding ducking his nose and switching his tail, smart and sassy at his own release. He'd have a fine taste of freedom and, when he got thirsty and hungry, he'd head for the one lone ranch off beyond the little dirt strip, he was already moving in that direction. No horseman, seeing the gray, would let him wander. As the plane passed over him he shied, bucked a little, and broke into a gallop.

When Mark banked sharply, lifting toward the mountains heading east, Lee leaned over scanning the foothills, but it was too dark among the massed rocks to see the higher pinnacle where he had buried the money. How long before he'd be back, to dig it up again? And what would happen to him, meantime? He began to worry about someone finding his stash, then he worried about the saddlebags and canvas bags rotting, or pack rats digging in and chewing up the money for nests. Sitting hunched under the blanket in the hopper of the front cockpit, he got himself all worked up worrying, like some little old woman.

Well, hell, the money was safe enough, it wasn't going anywhere. He was too edgy, he'd been nervous ever since he accidentally killed Zigler. He didn't like the thoughts he'd had, either, back there in the post office, wanting to hurt that young guard, he didn't like that it had even crossed his mind to kill him. That young fellow wasn't Zigler, he didn't deserve to die, he wasn't anything like that scum that Lee had wasted.

Mark had said they'd be following the Colorado River most of the way to Vegas but, looking out over the plane's nose, Lee couldn't see much but the night closing in on the deeper blackness of the low mountains, just their crowns catching the last gleam of daylight. Soon between the mountains they hit a patch of turbulence, the plane bucking, the wind so cold Lee pulled his jacket collar up, settled deeper in his seat, and pulled the blanket tighter. When he felt a tap on his shoulder, he looked back to see Mark shoving a wadded-up coat at him. He grabbed at it, the wind trying to tear it away. He got it into the cockpit and gladly pulled it on. Soon, bundled in the coat and blanket, he grew warmer—warm all but inside his chest where it felt like his breath had turned to ice. Hunching down in the coat collar like a turtle to warm his breath, he thought about the wagon trains that had crossed the desert and crossed those bare ranges below him, pioneers stubbornly heading west: a trip that took many months, where he and Mark were looking at just over an hour.

Some of the mountains those folks had crossed would take three teams of horses or oxen to pull one wagon up, with everyone pushing from behind. And on the other side, going down, trees had to be cut to use for drags to keep the wagons from getting away, from falling wheel over canvas, dragging their good teams with them. Those men and women, crossing a foreign land hauling their loaded wagons over the frozen mountains, they had had no idea what lay ahead, and they'd had only themselves to rely on. But they kept on, despite starvation, frozen limbs, despite sickness and death, despite the ultimate desperate measures that had kept some of them alive, that had shocked the generations who came after them, had shocked descendants who might not be here at all, if not for what they called, looking back, the most heinous of crimes.

Lee didn't know how to judge what was not his to judge, all he knew right now was, if it was cold in this open hopper, the winters during those crossings had been a hundred times colder, down there among the wild mountains.

As a kid, growing up in South Dakota, he'd thought there'd never be an end to winter. Every chore seemed twice as hard, his hands froze to any metal he touched, ropes frozen stiff, even the flakes of hay froze hard. Barn doors stuck, latches wouldn't work, ice had to be broken from water buckets several times a day and at night, too, so the animals could drink. He'd hated winter, and *he'd* had a home to live in, they'd had a fire at night to warm them and where his mother cooked, they'd had plenty of food, good beef from their own cattle, grain and root stores, but still he'd grumbled. Grumbled about splitting the firewood, grumbled about dragging hay over the snow to the waiting cattle. He'd even complained when he had to slog through deep snow to the barn to do his chores where he'd be cozy and warm among the warm animals.

Now, hunched down in the little airplane traveling in a way he had never imagined as a boy, he felt strangely unreal. The land below the wings humped away in darkness, a glint from the river now and then, and above the upper wing a glint of stars; and then far ahead Lee saw a cluster of lights, warm and beckoning, and that would be Vegas, a glittering oasis appearing and then vanishing between the low hills.

But where, all this time, was the ghost cat? Why wasn't he here beneath the blanket, warming Lee? Why had Lee not seen or sensed the cat during all his moves at the post office and then burying the money, turning the gray loose, getting in the plane and taking off—all without Misto?

Had the yellow cat abandoned him? Had even this crime of robbery, so removed from any betrayal of Jake Ellson, had even this transgression against the law turned the cat from him? Lee prayed not. He would feel a failure, he would feel betrayed if that were the case. To be abandoned so suddenly, without a word, without a last rub and purr, that couldn't make any sense to Lee.

Beneath him, now, the little city took shape, the land below brightened by colored neon, by palaces of yellow lights as the Stearman dropped down over the last ridge into Vegas. Mark circled the city lights, then put her nose down toward the valley. Warmer air washed over Lee. He sat up straighter watching the lights come up at him in sweeps of raw neon, the windows of the tall buildings crowded together and bright, and then a dark and empty space delineated by long straight rows of airport lights picking out the runways.

Mark banked the Stearman, coming around for a straight shot, a long approach. He set her down lightly and taxied to the far end of the runway, where he moved off toward a row of small planes tied down, and a few small hangars. The night was pleasantly warm, Lee pulled off the heavy coat as Mark killed the engine.

He was stiff, getting out. And he was still wondering about the cat, he still had that empty feeling, without the companionship of the ghost cat. Even when he didn't see Misto he could often sense him near, but now he sensed only emptiness. He felt lost, felt so alone suddenly that he might even welcome the goading presence of the dark spirit—if the cat would return, as well.

He helped Mark wheel the plane to a tie-down beside the hangars. Across the way, Lee could see the public terminal, and beyond that a parking lot, lines of cars reflecting the lights of the building. A commercial plane stood nearby, maybe from San Francisco or L.A. As Mark snugged the Stearman to the ground ties, looping the short lines through the metal rings, Lee fished a handful of bills from his pocket to pay for the gas.

"Hope you make a killing in Florida," he said, handing Mark the money, clapping the younger man on the shoulder. "And good luck in Wichita. Take care getting there."

Mark grinned. "Thanks, Fontana. I've enjoyed knowing you. Maybe someday we'll see each other again."

Lee nodded. "Maybe." Turning away, feeling strangely lost, he swore softly at his sudden loneliness. Then he straightened his shoulders and made his way across to the terminal.

He took the front taxi of three that were parked at the curb. The driver was maybe fifty, a Latino man, short hair, smooth shaven, pictures of his pudgy wife and three handsome kids stuck around the edges of the windshield, a small silver Virgin fixed to the dashboard.

"Take me to the best Mexican restaurant you've got," Lee told him. The driver smiled and took off, soon moving through a tangle of residential and small businesses, and then between the bright neon of casino signs that flashed along the street. At a small, noisy Mexican café, the man pulled over. Lee paid him and pushed in through the carved door to the good rich smell.

He found a small table in a corner away from the fancy-dressed tourists with their loud talk and laughter. He ordered dinner and two bottles of beer. He meant to take his time enjoying his meal. A few minutes wouldn't make a difference, and who knew when he'd eat Mexican again? Not where he was headed. He watched the bleached-blond tourist women in their low-cut dresses, the soft-bodied greenhorn men dressed in fancy Western wear, the creases still showing in their pearl-buttoned shirts, their brand-new boots and Stetsons that had never been near a horse or steer, their loud tourist talk and brassy smiles, their feverish partying.

And then, when again he missed the cat, he wondered suddenly what he was doing here. Was *this* why the cat had vanished? Had Misto left him because he found this whole plan repugnant? Because even this last robbery had been against what the cat wanted or approved of?

Frowning, he thought about changing his mind and sliding back to Blythe, of staying innocently on the job there. But that would mean some bad loose ends, would put him in Blythe at the time of the robbery, would put him in immediate danger. He needed this alibi, or he'd have the feds wide awake, coming down on him like buzzards on an injured calf. A new parolee in the area, known for his train heists. A bank robbery in the small town, such as they may never have known before. What else would they do but close in on him?

Even as it stood, they'd want to know why he'd taken off, leaving the state against his parole, at the exact same time as the robbery. Hell, he thought, maybe he should have kept the gray, hauled the money out with him right then, and beat it straight for the border. Maybe he could have made it into Mexico free and clear, could have vanished now rather than later.

He was still feeling uncertain about what was ahead when his dinner came, steaming on the sizzling plate, enchiladas ranchero, beans and rice and chile relleno. He ate slowly, savoring each individual bite as he went over his next moves, letting the noise of the tourists fade around him. At last, wiping up his plate with the one remaining tortilla, he felt better, felt easy and at peace. This plan was all right, he had it set up just the way it should be, he knew for sure that the next steps were exactly what he needed to do.

When the feds were convinced he'd been in Vegas during the post office robbery, when they received the police report that he would soon set up for them, why would they question that kind of proof? What were they going to do? Stop and interrogate every trucker who had taken that route? Every tourist who might have picked up a hitch-hiker? And how would they make the timing work out, for that long drive from Blythe up into Nevada? Smiling, he ordered a second side of corn tortillas and another beer. By the time he'd finished the third beer, a soft glow filled him. Feeling content, and full of good Mexican food, his worries evaporated. The plan ahead looked just fine. He paid his bill and left the café, smiling. Ducking into a liquor store at the next corner, he bought a pint of whiskey, and then found a deserted alley.

He broke the seal on the whiskey, took two swallows, swished it around and spat it out. He poured the rest of the cheap, dark booze over his shirt and pants, then tossed the empty bottle in a trash can, where it clanked comfortably against its brothers. Leaving the alley, he entered the first big casino he came to. At the main cage he bought a stack of chips with some of the money he'd carried in his boot.

He picked a roulette table, positioning himself across from the hard-eyed operator, bumping the player next to him, knocking some of the man's chips on the floor. The tourist wrinkled his nose at the reek of whiskey, picked up his chips, and moved farther down the table. The operator glared at Lee, then spun the wheel. Lee placed a stack of chips on seventeen and as the wheel slowed he weaved back and forth, picking his nose. When the ball dropped into sixteen he reached over the table and shoved the operator hard. "You son of a bitch. I saw you drag your thumb on the wheel."

The black-suited, hard-jowled operator slid around the table toward him, his pale brown eyes fixed on Lee. Lee stared at him, spat on the table, and threw the stack of chips in his face. He grabbed Lee, and Lee hit him hard in the stomach. People began shouting, dealers and security people came running, surrounding him. He grabbed up a stool, swung it hard, charging them, forcing customers to stumble over each other, getting out of his way. He glimpsed a man in Levi's leaning over a gaming table grabbing up a stack of chips and then the place was filled with cops, cops storming in. Lee paused, waiting, weaving drunkenly, ready to light into the bastards the minute they touched him.

When two of them grabbed Lee, he raked the edge of his boot down a uniformed shin so hard the cop swore, swung his nightstick and hit him in the kidneys. As Lee doubled over they hit him again across the shoulders, pulled his wrists behind him, and snapped on the cuffs. He fought and kicked as they dragged him away, he swore at them slurred and drunkenly as they hauled him out through the crowd, the tourists backing away opening a path for him, as wary as if the cops were leading a wild man.

Outside on the street the uniforms pushed him into the backseat of a patrol car, behind the wire barrier. He cursed them loudly all the way to the station, calling them every name he could think of. In the station, while they booked him, he managed to knock the sergeant's coffee cup off the desk and break it. He was booked for being drunk and disorderly, for fighting in a public place, for assaulting several officers, and destroying police property. When they searched him they found his parole officer's card in his hip pocket, folded in with the address of Delgado Ranch, and Jake Ellson's phone number. The booking officer, a short, heavyset sergeant, studied Lee.

"You're under the feds?"

"That's what they like to think. If I want to leave the damn district and have a little fun, that's my business."

"Where and when were you released?"

"McNeil. March eighth, this year."

Sergeant Peterson raised an eyebrow. "Not long. Mr. Raygor will be interested to know how you feel about his supervision. Any message, when we call San Bernardino?"

Lee scowled at him, and said nothing. He watched Sergeant Peterson seal his pocketknife, his savings book, three hundred dollars in loose bills, and Mae's picture into a brown envelope. "I want the picture back in good shape, not broken."

Sergeant Peterson looked at the photo of the little girl. "Granddaughter?"

"My sister."

Peterson studied the yellowed, faded photograph. "Long time ago. Where is she now?"

"I have no idea. Haven't seen her since she was little."

Peterson looked at him a long time. "No other family? Anyone you want us to contact?"

"If there was, my PO would do that."

Peterson said nothing more. He nodded to a young, redheaded officer who ushered Lee on back to the tank, walking behind him, very likely his hand resting on his weapon. He unlocked the barred door, gave Lee a shove, and locked him in. The big cell was half full, mostly of drunks, the place smelled as sour as a cheap bar, that stink mixed with the invasive smell of the dirty latrine. Lee picked a top bunk at the far end of the long cell, stood with his back to the ladder glaring around him, looking for trouble, for any challenge to his chosen space.

There wasn't any, most of the men were asleep or passed out. A sick young man lay curled on the floor in one corner, shivering. Lee climbed to the upper bunk and stretched out. He checked the ceiling for roaches, then rolled onto his side with his face to the wall. The mattress and thin blanket stunk of stale sweat. But in spite of the depressing atmosphere of another lockup, Lee lay smiling.

His moves had come off just as he'd planned. All he had to do now was wait. If he got lucky, he'd do his time right here in the Vegas jail, and he could think of worse places. Why would the feds bother to send him back to the federal pen just for drunk and disorderly? They sure wouldn't send him back to McNeil for such a small infraction. Maybe they'd tack some extra time on his parole, but what was the difference? As soon as he was out again, he meant to jump parole anyway. No one would come looking for him in Mexico, or be likely to find him, if they did. The money was there in the desert waiting for him, and they sure wouldn't get him on the post office charge. What court or jury could put him in Blythe when he was nearly three hundred miles away at the time, tearing up a Vegas casino?

Turning over, ignoring the stink of the cell, Lee drifted off toward sleep, quite content with his fate. Unaware, as yet, of the long, dangerous, and tangled route he had chosen, oblivious to the precipitous road he had embarked upon. He hadn't a clue to the tangled connections he was yet to encounter and to the many long, dangerous months before he would return to Blythe to claim his bounty and head for the border. And if, three thousand miles away in Georgia, a young man waited, puzzled, for the old cowboy's fate to play out, for the cowboy's future to join his own, Lee did not know that, either.

If Morgan Blake, sitting hunched on his sagging bunk in the Rome jail, waited with a desperate hope that indeed a miracle was in the making as predicted by Sammie's dream, if he clung to his wild belief that his little girl had seen truly, who could blame him? He had nothing else to hang on to. If their attorney failed to free him, Sammie's prediction was the only hope Morgan had.

Maybe only the cat, sitting unseen in Lee's jail cell in Vegas, saw clearly the direction the two men were headed, saw how they were connected, saw how their futures were drawing together. Crouched invisibly at the foot of Lee's bunk, so weightless now that Lee was unaware of him, Misto looked around at the human scum that occupied Lee's cell—a worse lot, by far, than the men in the Rome lockup where Morgan waited. Though, in Rome, Morgan's view of the future was far more agonizing than the future that Lee envisioned.

For Lee, the dark spirit seemed to have pulled back, his aura of evil to have thinned, easing off the pressure on Fontana. Perhaps, Misto thought, Satan had grown bored with Lee, maybe he was soured at the effort he'd made that had garnered no satisfying results. Whatever the cause, Misto sensed that, at least for the moment, the devil had stepped back, that all was well with the world; and the invisible cat twitched his tail with pleasure.

Lee and Morgan and his family would keep Misto tethered to this time, to the drama that was only now unfolding and that would lead ultimately to the cowboy's final fate. One day, not far off, the cat must return to the world as a living part of it, as a mortal beast only, without the powers and the freedom and vision he presently enjoyed. But, the great powers willing, he meant to remain close to Lee, as spirit, until Lee broke Satan's curse for good and forever, until Satan gave up the chase, admitted defeat, and turned to tormenting other men, weaker souls who would be more amenable to his wiles.

You are the loser, the ghost cat thought, sensing Lucifer watching now, curious and waiting. *You are the loser,* Misto thought, *soon Lee will drive you away and the child will drive you away, forever. You are wasting your time in this quest of Dobbs's heirs, you will fail, you will finally and ultimately fail.* And, smiling, the ghost cat rolled over across Lee's feet, making himself heavy suddenly, purring mightily, jarring Lee awake. Lee looked down at him, and laughed. And in that moment Lee knew the cat would stay with him, that Misto wouldn't leave him. In a rare instance of half-dreaming perception, Lee knew the ghost cat would remain beside him as Lee wove through a longer and more complicated tangle than he had imagined, as he fought through the encounters and trials that were laid out for him; as he was united with the child he had dreamed of and, surprised by the relationship, he discovered new partners and, with them, fought his way to his final and eternal freedom.